THE SEVEN EXPERIMENTS

STEPHEN KANICKI

Black Rose Writing | Texas

ISBN: 978-1-68433-337-0
PUBLISHED BY BLACK ROSE WRITING
www.blackrosewriting.com

Printed in the United States of America
Suggested Retail Price (SRP) $18.95

The Seven Experiments is printed in Traditional Arabic

To Courtney, Stephen and Kyra.
I could not have written a better story than you.

THE SEVEN EXPERIMENTS

CHAPTER ONE

What Bobby saw did not belong to the natural world. It sent chills through him and made him question everything he thought was real.

The boy wasn't prone to hallucinations, nor exaggeration. He was a reasonable young person, intelligent and grounded in reality. The ordinary life-forms found by the river's edge were good enough for him. He loved the Chadakoin River, its fast-moving murky water, the brightly-colored frogs sunning themselves on the bank, minnows and sportfish breaking the surface as they chased Mayflies. These were the normal things, the things he expected to see, and the things that made his heart race. What he saw this morning was something different.

It began like any other trip to the Chadakoin, a hike through a secluded trail tucked away amidst large oak and maple trees that lined either side. It was covered in dense brush, which tugged at his insteps and deposited sharp stickers onto his jeans as he strolled past. This was the old part of Falconer, New York, a part that people forgot about or never knew existed in the first place. It was a place where few ventured, preferring the modest comforts of town as opposed to this patch of rugged land. The only other people Bobby saw this morning were two stoners heading towards town after completing a pot transaction. The older boys recognized him from school and said hello to him as they walked by. Bobby quickened his pace. He didn't have much time to explore. Lunch would be waiting for him at home in an hour.

As he neared the river, Bobby heard the fast-moving current followed by the high-pitched cries ringing from the treetops like a chorus of analog alarm clocks. They were birds startled to life by his presence, but the awful noise elevated his heart rate and made goose bumps swell on his arms.

He moved gingerly along the river's edge, being careful not to step into a divot that might pitch him into the murky river. Suddenly, the water next to him exploded. A prehistoric-looking bird unfurled its six-foot wingspan and slowly lifted off. The loud thrashing and the sight of its massive body caused him to jump back. Once he realized what it was, he caught his breath, gathered himself and marveled at the Blue Heron's graceful flight as it slowly disappeared into the morning haze. *Nothing that big should fly without an engine strapped to its back*, he thought to himself as he continued down the path.

The natural sights and sounds made him forget about his drab middle-class life. Video games were fun, but the Chadakoin River was real, not just animated pixels; it was nature, fully alive and wild, or wild enough to suit his tastes. The river caused his hair to stand on end, and he liked that feeling.

It happened as he walked onto the cement footbridge that spanned the river. Halfway across, he paused, leaned against the metal handrail and peered down at the fast flowing water. The Chadakoin ran muddy, and visibility was poor making it impossible to see the bottom in the deeper pools. But in the shallower eddies, where the sun penetrated, he marveled at the assortment of wildlife swimming beneath the surface. From his perch looking down at the water, he saw minnows swimming in large schools. He watched as a school of Crappie moved in and dive-bombed the baitfish. The minnows scattered in all directions at once and leaped from the water like popcorn.

As Bobby watched on, something downstream caught his eye. It was a black-clad figure, long and wiry; his ashen skin wrapped tight against his skull like cellophane, and a tuft of jet-black hair rested on his lip and chin. Bobby's heart raced as he watched this man. The boy's eyes narrowed; his smile disappeared, and he felt unusually cold despite the summer heat.

Bobby's brain searched for answers. He had a series of images that contradicted each other and conflicted with his knowledge of the world around him, and though his twelve-year-old mind had limited understanding of science, he knew what he saw was not right. Humans cannot walk on water.

And the fact the stranger was walking on water wasn't the oddest part of the scene. It was how he walked. He moved without a care, in a perfectly reasonable manner, placing one foot in front of the other with his arms crossed over his chest in a matter-of-fact fashion. His face was placid and without emotion. There was no hesitation, and no balance issues. The man's feet appeared to float on the surface, and he strolled along as if he were on a Sunday jaunt in the park.

Bobby's jaw dropped as he gulped the stifling, thick air. His eyes moved from the man to the water, and then back to the man again. There had to be an explanation, something he had missed, a wire perhaps, or special shoes. *That's it*, he thought. The man was wearing special shoes. But on closer inspection, his footwear appeared ordinary. Bobby looked for another answer. He recalled fragments of grade school science lectures about water, and ice and the pull of gravity. There was something about solids, liquids and gasses, and how one element could take on three different forms, but that didn't make sense either. It was summer, and the Chadakoin was water, pure unadulterated free-flowing liquid. Even during the winter months the fast-moving river never froze. *What the Hell is this*, Bobby thought?

Once again, Bobby felt the goose bumps on his arms. This wasn't like the Blue Heron startling him. This was a different kind of fear. He wanted to turn and run, but he was compelled to stand his ground and watch.

The man turned suddenly and looked up at Bobby. The two locked eyes, and the boy immediately recognized something sinister in them. Bobby grasped the metal rail tightly. His first thought was to look away as if by quickly turning his head he could fool the man into believing he saw nothing. But even this simple act was impossible. Instead, he was forced to return the man's uncomfortable glare. Bobby found it impossible to resist.

The man spread his palms towards the sky and Bobby heard his voice. It was not an audible sound, but he heard it in his head. "Look at me," the voice commanded. "Have you ever seen anything like this?"

Bobby shrugged his shoulders and returned a nervous smile. The man smiled back. Bobby wanted to run for home, but his feet were planted, and he was unable to move. The staring contest seemed to last forever, until the man's smile faded. It began with an involuntary twitch on one side of his face, and continued with more twitches that followed in close succession as if he were having an epileptic fit. The man looked down at his feet and that appeared to seal his fate. The spell was broken. His body reacted accordingly by pitching forward, and then back. His legs wobbled violently beneath him. His jaw fell open and his eyes grew dark and wide. His once relaxed gait was now replaced with the flailing arms of a high wire act gone horribly wrong. Then, with one downward flush, the river swallowed the man into the deep hole over which he stood.

Bobby squinted, but he was too far away. The angle and the silted water made it impossible to see beneath the surface. He waited for the man to resurface amidst the bubbles and churning water, but he grew impatient. His legs were working now, and feeling somewhat responsible, he hurried toward the river's edge.

CHAPTER TWO

The scent of musty books made Gary's nostrils flare. There were north of a thousand titles by his estimation, a private collection that surpassed any he had seen before.

Many titles were scholarly texts; biology, chemistry, physics, mathematics, evolution, primate development, physiology, and human behavior were just some of the disciplines represented. There were titles of a dubious scientific nature as well; books on psychics, ghosts, Bigfoot, Yeti, and the Lochness Monster made Gary cringe at his friends' bizarre tastes.

Gary's eyes widened when he saw the religious and spiritual texts. Books on Christianity, Taoism, Buddhism, and Judaism lay side-by-side in disheveled rows without any apparent organization; Z's stood with A's. Judaism mixed with Christianity and sprinkled amongst them were healthy doses of Buddhism and Taoism. There they stood, coexisting peacefully without fuss or muss. *Huh*, Gary thought, j*ust as it should be.*

An adjacent shelf was full of self-help texts on weight loss, happiness, wealth building, and getting laid. Gary scanned the spines and shook his head as he read out loud. *Feed Your Addiction; Get What You Want, The Origin of Species, The Law of Attraction, Chemistry 101, The Secret of The Tao?*

"What the Hell?" Gary whispered to himself. He was happy to see Bob taking an interest in spiritual matters, but it appeared as though he was searching and hadn't yet found the answers. Gary thought about offering spiritual advice, but remembered Bob was offended by conservative Christian beliefs.

Gary turned his attention to the room in which he and Doctor Robert Harris sat. It served as a library, complete with black leather chairs, and oak furniture sprawled out over a spacious open layout. A brilliant ornate carpet partially covered the hardwood floor and added a splash of color to an otherwise drab ambiance.

Off to his right, Gary saw a pool table, or more accurately, a billiard's table. On top of its pristine green felt sat several brightly colored balls frozen in midgame between two nameless and faceless players.

Gary shot an index finger in the direction of the table. "You play?" he asked his friend.

Bob shook his head and said, "Nope."

A new scent now grabbed Gary's attention. He breathed hard through his nose and inhaled a dark, earthy mix of furniture polish, leather and cigar smoke. Gary closed his eyes and imagined Bob lighting a cigar while reclining peacefully in his chair, a wisp of his short, white hair contrasting with the black leather, living the good life, or as good a life one could ever hope for.

Gary imagined owning this castle; he saw himself sipping Bourbon, a beautiful woman hanging on his arm and smoking a fine cigar. It was a pleasant vision, one that brought a smile to his face. When he opened his eyes, however, he saw the real owner sitting in front of him, sipping a drink and wearing a smug smile.

Gary shook his head. A big-ass house, a Tesla parked in the garage, and the beautiful Belle, no doubt lying naked in the upstairs bedroom—It was beyond the means of a retired two-year college professor. He and Bob weren't so different; were they? They had been professors at the same Catholic college, earning meager salaries, living paycheck-to-paycheck. Yet Dr. Harris' enjoyed retirement, living a comfortable lifestyle while Gary struggled. How did he manage this? Lucky bastard, Gary concluded.

A part of Gary was happy for his friend, or he pretended to be out of obligation. Another part was envious and more than a little jealous. Bob was smart; there's no denying that. Bob was also older and perhaps a bit wiser than Gary. More importantly, people liked Bob. They gravitated toward him and were drawn to his large personality and his infectious laugh. When Bob entered a room, it lit up and came to life. With Gary, well, his presence or absence was inconsequential, or at least that's how Gary felt.

Gary wished he could be that carefree, that likable, but he knew this was impossible. Since he was a boy, Gary felt awkward and different. Making friends was difficult for him and at times, painful.

Gary once again focused on the stacks of books. "All these books," he said. "Have you read them all?"

"Yes," Bob replied without hesitation or a hint of emotion.

"And what about the Bible? In this entire collection of yours, do you even own one?"

Bob jerked his head around and quickly scanned the book stacks. "Yes," he replied. "Many versions. Some, very rare. I believe there's one signed by Jesus Christ himself."

Gary rolled his eyes. "I'll get you one. I have extras."

"I have a Bible," Bob insisted.

"Perhaps you should read it."

"I have read it."

Gary raised an eyebrow. "You have?"

"Yes," Bob said. "When I was fourteen. I read the entire thing over a single weekend, cover-to-cover, starting with Genesis in the Old Testament and ending with Revelations in the New Testament. Sixty-six books in total if memory serves me right. Thirty-nine in the old and twenty-seven in the new. Is that right?"

Gary removed his wire-rimmed glasses and placed the earpiece into his mouth as he was in the habit of doing. Then he ran his hand over his short, dark hair while he contemplated Bob's claim to have read the entire Bible—in one sitting, and at age fourteen no less. Gary had yet to meet a person who had slogged through the entire text, reading scripture from cover-to-cover as if it were a seamy crime novel. Gary himself, a graduate of divinity school, had not read the bible in its entirety.

"Sixty-six?" Gary finally answered. "Yes, I believe that's right. What have you learned from it?"

Bob jerked his head back. "A lot," he said.

"Yeah? And do you have any questions for me?"

"Nope. I read it and understood it nicely on my own. But thanks anyway."

"So, what do you think?"

Bob paused a moment and cast his soft blue eyes into the far corner of the library as if his reply dangled from the vaulted-beamed ceiling that stood aloft.

"Well, Jesus was a good guy," Bob finally announced with a satisfied smile.

Gary nodded his head slowly and echoed his friend's sentiment. "Jesus was a good guy? Indeed. Is that all you got from it?"

"Oh, fuck," Bob said raising his voice in mock anger. "I didn't ask you here to preach to me. This is a non-fundamentalist-Christian-zone. No

Fuckin' Fundies allowed. I called it. Only science and spirituality are allowed in the Harris household. Here, have some more Bourbon."

Gary placed his hand over his half-full glass. "Oh, for Christ's sake, Bob, it's early morning; I don't need any more. I shouldn't be drinking. I have class soon."

"Jesus Fuck," said Bob. "You need a drink more than anyone else I know. C'mon, it'll loosen you up a bit." Bob moved forward with the decanter and tried to pour the liquid right through Gary's hand and Gary finally relented.

The two men eventually settled down and sat quietly across from each other while they sipped their drinks. Gary was in poor spirits before now, but the laughing and cajoling made him forget his worries. Bob had that effect on him even though the two were polar opposites; Gary was reserved and thoughtful while Bob was loud and crude. Gary thought Bob was a buffoon—a smart, funny and well-educated buffoon, but a buffoon, nonetheless. And while he infuriated Gary at times, it was Bob who pried Gary from his shell and made him feel good. They became friends despite or even because of their differences. With Bob, Gary didn't have to try. He could be himself. He could tell Bob anything, things he would not tell another soul, and he could always trust his friend to listen and to never judge.

"Remind me," Gary said. "Where did you get your degree from?"

"Undergrad, grad or Ph.D.?" Bob replied.

"Let's go with Ph.D."

"The University of Fucking Chicago," Bob announced with more than a hint of pride. "They split the atom there, ya know."

"Oh, now I remember," Gary said. "You've lived an interesting life, my friend. A professional ballplayer, a Ph.D. in physical sciences, a retired college professor—I wonder how many people can lay claim to all of that."

"Not many," Bob concluded with a smile. "Did I ever tell you how I struck out Thurman Munson?"

"You have, but it's a good story. Tell me again."

"Yeah, I struck him out," Bob said before shaking his head and downing the rest of his drink. "He died."

"Yes, I know."

"Plane crash. What a great athlete; what a loss."

"Yes," Gary agreed. "Very unfortunate, but how about you? How have you been, my friend?"

"I'm fine."

"The Cancer?"

"It's gone," Bob replied staring into his empty glass. "They cut it out. They cracked my chest open like I a fuckin' lobster and cut the tumors out; I take drugs to make sure it doesn't come back. I have a six-inch zipper-scar running vertically down my chest as a constant reminder. Would you like to see it?"

Gary held up his hand. "Thank you," he said. "Perhaps another time."

"Okay. Your loss."

Gary took a sip of his Bourbon. "I'm happy for you, Bob. You know you were in my thoughts and prayers."

"I know," Bob said nodding his head. "I know."

"I hope you don't mind—me praying for you."

Bob furrowed his brow. "Mind? Why would I mind?"

"Well," Gary reasoned. "I know you're not big on religion—my religion at any rate."

"Oh, I'm okay with Christianity. I'm okay with all religions. It's just that—well, what's become of it?"

"What do you mean?"

"I mean I don't even recognize Christianity anymore. What is it? I used to think it was a message of love, forgiveness, and kindness, but now I don't know what it is. Do you?" Gary didn't respond; he sat stone-faced while Bob ranted. "It's more akin to a conservative, right-wing, political movement than it is about the teachings of Jesus Christ. It's more about bashing homosexuals or protecting the second amendment than it is about spiritual truth. And where are people getting this shit from? Show me in the Bible where it says to arm thyself to thine teeth and protect yourself from thine enemy? C'mon, you're the expert. What book, what verse?"

Gary threw his palms up and shrugged his shoulders. "I cannot," he replied.

"C'mon," Bob said. "What's wrong with you? You're sitting there like a sad sack. Wave the Christian flag at me and tell me how much I need Jeeezus in my life."

Gary stared blankly at his friend. Bob was right to expect a more volatile reaction. The old Gary would have fought back. He would have defended his faith with a fury that undermined his placid appearance. Today, however, he sat slumped and timid as he sipped his Bourbon.

"C'mon," Bob persisted. At least call me an asshole or something."

"Well, you _are_ an asshole," Gary said laughing. "Make no mistake about that, but your assessment of Christianity seems reasonable. I don't have any argument with you, if I'm being honest."

Bob looked concerned. "Oh, shit," he said. "What's going on with you?"

"Nothing. It's just that I'm having a crisis of faith; that's all."

"Oh, no. I'm sorry to hear that."

"Don't be," Gary said taking another sip. "It's not such a bad thing, is it?"

"It's not?"

"Well, I don't know. For years, I was told what to believe, how to think and behave, and now I'm thinking for myself, that's all. It's just— it's just a little scary, you know, reexamining oneself, and asking what I believe and more importantly, why I believe it?"

"And why do you believe in what you believe?"

"That's just it," Gary said shaking his head. "I don't know anymore. I was brought up Catholic, and I guess I was too afraid not to believe for fear of burning in Hell and the Devil and all that. Perhaps I wouldn't get any Christmas presents if I wasn't a good Catholic, or a good little boy."

"So, you were raised Catholic?"

"Well, there's a story."

"Yeah?"

"Yes. I must have been seventeen or eighteen, there was this incident at my local parish."

"What kind of incident?" Bob asked.

Gary averted his eyes. He had a big mouth and sometimes let things slip. "Uh—it was nothing," he said. "I got into an argument with a priest. At any rate, I was fed up with Catholicism, but I was still very spiritual and very much into learning about God. So I latched on to this evangelical church in my hometown. Well, they had this Tuesday night bible study, and I decided to attend one day. They seemed very nice; we sang songs, read the bible and prayed. That sort of thing."

"Sounds riveting."

"Yes, well, it gets better. At the end of this Bible study, the leader, a pretty blonde named Lyndsey, closed the meeting with a prayer; she tells us that people have let her down, but God has never let her down. You know, the standard born again platitudes. Well, everyone else in the room nodded their heads in agreement, and I was like what the fuck is she talking about? God had always let me down, and I made the mistake of sharing my views with the room and telling them about all the times I've felt let down by God."

Bob laughed and clapped his hands rhythmically. "Ah," he said. "I love it, God has always let you down."

"I wasn't trying to be an asshole, Bob." Gary paused and finished his Bourbon before continuing. "I was young and opinionated and was expressing my feelings in a way that was honest and forthright. I just sat through an hour-long meeting where a group of young people closed their eyes and waved their hands in the air in praise of Jesus. I suppose many were sincere in their beliefs, but I also knew there were others who were frail and hurting and for whom praise to an unseen god rang hollow and felt trite. I knew this because I was one of those people, and that's why I said what I did, to keep things real and to give a voice to those who were too afraid to speak their own mind."

"So, what did they say?"

Gary's sweaty palms grasped the chair rest as he relived the incident. The memory was fresh in his mind causing a chill to race up his spine and his neck hairs to stand on end. He regretted telling Bob all of this, but he was in too deep to stop.

Gary's eyes turned black and vacant as he continued the story. "Well," he said. "The entire mood shifted. No one said a word; everyone just— well, they just stared at me. You would have thought I said Jesus was as fake as a three-dollar bill, or something."

"Wow, that must have been awkward."

Gary smiled. "Yes, it was," he said. "But it gets even more awkward."

"Yeah?"

"Afterwards, at the refreshment table, no one talked to me; no one even stood next to me. Instead, they huddled together and connived, jabbering like the little weasels they were. They were talking about me, the new guy, the stranger with the strange ideas. They made me feel like a real asshole just for expressing my feelings. I was ready to leave when I saw Lyndsey approach me. She was smiling, and I thought for sure she was going to offer up some kind words." Gary grimaced, and shook his head. "Do you know what she said to me?"

"No, what?"

"She said they had talked it over and decided I shouldn't come back."

"What? No shit?"

"No shit. I told Lyndsey, see, this is yet another example of God letting me down."

"And what did she say?"

"She said, no. This is an example of you letting yourself down."

"Jesus Christ," Bob said. "What a fucking bitch, and from someone who professed to be a Christian?"

"Yes, what a bitch alright."

"I hope you told her off."

Gary's hands were wet as he gripped the armrest tighter. He shut his eyes and had a bird's eye view of himself talking to Lyndsey. The pretty blond wore a big smirk, and was ogling him, waiting for his next move. He should have turned, he thought—turn and get out. No one would know. No one would care, except for him. He probably would never see these assholes again.

He didn't turn, however. He stood his ground, cocked his head, and lurched forward like a Cobra. He watched Lyndsey's pale skin turn three times lighter as drool ran down her cheekbone before falling off her chin in a single, sparkling strand.

When Gary opened his eyes, he saw the shock on Bob's face. Had he said too much? What did he say? It didn't matter now. It was out there and there was no taking it back.

The two friends sat silently for several seconds before Bob spoke. "For real?" he said. "You spit in that girl's face. Like spit, spit?"

Gary laughed and shook his head. "You know I was young and stupid, and angry, and, and… I regretted it as soon as it happened, even before it happened. God, I wish I could take it back."

"What did she do after that?"

"I don't know. She was no longer smiling; I remember that much. I just turned and walked out of there. Maybe I ran out; I don't remember."

"Holy shit, Gary."

"Yeah, I know."

"That blows my Thurman Munson story away."

"I know, right?"

"But I don't understand. This is how you turned evangelical, by spitting in a girl's face?"

"No, you idiot. About two weeks later, I was in a grocery store, and I saw someone from the bible study, not Lyndsey, but another girl, a plump blonde, green eyes. We spotted each other and there was this moment of recognition. I was embarrassed, so I turned and walked the other way, but she called out to me and I stopped. Then she approached and told me how sorry she was."

"How sorry she was?"

"Yeah. Can you believe that? She apologized for her Christian friends. She told me she had no part in their decision, and that she had tried to stick up for me. She said she had found another church and invited me to attend."

"Did you?"

Gary smiled. "I did," he said. "We went together, and these church people were much nicer to me; of course, I learned to keep my mouth shut by this time. We went every week, and attended Bible study, and this young lady and I became—well, we became sort of an item."

"Sarah?"

Gary nodded his head. "Yep, my future wife, Sarah."

"Oh shit. That's fantastic. Sounds like you owe Sarah a lot."

"I don't know where I'd be without her. Probably in a ditch somewhere I suppose." Gary placed his empty glass on the table. "More please."

"How is Sarah?" Bob said while filling Gary's glass.

"She's fine. She talks about you all the time. If I didn't know better, I'd swear she has a crush on you."

Bob smiled. "You better be careful because the feeling is mutual. Send her my love, will you?"

Gary nodded.

"Tell me about work," Bob continued. "Did the faculty get a cost of living raise yet?"

Gary smirked. "We get our contracts soon. I'm hopeful."

"How long has it been?"

"Four, five years? I don't know. I've lost count."

"Five years without a fucking raise. What a shame. I'm so glad I'm out of there."

Gary looked around the library. "Well," he said. "You seem to be doing well. The school must treat their retired professors better than their current ones. This place—well, I'm a little jealous."

"Jesus fuck," Bob scoffed. "Like I'm waiting for St. Mary's to help me. I'd be dead before they lifted a finger to help me."

"But how did you get all of this?"

Bob leaned in and said, "The answer to that question is why I invited you here."

Gary smiled and waved off his friend. "No, no, no," he said. "I'm okay. I don't need money. Sarah and I are doing fine. Well, fine enough I suppose."

Bob shook his head. "I wasn't talking about money," he said. "But of course, if you needed it. I would gladly help you."

"Then what is it?"

"I want to give you something, the ability to get anything you want out of life, and I'm not just talking about money. I'm talking about money, health, promotions, respect…" Bob paused dramatically, and a grin spread across his face. "Belle?"

Gary looked disgusted. "Oh for God's sake, Bob. Have you—have you not an ounce of decency in that body of yours, just an ounce of decency?"

Bob laughed hard and clapped his hands. "Ah, you know it's true, Gary. You know you have a crush on my wife. Don't deny it."

"Of course I won't deny it. Every man has a crush on Belle, some women too, and why wouldn't they? She's gorgeous. Besides, you like my wife so I should be able to like yours."

"Exactly."

"Where is your wife?" Gary asked.

"She's probably still sleeping."

"Aw, that's too bad." Gary looked at the imaginary watch on his wrist. "Well, I got an early class," he said rising from his seat. "I should be going."

"You sit down," Bob ordered. "I haven't even told you the reason why I invited you over."

"I thought you invited me over because we're friends and you enjoy my company."

"No, that's not it," Bob said laughing. "But seriously, what if you could have anything you want?"

Gary sat down and contemplated the question. "I would tell you I want more money," he said after a few moments.

"More money?"

"Well, of course, I could always use more money."

"Okay, let's stop there. What if I said you could have more money?"

"Oh for Christ's sake, this isn't one of those Amway scams? People at my church are always trying to—"

Bob waved Gary off. "No, you idiot. This is not Scamway. It's science."

"Science?"

"Yes. I devised a system that will help you achieve your goals, your aspiration, needs, wants, desires—anything."

"Is it legal?"

"Well, of course it's legal."

"I'm listening."

"Well, it works like this. Do you realize that anything and everything in this world, began as a thought?"

Gary shrugged. "Okay, I guess."

"Well, it's true. You owe your life to a single thought. Your dad thought about fucking your mom, and he did, and nine months later— well, here you are."

Gary buried his head in his hands and in a muffled voice said, "Yes, I'm well aware of how human reproduction works, Bob."

"Of course you do, but my point is this; we began as a thought. Agreed?" Gary nodded. "Good. Well, I devised a method to concentrate your thoughts, to magnify them if you will, make them more powerful than they would be otherwise. I call it the Seven Experiments."

"The Seven Experiments?"

"Yes."

"Is this what retirement does to you, Bob, turn you into a raving lunatic?"

Bob momentarily contemplated the question, but decided it warranted no further merit. "As the name implies," he continued. "There are seven in all. Each one builds confidence in your ability to manifest your thoughts into the material world, starting with very small things and gradually building to bigger things."

Gary held his glass to the light. "This is good Bourbon," he said. "Where did you get it?"

"Do you like it? I'll get you a bottle."

"Yes, yes I do," Gary said before downing the rest.

"So, what do you think?"

"I'm sorry?"

"About the experiments? Are you willing to give them a try?"

"Excuse me. I'm a bit fuzzy here. There are seven experiments and their purpose once again?"

"Look at it this way. Our thoughts are powerful, more powerful than what we give them credit for. I already cited the example of how we came into being. Now we can apply this concept to everything in our lives. My

Ph.D. started as a thought; so did my baseball career; you're a professor and a minister. All these things, everything you achieved or owned originated from a solitary thought, and this thought brought our world into existence. Do you understand this?"

Gary squinted his eyes and wrinkled his forehead. His brain was soaked in Whisky and he was having trouble following Bob's logic. Despite this, he did his best to play along. "I—I suppose," he said.

"Okay, good. This concept is nothing new. It's called attraction. Some people call it the law of attraction; even though it's not technically a scientific law, but the principle is sound—we humans attract things into our lives, both good and bad, through our thoughts."

"Okay?"

"Gary, your mind can give you anything you want."

Gary leaned in as he spoke. "Anything I want?" he said.

"I asked you before and I'll ask you again, what is it you want, Gary? And don't tell me money; that's a bullshit answer; everyone wants that. Tell me what you want. What does Gary Miller really want?"

A single word slipped past Gary's lips. "Power," he said. He didn't remember forming the word with his mouth. It was as though someone else spoke for him, and he merely heard it as a whisper.

"Power? That's what you want?"

"I don't know. Yes, I guess. I said it, didn't I?"

"Well, what if I said you can have that power?" Gary's eyes lit up. "Would you like to try it?"

"I don't know," Gary said gritting his teeth.

"What are you afraid of?"

Gary knew the answer to that question all too well. "Disappointment," he said. "It sounds like another empty promise; people make big claims, but seldom deliver."

"But this is not an empty promise. I created the experiments," Bob said pounding his index finger into his chest. "I was my own Guinea Pig. Everything you see in this house, in fact the house itself, the Tesla, my health, my life and my wife, came from these experiments. I owe everything—"

The double doors slid open and interrupted Bob. The two men immediately turned their heads and gawked at the stunning brunette walking towards them.

"Gary," the Brunette said smiling. "It's so nice to see you."

Gary sprang to his feet; his heart raced. "Belle," he said. "I'm sorry. Did we wake you?"

"No," Belle replied.

The two of them hugged, and Gary pushed his nose against the nape of her neck. He smelled lavender mixed with a hint of Cannabis; his body tingled, and he conjured an image of their nude bodies pressed together. After a long embrace, Gary reluctantly pulled away.

"I was trying to talk some sense into this ass," Bob said to his wife. "Maybe you can talk to him, Hon."

"Oh hush, you," Belle replied. "Gary, you let me know if he's bothering you. I'll take him over my knee."

Bob's face lit up. "Ooh. That sounds like fun."

"That's quite alright," Gary said to Belle. "I can handle your obstinate husband well enough."

"Well, just let me know if you need backup," replied Belle. "I have him on a short leash you know."

"That's probably a good thing."

"You're staying for breakfast, I hope?"

Gary shook his head. "No," he said disappointed. "I have a ten A.M. class. I really should be going."

"Oh, must you?"

"Yeah," Bob said. "I haven't even told you about the experiments. Call in sick."

"No. I can't," said Gary. "My students have a test next week. I need to prepare them."

"But Gary," Bob pleaded. "This could really help you."

"Of course. I'll be back. We can talk then."

"Well," Belle said. "I need to make breakfast for this old man. It was nice seeing you again, Gary."

"The pleasure was all mine," Gary said.

Gary turned to Bob and said, "See me out?"

When the two men reached the front door, Gary stepped outside, took a deep breath and exhaled a cloud of smoke into the February air. "God, this weather," he said. "I can't wait till spring."

"Summer will be here soon," Bob assured him.

"I know. I need the break; these students are starting to get to me."

"I know. I remember what it was like."

"Thank you for having me over, Bob. I do enjoy our talks, and I'm glad to see you are doing well."

"Thank you, Gary. I feel the same."

"I'll continue to pray for you."

"I'm counting on it."

"Well, I'll talk to you later, Bob. Goodbye."

Gary turned to leave, but Bob's voice stopped him. "Gary," he said.

"Yes?"

"Today, you're going to find a shiny penny. That's experiment number one."

Gary opened his mouth to protest but was cut short by the door closing in his face.

CHAPTER THREE

Gary's heels clacked against the decorative stone tile floor as he made his way to his office. The school's low enrollment kept the hallways empty and quiet these days.

Though he taught at St. Mary's for ten years, Gary never grew tired of its architectural beauty. There was nothing pedestrian about the campus. It was magnificent, and tasteful as any educational institution twice its size. Built in the mid-1800's from quarry-mined stone and fashioned after European gothic architecture of the 18th century, its structures were worthy of their Catholic tradition.

Two glass doors partitioned Christ the King Chapel from the hallway; to the left of this doorway stood a white-stoned Virgin Mary holding the baby Jesus. Although Gary was no longer a practicing Catholic, he hastily made the sign of the cross as he walked past. The gesture was a habit, a remnant of his youth where he spent Sunday mornings as an altar boy for St. James church. It was also a tribute to his late mother—a devout Catholic woman who was embittered by her son's defection to the evangelical church, an act tantamount to treason in some Catholic families, and the Miller household was no exception.

Gary looked through the glass doors and saw the dark sanctuary partially lit by an array of white votive candles. Someone had died, a student or a former student, he couldn't remember what the email had said; the candles were offered as a blessing to her departed soul. The chapel's interior, replete with stain-glassed windows, votive candles, religious statues, and hard wooden benches, brought back bittersweet memories.

Gary could see himself as a child wearing the altar boy's uniform, his white laced, oversized sleeves drooping at the elbow as he carried a wine-filled golden goblet towards Monsignor Callagollia. He smiled faintly and recalled the fear the Monsignor instilled in him and the other boys. Unlike the other diminutive priests, the Monsignor was a big man and physically imposing. Large, muscles swelled beneath his priest uniform like a heavyweight prizefighter.

And if there were any question as to his physical prowess, one handshake from the good father would erase this doubt forever. His grip was an iron vice, which left your hand numb and tingly several minutes after initial contact. Word on the street had the Monsignor working as a bouncer before entering the seminary. Everyone knew you crossed the Monsignor at your own risk. No one dared cross him.

When Gary was seventeen, and still a devout Catholic, the Monsignor caught him and another boy kissing on a pew in the empty church. The Monsignor lit into Gary with a string of profanity he had never heard before. It would have been hard to take from a normal citizen, but it was especially frightful coming from this supposed man of God. Gary's body quivered in the pew; he looked around for his mom, but she wasn't there, and she'd probably take the priest's side if she were.

It was Gary alone who was the target of the Priest's rage and not the other boy. Gary reasoned it might have been the age difference—he was, after all, six years older. But when Gary turned around looking for some help, the boy had vanished, and was nowhere to be seen. He was smart, Gary thought. He escaped before the storm.

When the Monsignor had finished his rant, Gary's body shook; tears ran down his cheeks. He was ashamed, and when he couldn't bear another moment, he bolted forward, aiming a forearm to the priest's jaw only to have it miss and land with a thud against his chest.

Several weeks passed. Gary's mom asked him about his depression and wondered why he didn't attend Mass. Gary could no longer ignore his feelings, so he went in and talked to the Monsignor. He explained that the other boy had kissed him and that it was an act of curiosity more than anything else. The Monsignor listened calmly, but he wasn't buying it. Instead, he explained that homosexuality was a heinous and unnatural act and he should seek God's forgiveness and resolve to never act on his impulses again. When Gary asked the Monsignor what he could do to fix things, he was told to go to the church, light a candle to the Virgin Mary and say one hundred Hail Mary's. *Christ*, Gary thought. One hundred Hail Mary's was ludicrous. The most he was ever asked to say was twenty, or twenty-five.

After much self-debate, Gary decided to make amends and perform his penance at the Virgin's alter. After about ten Hail Mary's he stopped and thought how ridiculous this was. How was praying the rosary going to help him? His feelings were his feelings and the only shame he felt came from the outside world, not his own personal convictions. Fuck this shit, he thought. Fuck 'em all.

Gary stared at the lit candles through teary eyes; He was mesmerized by the blurry, dancing flames. A thought popped into his mind. One candle is all it would take. Tip one over, and it would set the white cloth on fire. The flame would devour the Virgin; it would spread and fall to the carpeting setting it on fire. Within minutes, the entire church would be engulfed, and no one would know who had started it. If he were lucky, the priest would end up getting his just punishment for treating him so poor.

Gary stood up, wiped his eyes and made the sign of the cross out of habit. Then he left without acting on his impulse. He never returned to St. James Church.

The memory was a bitter one for Gary, but he forced a smile as he moved past the chapel, down a flight of stairs and through a long corridor towards his office. He walked past several closed doors before reaching the first open one. It belonged to his department chair, Ryan Rupprecht. Gary popped his head in and saw Ryan sitting behind his desk with his nose buried in paperwork. Gary's heart rate quickened, and his mouth grew dry as he raised his voice to speak.

"Hello, Ryan," Gary said tentatively.

Ryan slowly lifted his head and peered at Gary over his plastic-rimmed glasses.

"Oh, hello Gary. How's it going?"

Gary studied Ryan's face for a clue, a hint of cheer that may give him the answer he hoped for, but Ryan's blank expression, while friendly enough, gave nothing away.

"I was just wondering about our contracts," Gary said.

"They're done. They're in the Dean's office; you'll have to stop in and sign for it."

Gary paused and waited for him to expound, but Ryan was silent, and his face grew sullen. It was a subtle shift, barely perceptible to most eyes but still enough to tell Gary what he needed to know. Despite this, Gary persisted.

"And the raises?" Gary asked.

Ryan slowly shook his head while biting his lower lip. "Not this time," he said. "Without a balanced budget, the school couldn't give raises this year."

"No raises?" Gary repeated. "It's been five years. Well, I've got to go. I have a—"

"They were talking about doing something in March. If they get the budget balanced, they will offer small raises retroactively, but for now, I wouldn't count on it."

Gary smiled. "Yes, well maybe next year then?"

"Yeah, Maybe."

Gary did his best to hide his disappointment, but he wore his emotions on his sleeve. He turned to leave, but Ryan stopped him.

"I'm sorry," Ryan said. "You know none of us got raises. Enrollment is down, but the new administration is hopeful they'll have a balanced budget soon, and we'll start getting raises again. Okay?"

Gary's eyes narrowed, and his tone grew curt. "Oh yeah?" he said. "And how soon will that be?"

Ryan shrugged. "I don't—"

"And when we do get raises, how much will they be, two, maybe three percent if we're lucky?"

"Yeah, probably."

Gary felt the blood rushing in his ears. He knew he should stop but was powerless to do so. It had been building up for some time; the lousy pay, the mismanagement, and the ever-decreasing quality of the student population took their toll. Most days he managed his frustration. Some days he could not.

"It's funny," Gary continued. "The school always seems to have enough money for new construction and campus beautification. How much did the renovations to the student union cost, one million was it? What about the new field house? How many millions were spent on that?"

"Well," Ryan said. "A new union and field house will attract more students and increase revenue over the long term that will help pay for salary increases."

Gary was no longer able to force a smile. "Oh, yes. Of course, or it just might help pay for more renovations," he said. Gary turned to leave, but a pang of remorse stopped him. "Ryan, you will keep me informed of any overload opportunities, right? Sarah and I—we have expenses—we could use the extra money."

Ryan smiled. "You know I will, Gary."

"Thank you."

Gary took a seat at his desk and stared silently into the blank computer screen in front of him. Bob's Bourbon was slowly wearing off, but he still felt its pleasant aftereffects. He wasn't used to drinking so early in the morning, but he knew he could grow accustomed to it. It helped to calm his nerves and alleviate his ever-present anxiety.

A knock on the door startled him out of his trance.

"Come in," Gary said.

The door slowly swung open, and Brandon Roache, stepped in.

"Dr. Miller," Brandon said. "Sorry. The door was closed."

"Yes, come in, Brandon."

"But you have office hours now so—"

"Yes, Yes," Gary said while motioning Brandon into his office and towards the empty chair. "What can I do for you?"

Brandon walked in and sat in the chair next to Gary. "I had some questions for you; about class."

"Yes, of course. Let's see. You're in Intro. to Christianity, correct?"

"Yes, ten A.M."

"Ah yes, the one I should be prepping for," Gary said smiling.

"Oh, I'm sorry. I didn't mean to bother you."

"It's quite alright young man. I always have time for my students."

"You do?"

"Yes, of course. Now, what can I do for you?"

"Well, do you remember your lecture on moral theology last class?" Gary nodded. "Yes, well, I guess I'm a little confused. I was wondering if you were going to go over it before our exam?"

"And what confuses you?"

"Uh, well, I guess I don't understand how with one God and one Bible we end up with so many different views within the Christian faith?"

Gary smiled and nodded his head. "It's interpretation. Yes, we have the divine word of God, but God saw fit to give us a choice, to read scripture and interpret it for ourselves. Does that make sense?"

"Yes, but if the Bible is divine shouldn't everyone be reaching the same conclusions?"

"Well, first off there are not as many differences within the Christian faith as you might think."

"There isn't?"

"No. Not when it comes to the major issues." Gary crossed his legs and then leaned in close to Brandon while he spoke. "For example, Christians believe Jesus was both divine and human, and that he was the incarnate God sent to this earth to absolve humanity's sins and that he was crucified at Calvary for our sins, and that anyone who believes in him will have everlasting life. Agreed?"

"Yeah, I guess, but that's where the similarities end."

"No, I don't believe so. You're a Christian?"

"Yes."

"Okay, then, you and I can agree on things like murder, stealing and lying. They are sinful. And that love, kindness, and forgiveness are righteous. Right?" Brandon nodded his head. "See?" Gary reclined back in his chair with a satisfied posture.

"Yes, but what about all the other things?"

"What other things?"

"Like sex outside of marriage, or abortion in case of rape, or war, or liquor, or gambling, or—" Brandon paused for a moment and stared blankly out the window. "Or homosexuality?" he continued. "It seems like you can put ten Christians in a room, and you'll get ten different opinions."

Gary pursed his lips together; a slight smile waxed over his face. "Yes, it does seem that way, sometimes. I'll tell you what, Brandon. I'll be going over these topics in today's lecture. Then, if you still have questions..."

Brandon turned his attention back to the room and locked eyes with Gary. "You're a Minister?" he asked.

"Uh, yes. I'm ordained in the Baptist church."

"Well, I had some other questions too, they're sort of related to class, but they're more personal questions. I—I was wondering. Maybe not today—but could we make an appointment?"

"Yes, of course," Gary said. "My door is always open. You know that."

"I'm a Catholic."

Gary waited for his student to expound, but after a lengthy silence, he finally caught on. "Oh, well, that's okay, Brandon. I was raised Catholic, and besides, I'm trained to counsel individuals of all faiths."

Brandon smiled. "Oh—oh good," he said. "I was thinking about seeing the school's chaplain, Father Joe. Do you know him?"

"Father Joe? Yes, I know him. He's a good guy."

"I was thinking about seeing him."

Gary saw a lot of himself in Brandon; what the young man needed was a sympathetic ear stripped free of the company-line bullshit that priests are trained to spew.

"No, don't bother him," Gary said. "I mean, come and see me. I can help you. How about nine A.M. on Friday?"

"I don't have class then, so yeah, I can make it."

"Very good. I'll see you Friday."

"Well, actually, you'll see me in ten minutes. Religion class is about to start."

Brandon stood up from his chair and was ready to leave when Gary stopped him.

"Brandon," Gary said. "You're okay, right? I mean you're not depressed, are you? You have no intention of hurting yourself?"

"No," Brandon replied. "It's nothing like that. It's not that bad."

"Good. I'm glad to hear it. You know whatever it is; it's never as bad as what you think. Trust me; I know."

Brandon smiled. "I'll see you in class, Doctor Miller."

• • • • •

Gary wasn't in the habit of being late. Generally, he made it a point of arriving five minutes early to the start of his lecture.

"All right," Gary announced in a loud voice that startled his students to attention. "Open your texts to chapter three. Last time, we were discussing moral theology. Today, we're going to review the seven areas of applied Christian ethics. Does anyone remember what they are?"

Gary scanned the room and saw a generally disinterested audience staring into space or texting on their phones. A few students opened their texts and notebooks in search of an answer. An arm went up. It belonged to Dylan. Gary tried to ignore him but finally had to relent to Dylan's unwavering persistence. "Yes, Dylan?" Gary said in a monotone voice. "What is it?"

"Hey," Dylan said enthusiastically. "I beat you. Normally I'm late, but today, I'm on time, and you're late. What's up with that?" Dylan wore his giddiness in the form of a broad grin.

"Yes, Dylan. Congratulations, young man. Four weeks into the semester, and you've finally shown up on time. Everyone, let's give Dylan a round of applause." Gary led the hand clapping and was joined with a weak effort by a few of his students.

"Oh, I've been on time before. It's just that when I'm off my meds, I tend to have trouble getting out of bed in the morning."

"Dylan, if you know you need your meds to make it to class on time if at all, why do you ever stop taking them?"

Dylan shrugged but still wore his grin proudly. "I don't know."

"You don't know?"

"Nope."

Gary scanned his half-full classroom. He had a few exceptional students, but the class was mediocre at best. Many were underachievers with poor study habits and even worse attitudes. They had barely survived high school, and many could not hack the rigors of a post-secondary education. St. Mary's open enrollment policy scraped the bottom of the barrel looking for students to fill its classrooms, and because of this, the school developed the reputation as the second-chance college, a place where poor students could attend and earn a two-year degree.

"Okay," Gary continued. "Does anyone else have anything else to say, before we begin?"

Another arm went up. It was Emily Saunders, a pretty, but dull blonde who sat in the front row. "Dr. Miller," she said. "Are we still having the test on Monday?"

"There's a test on Monday?" Dylan said.

"No," Gary said. "I'm afraid I didn't go over Christian ethics well enough, so I'm pushing the test back to Wednesday. Monday will now be our review day."

A collective buzz permeated the classroom. When it died down, and all was quiet again, Gary began. "Okay, the seven areas of applied Christian ethics. Who can tell me what they are?"

Brandon raised his hand. "I wrote them down," he said before he was called on.

"That's fine," Gary said.

Brandon began reading from his notes. "Abortion, Alcohol, Divorce…"

Gary's attention drifted toward the window. There wasn't much to see outside except for the cold, gray campus covered in its February blanket of snow. It was a pleasant enough distraction while Brandon droned on. "…Celibacy, Homosexuality—"

As Brandon neared the end, Gary returned to the class; his eyes scanned the room, looking for a glimpse of life amongst the bored faces. He glanced down and saw a bright copper coin near his shoe. The room disappeared and grew silent as the shiny object seized Gary's attention. It drew him in like a beacon of light. He bent down, picked it up and held the coin up for examination. He flipped it once to check the date, and then flipped it again, and then once more for good measure. A strange feeling came over him as he recalled his conversation from this morning. His heart beat faster, and he felt a rush that he hadn't felt in a long time.

"Dr. Miller?" a voice said.

"Yes?" Gary replied, his eyes still glued to the coin.

"Was that right?"

"Uh, Yes, Brandon. That's quite right."

CHAPTER FOUR

When Gary arrived home that evening, he was greeted by a stray cat named Snowball. Gary's wife named him Snowball because of the white, downy fur that made the stray look like, well, a snowball.

During the day Snowball made himself scarce, preferring the dank quarter under the porch to the sunlight of open air. He would come out of hiding whenever he heard Sarah's footsteps pounding the porch boards from above. That meant suppertime.

Snowball owed his life to Sarah. As a newborn kitten, he and his unnamed twin sister had been viciously assaulted in a weed-whacking incident that left them both slashed and bloodied—the Miller's neighbor had unwittingly weed-wacked the stray kittens as they hid amongst the tall grass. After hearing their terrified shrieks, Sarah ran next door to see if she could help. Snowball's sister was too far-gone, but Snowball, while badly mangled, was still salvageable. Sarah rushed him to the veterinarian's, and by some miracle, his life was saved.

Sarah was an excellent cook and a kind, nurturing soul who used both assets to nurse Snowball back to health. Under Sarah's watch, Snowball gained weight and transformed from the scraggly bag of ribs he had once been into a healthy—if somewhat paranoid—cat. While Sarah was Snowball's true benefactor, it was Gary whom Snowball loved. It's hard to say why Snowball was attracted to his disinterested owner, but the feeling was pure, the heart of one animal gravitating towards the heart of another. Sarah never quite understood Snowball's affection for her husband, but she gladly welcomed it.

"Oh my, God," Gary shouted at the fury, white ball barreling towards him.

Snowball ignored Gary's rebuke. The cat clamped its teeth around a shoelace and held it firm between his teeth where it hung from its mouth like a Fu Manchu mustache. Though the routine had grown tiresome to

Gary—this, after all, occurred every day after work—he couldn't help but laugh at the mischievous Snowball.

"What is your fascination with my shoelaces, young man?" Gary said. Snowball looked up at Gary with his big, blue eyes and replied with a soft meow.

"It's no wonder, Sarah loves you so much," Gary said while patting Snowball harshly on top of its head.

Snowball closed his eyes and purred; he let go of the lace and escorted Gary to the front door, darting in and around footfalls, while artfully dodging Gary's hard heels. The death–defying dance would continue until Gary disappeared behind the front door. Snowball waited outside to see if Gary would reemerge. He never did. After a few minutes had passed, Snowball quietly retired to his dark space beneath the porch.

"Sarah," Gary called out. "Have you been feeding that stupid cat again?"

"His name is Snowball," a voice from the kitchen called back. "And no, I haven't been feeding it. He's quite capable of feeding himself."

Gary stepped into the kitchen and found his wife prepping dinner. He sniffed the air and recognized the aroma of garlic intermingled with Italian spices. Sarah was making spaghetti and meatballs, one of his favorite dishes.

"Well, Snowflake seems to have taken a liking to me. You know I swear that cat lies in wait every evening and then pounces on my shoes the moment it sees me."

"Snowball, Gary. His name is Snowball, and he has grown quite fond of you though I honestly don't know why."

"You should have named him striper or stripe. Remember, when he was chewed up by Johnson's weed eater?" Gary said laughing. "He had those red stripes running across his face."

"Yes, I remember. I'm the one that drove him to the vet."

"Yes, how fortunate for the little mongrel."

Sarah smiled. "How was work?"

Gary remembered the penny and took it out of his coat pocket. "Look," he said. "Look what I've found."

Sarah leaned in and studied the coin. Then she looked into her husband's green eyes and threw her hands in the air.

"It's a penny," Sarah said.

Gary's voice rose with excitement. "Yes, yes. It's a penny."

"Okay?"

"Yes, well, don't you remember? I texted you about the experiments."

Sarah knitted her brow and slowly shook her head. "No. You didn't text me about any experiments. In fact, you didn't text me at all today. You were very quiet."

"Was I? It's silly, actually. What's for dinner?"

Sarah didn't reply immediately. She crossed her arms over her chest and shook her blond curls. "No," she finally said. "You can't come home from work, hold a penny in front of me like it's the Holy Grail and then ask me what's for dinner."

Gary flashed a surprised expression designed to coax a laugh from Sarah. "No?" he said.

"No."

"Oh, dear. I'm afraid I just did." Sarah stood motionless and stared at Gary through two cold, grey slits. "Okay," Gary relented. "I'll explain."

"Yes, please do."

"Well, this morning, I went to see Bob. He had asked me over. You knew that. I told you that much."

"Yes," Sarah agreed. "You told me that, but what about the experiment?"

"It's silly, actually. I don't even remember everything he said, but it had something to do with getting things you want simply by thinking of it."

"What kinds of things?"

"Oh, I don't know. Anything, a new car I suppose."

"That's good. We need a new car. Ours is about ready for the junk pile."

Gary nodded his head. "Indeed."

"So, how does the penny fit into all of this?"

"Yes, I was getting to that. You know Bob is a scientist? Well, I guess he has to fill his free time with something useful, so he came up with these experiments—the seven experiments he called them—and he wanted me to participate in them, sort of as a guinea pig."

"And what did you tell him?"

"That it sounded like a bunch of rubbish. I told him that God provides me with what I need."

"Good for you."

"But it would be nice to have some extra money at the end of the month." Gary rolled the penny between his thumb and forefinger with the dexterity of a magician. Then he stopped, held the penny up to the light and studied it with exaggerated concentration. "He sort of forced the first experiment upon me, Sarah. Before I left, he told me I would find a penny today, and I found this one during my morning class."

Sarah tried unsuccessfully to stifle a laugh.

"What's so funny?" Gary demanded.

"I'm sorry, but it's a penny."

"What's wrong with it?"

"Well, I got news for you, Gary. It's going to take a lot more of those pennies to help us with our financial mess."

Gary closed his fist hard over the penny and shoved it back into his pocket before walking away. "Sorry to have mentioned it," he said. "I should have known better."

"Oh, come on. Why are you getting angry?"

"I'm not angry."

"Yes, you are. I can tell."

Gary opened the fridge and stared absentmindedly at the empty shelves. "I know it's only a penny, but it was something. He told me I was going to find a shiny penny, and I did."

"I'm sorry, Gary. I didn't realize it meant so much to you."

Gary turned to his wife and said, "It doesn't, really. I had a shitty day that's all."

"Tell me."

"Next year's contracts are out. Well, I got one. I've been asked to return for at least one more year. So that's good."

Sarah placed her hand over her chest. "Thank God."

"Yes," Gary agreed. "But no raise."

"Again?"

Gary shook his head. "No. The budget still isn't balanced."

Sarah's face turned flush. "Well, I suppose if they didn't overpay the President, then they would have a balanced budget. Sorry."

"No," Gary laughed. "You're right about that."

"It makes me angry, Gary. You have a doctorate's degree in philosophy and religious studies, and you work so hard, as hard as anyone, you and your colleagues, and just because you teach at a two-year college instead of a four-year college, you get so much less. It's not fair."

"Life isn't fair, Sarah."

Sarah gave her husband a sharp look. "That's just an excuse to treat people like crap."

Gary paused as he considered Sarah's comment. "Maybe," he said. "But there's no point in blaming others. I could have done something else, found another school to teach at, or something."

"You could have, but you love teaching at St. Mary's."

"Yes, but at what cost?"

Sarah stood quiet for a moment, hugging herself. "Put your arms around me," she said.

"What?"

"I'm your wife. I like it when you hold me. I like to be held."

"Yes, of course."

Sarah walked into her husband's outstretched arms; he pulled her in tight and gently lowered his chin to meet her head and breathed in her vanilla–honey scent. "You smell good," he whispered.

"I like being kissed too," said Sarah, her voice muffled by his corduroy lapel.

Gary took the cue and placed a kiss on Sarah's forehead. She lifted her eyes and smiled. After some hesitation, Gary kissed her full on the lips. "Thank you," Sarah said. "You should do that more often."

"You're right. I should." Gary rested his chin on Sarah's forehead, and when he spoke, his breath rippled through her hair. "It's not all about the budget you know."

"What?"

"I was told as much. A friend of mine in administration said there were other things, malfeasance, an old boys' network, and million-dollar expense accounts. Administrators were renting Cadillac's and Mercedes's while on conference trips. They were staying at four-star hotels, dining at the most expensive restaurants." Gary shook his head and laughed. "That's where our raises went you know."

"Yeah?" said Sarah with closed eyes. "What a shame, and a Catholic college too."

"It's not the Catholics; it's the people running the place, Catholics and Protestants alike. People are inherently bad, and greedy."

"Yes, I think so." Sarah patted her husband on the backside. "C'mon, dinner's ready."

"Yes, I could smell it when I walked in. Meatballs, right, and spaghetti?" Gary broke the embrace, walked to the stove and opened the lid of a large pan oozing with thick, tomato sauce. "You really are a good cook."

Sarah forced a smile. "Gary, I was wondering if maybe we could eat dinner and then make an early night of it." Sarah sauntered up to her husband and placed a gentle hand on his shoulder. She leaned in close and whispered in his ear. "What do you think?"

Gary smiled nervously at his wife. "And garlic bread? Did you make garlic bread too?"

· · · · ·

Sarah would drop subtle and not-so-subtle hints. Some evenings she'd wear a seductive top showing off her ample cleavage. If she went topless there would be a full-on assault that Gary would have to fend off. On this night, Sarah wore a flimsy t-shirt which highlighted two nipples outlined within the soft fabric. It was an open invitation to taste, an invitation few men would turn down.

It wasn't just her manner of dress that Gary could read. Sarah broadcast her emotions like a trail of breadcrumbs. Her half-closed, bedroom eyes, a provocative toss of her long, blonde hair or the slightest upturn of the lips told Gary she was in the mood. Tonight, all the non-verbal-cues were there. He was afraid of this. She wanted to go to bed early, and this was why.

Gary pulled back the covers on his side of the bed, and after giving Sarah a light peck on her cheek, he announced his intentions. "Good night, Sarah." Sarah let out an audible sigh. Her disappointment was palpable, but he remained unapologetic. "I have an eight am, tomorrow morning."

"So what?" Sarah argued. "So you have an eight am class tomorrow. Does that prevent you from making love to your wife?"

"I'm tired, Sarah. You know how I get. I'll be a wreck tomorrow. I'm a wreck now."

Gary felt Sarah's big toe running up the side of his leg. When she reached his crotch, she stopped. From there, Sara pressed down slightly using the pad of her big toe. "You feel that?" Sarah whispered.

"Yes—yes of course I do," Gary stammered. "How could I not?"

"You like?"

"I do."

Gary pulled Sarah on top of him and the two kissed hard before Gary pushed her off.

"Are you forgetting something?" he said.

"What?"

"The stockings?"

Sarah rolled her eyes. "Do I have to? Can't we just skip it for once?"

"Sarah, you know I love those black stockings. There's nothing wrong with it you know."

Sarah let out a sigh. She stood up, walked to the dresser, and removed a pair of black stockings from the bottom drawer.

"I'll be home late tomorrow," Gary said while Sarah slipped into the stockings.

"How come?"

"I'm going to visit Bob after work."

CHAPTER FIVE

Gary looked up and past Bob. As on his previous visit, he found himself drawn to the rows of books that lined the wall. They were a testament to Bob's incredible knowledge and seemed to mock Gary's own limited understanding of the world. Gary knew a lot about religion and God—well, religion at any rate.

Lately, however, he asked himself questions, the hard questions that challenged everything he once believed, and the questions that flew in the face of Evangelical Christianity. If there is a God, isn't this God responsible for science? Did he not create mankind to think and wonder and study and experiment and discover the world around him? Of course he did and if these discoveries contradict the Bible or two-thousand-year-old folklore, then so be it. We don't live in the dark ages. The world isn't flat. Man can fly; we've conquered space and the moon; Mars is next. Gary's mind awoke to new possibilities, and these possibilities both challenged and excited him.

Bob's voice stirred Gary from his daydream. "One thousand volumes," Bob announced proudly.

Gary's eyes grew wide. "One thousand? For real?"

"Yup, and another thousand in storage. I couldn't fit them all. I'm going to have the Amish build more for me. They're very good at carpentry you know."

"Yes, I know. And you say you've read them all?"

"Yes. Shakespeare, Kipling, Twain, Tolstoy, Hemmingway, Bronte, Shelly, Verne. Many are first editions."

"You have a remarkable mind, my friend."

Bob smiled. "Yes I do, plus a powerful thirst for knowledge. I want to know things, Gary—how things work, and how the world works, and the universe. I want to know what these authors knew." Bob scanned the rows of books. "Those authors, Gary, they had knowledge, intelligence, wonderful stories to tell, and a treasure trove of art stored deep within them." Bob paused a moment to reflect. "And now, by reading their work, I have it. It's all inside me. You see?"

"Yes, I see that."

A broad smile waxed over Gary's face. He reached into his pocket, pulled out the coin and slapped it onto the coffee table. It resonated with a loud clack that reverberated throughout the library leaving a tin echo in its wake.

Bob, laughed uncontrollably, his body shaking in his leather chair. "See?" he said. "See, you Somnabitch?"

"I see a penny," Gary relented. "I see that much."

"But you're still not convinced?"

"I am not."

"And yet here you are presenting me with this penny, a mere coin hardly worth anyone's time?"

Gary leaned back in his chair. He knew a penny wasn't about to change anyone's life let alone his and yet this coin, well, it made him think. In fact, he could barely concentrate on anything else. Even while making love to Sarah, he couldn't get his mind off the damn penny. Finding it proved nothing to him; people find penny's every day. Most never bother picking them up. But the mere suggestion he would find it, coupled with the fact that it came true, had piqued his curiosity. In fact, he was beyond curious; he was obsessed.

"Well," Gary replied trying to sound nonchalant. "Let's say I couldn't stay away from the stimulating conversation you provide."

Bob smiled and nodded his head. "Would you like Belle to fetch us some coffee?"

"I'd like some coffee, but don't bother Belle. I can get it myself." Gary made a motion to stand up. "Where's the kitchen?"

"Sit down. She won't mind, and she'll be happy to see you."

Bob reached out to his left and grabbed hold of a thick, gold silk chord hanging from the wall. He gave it a quick, jerk and then sat back with a satisfied expression.

"What's that?" Gary said, pointing to the chord.

"You'll see."

A few silent and awkward moments passed before Belle entered through the double-doors and sauntered up to where the men sat. Out of habit, Gary stood up and was rewarded with a warm hug and a kiss on both cheeks. He breathed deep anticipating a reward of sweet Jasmine, but instead was jolted by the skunk-like odor of Cannabis. It took him off guard at first, but his smile returned as he felt Belle's soft bosom pressed tight against his chest.

"Gary, it's so nice to see you," Belle said.

Gary's eyes traveled the length of her neck, stopping at the crevice formed by her plump breasts. He stole a glance, then quickly averted his eyes so as not to appear conspicuous.

"Ah, Belle," he said. "I told your husband not to bother you."

"Oh, nonsense. I'm glad he did. I'm always glad to see you, Gary."

"Honey," Bob interrupted. "Would you be kind enough to bring us some coffee?"

"Oh, and you'll join us too," Gary said to Belle. "We're going to discuss your husband's little project."

Belle smiled and gave her husband a questioning look. "Well, I was actually thinking about heading out and doing some shopping. Carnahan's has a sale on blouses."

"Do you need my credit card?" Bob said.

"I already have it. I'll make some coffee before I leave."

Gary and Bob watched intently as Belle turned and strolled out of the room. "Honestly," Gary said as he returned to his seat. "We can get our own coffee."

"What a fine ass she has," Bob said with an approving smile.

Though he was inclined to agree with his friend, Gary rolled his eyes and shook his head. "Jesus," he said.

For the second time that evening the room quaked with Bob's sharp cackle and clapping hands. "Ah, Gary. You should see the look on your face."

"Really?"

Bob's face abruptly grew stern. "You know I fucked that ass."

Gary's ears perked up. He never had anal sex, but he was always intrigued by the possibility. It was the one thing he wanted to try with Sarah, but her conservative attitude made its reality doubtful, so he simply never tried.

"For Real?" Gary said.

"Yep, it's true. I stuck my cock right up her ass."

"And she likes it?"

"Oh, she loves it. It makes her come, and then she howls like a coyote."

"A coyote?"

Bob nodded his head. "Oh yeah. When she comes with my dick in her pussy, she's loud, but in the ass…" Bob paused, looked side-to-side and then whispered, "…the walls shake."

"Does it hurt her?"

"Well, you gotta use lube. Have you never tried it?"

"I've never had that pleasure."

"You should."

"Bob, may I ask you a rather personal question? How often do you and Belle make love?"

"Every day," Bob answered without hesitation.

"Every day?"

"I fuck Belle every single day, sometimes twice a day."

"Really?"

"Yes. Why do you ask?"

"Oh, I don't know. Just curious is all."

"And how often do you and Sarah have sex?"

"Well, I can tell you it's not every day."

"No? Sarah is cute. She's got big tits like Belle."

"She has a big belly," Gary added.

"That's okay. People can lose weight."

"They can gain weight too. When we were first married, Sarah was pleasantly plump, but she's been gaining weight every year after that. I mean, I don't mind so much, but she has lost her shape."

"Does she like sex?"

"She loves it."

The two men sat silently for a few moments before Belle walked back into the room. "Your coffee is brewing," she told Bob. "I'm off to do some shopping now."

Belle walked over to Bob and planted a kiss on his lips while Gary watched intently. An image of the couple having sex flashed into Gary's mind. He was a fly on the wall watching Bob standing behind Belle.

"Goodbye, Gary," Belle said.

"What?" Gary replied. "Oh yes, goodbye, Belle."

After Belle left, Gary exhaled a huge pent up breath. He turned to Bob and said, "Okay, these seven experiments, tell me more."

"Well, you manifested a penny, so that concludes the first experiment."

"What do you mean manifested? I found a penny."

"That's just it. The pennies are there; they always have been. You never took notice, not until I planted the thought in your brain." Gary stared blankly at his friend. "You see," Bob continued. "All the things you ever wanted, everything your heart desires, already exist. They're right here, beneath your nose. You just needed a mechanism to train your mind and bring them forth."

"The experiments?"

"Exactly."

"I still believe its nonsense, you know."

"And yet here you are, sitting in my library wanting to know more."

"What do I have to lose?"

"Nothing. Not a goddamn thing. Shall we continue?"

Gary clasped his hands together and lowered his head. "I am your servant Dr. Harris."

"No," Bob corrected him. "That's the thing, the Universe is your servant. It is here to serve you."

"Here we go," Gary said rolling his eyes. "Can you kindly leave out your spiritual mumbo jumbo? I'm a Christian. I am here to serve God. I don't believe in the Universe. I believe in God."

Bob waved his hand. "Call it what you wish, God, the Universe, Allah, Eloah, Jesus Christ. It really doesn't matter; by any other name, they all lead back to the same source."

"Yes, but I'm here to serve God. He is a good God, a just God."

Gary cringed at his own reply. Words that once felt so Godly and righteous now rung hollow and sounded trite.

"Yes, I believe that too," Bob said. "But I don't think you realize just how good he is. You've been underutilizing him all this time. You can serve God if you wish, but he will serve you too."

"I pray to God. Lord knows how much I've prayed."

"Prayer is fine, but my experiments differ from common prayer by tapping into the power of your mind; you don't ask the universe for what you want; you tell it what you want."

"Oh, God," Gary said with a pained tone. "This is blasphemy."

"It's not blasphemy. It's simply utilizing this power that both you and I believe in. Right?"

Gary shrugged. "I'm not so sure."

"Look, you worship Jesus, right?"

"Well, of course I do. I'm a Christian."

"Okay, then, he's the perfect example. Jesus Christ himself tapped into the power of the universe—or God, or whatever you want to call it—over two thousand years ago."

"Yes, but he was Christ. He was God. He didn't need to tap into anything."

Bob's face broke into a broad, eat-shit grin. "Except for Mary Magdalene."

Gary stared at his friend and shook his head coldly from side-to-side. Bob pointed at him and exploded into a chorus of laughter and hand clapping.

"Oh God, I knew this was a bad idea," Gary lamented. "Sarah—she tried to warn me, but I wouldn't listen."

"Oh my God," Harris said after finally regaining control. "Sorry, man, but you set me up."

Gary looked at his friend with a mixture of disgust and intrigue; then he took a quick glance at his imaginary watch. "Oh, look at that," he said. "I must be going. Give me a rain check on the coffee, old man."

"Ah, ah ah. You sit down. I'll behave. I promise."

Gary settled back into his chair and drew a long breath. "Continue," he said.

"Just think about this, Gary. When Jesus Christ stepped out of the boat and onto the sea, what held him up?"

"God?"

"Belief," Bob announced. "Or call it faith or call it whatever you like. But I'm telling you Christ knew he could walk on water and it was this belief that allowed him to do so. Do you think that Christ had any doubt, even a smidgen, that he would not be able to walk on water?"

Gary knew what Bob wanted him to say, but the old Gary, the part of him that clung to the belief of a divine Christ was uncertain. If he understood his friend correctly, Bob wanted him to believe the impossible—that a man who was not a God, could walk on water through simple belief alone.

"I don't know," Gary said shaking his head. "Probably not."

Bob sat at the edge of his seat and spoke with hands. "Probably not? Most definitely not. Every fiber of Christ's being knew that when he stepped out onto the water, it would hold him up and that he could walk across it just as you and I can walk across this floor."

"Yes, Bob, but Christ was divine. We are not."

Bob pointed at Gary. "No," he said. "We are all divine."

"But we're not divine. We're human. We're not God."

Bob sat up in his chair and recited a bible passage verbatim. "Jesus answered them, is it not written in your law, I said, you are gods? If he called them gods, to whom the word of God came, and the scripture cannot be broken; say you of him, whom the Father has sanctified, and sent into the world, you blaspheme; because I said, I am the Son of God?"

Gary felt lightheaded and the library seemed to be spinning. He was familiar with the verse, but Bob's robotic recitation and Gary's swimming brain made it impossible to comprehend. "What?" Gary said.

"Translation, we are Gods. Jesus was answering the Jews who accused him of blasphemy for calling himself, God. He was simply telling them that God himself declared us Gods so that we are all gods, you, me, Jesus, everyone."

Gary sat quietly while he contemplated Bob's claim. His instinct told him to argue. After all, calling oneself God flew in the face of evangelical doctrine. But his fading convictions made arguing pointless, and besides, Bob was the one with the big house and Tesla. Gary remained silent and listened.

"That's all this is," Bob continued. "We're tapping into this power that exists all around us by strengthening our belief, our faith that all things are possible."

"Like walking on water?"

"Like walking on water, turning water into wine, good health, money, success—anything you want, actually. Well, there it is."

"And this won't damn you to Hell, or me, or everyone we know?"

Bob laughed. "No, of course not. That's just crazy talk. There is no heaven. There is no Hell."

With a stone-cold expression and a deadpan delivery, Gary said, "Fine. What's experiment two?"

Bob laughed and clapped his hands raucously, and rhythmically. "So, you're willing to move ahead?"

"I suppose. What do I have to lose, only my eternal soul to the eternal damnation of eternal hellfire I suppose?"

"Well, that doesn't sound so bad, does it?"

Gary covered his face with his hands and said, "Oh God, what fools these mortals be?"

"Ah Shakespeare, Midsummers Night's Dream. I have that in my collection too."

"Of course you do."

"So, you're ready for experiment two?"

"Lay it on me."

"Green cars and yellow butterflies."

Gary waited for Bob to expound but was greeted only with a broad, stupid grin. "Green cars and—okay, what?"

"Green cars and yellow butterflies," Bob repeated. "In the next forty-eight hours, I want you to take note of the number of green cars you see. Count them."

"Why?"

"Because what we expect to see will actually appear in real life. So if you look for green cars, that's what you're going to see."

"Yes, but I see green cars all the time."

"Exactly. But you never pay attention to them. So now I want you to open your eyes and see how many there are, keep a running total. Write the number down and remember this. If it works for green cars, it will work for everything else."

"Okay?"

Bob was now sitting at the edge of his seat. "You see, Gary. There are so many things, wonderful things all around us, and all we have to do is open our eyes to them. Once you're fully aware of the world you live in, you'll see all sorts of things; blessings will appear as if by magic. You'll be able to pluck them from thin air like picking apples from a tree."

"And yet they were there all along?"

"Exactly."

"Okay, that makes sense, but you said something about yellow butterflies?"

"Ah, yes, experiment two is a two-parter. After the green cars, I want you to look for yellow butterflies. You have forty-eight hours to find both."

Gary sat stunned, and motionless for several seconds before replying. "It's February," he announced.

"Yep."

"Okay, its like twenty-degrees out there. There are no butterflies, yellow or otherwise to be had."

Bob shrugged his shoulders. "That's experiment two. Take it or leave it."

Gary drew a long breath and then blew it out forcefully between his lips. "Why not?" he said.

"Good, you have forty-eight hours to complete the experiment. Record your findings."

"That's it? All I have to do is look for green cars and yellow butterflies in the next forty-eight hours? This seems a bit underwhelming."

"And then record your findings. Do you own a journal?"

"No, I do not."

"Get one. It will help you manifest bigger things when we get to them."

"And all this will help me get what I want?"

"It will my friend. We're slowly building confidence in your ability to manifest. We started with a penny. Now we move to something bigger; next time it will be bigger still. With each successful iteration, your faith will grow-and-grow until you can visualize anything and get it."

"A pay raise?"

"Oh," Bob exclaimed. "Much bigger than a mere three percent cost of living raise."

"That three percent raise would come in handy right now."

"I know my friend. As I told you before, I've done these experiments myself, and I can tell you, the very room we're sitting in, in fact, my entire house was visualized in my mind even before I set eyes on it. I even drew pictures of it."

"You drew pictures?"

"Yes, of the house I wanted. I wrote it down in my journal."

"And?"

"And? You're sitting in it. This is the exact home I visualized."

Gary opened his mouth and cocked his head to the side. "Really?"

"Here, I'll prove it." Bob stood up and hobbled over to a roll top desk sitting across the room. He opened one of its drawers and returned with a book. It was bound in black leather and had a latch mechanism, which held the cover shut. Bob undid the latch and slowly leafed through its pages one at a time, reading for a brief moment with a studied expression and sometimes breaking into a grin. After several moments, he found what he was after.

"Here it is," Bob said handing the journal to Gary. "My entry from June 2015, one year before my retirement, and one year before I purchased this house."

Gary took the journal from Bob and started reading. Sure enough, the entry for that date laid out a detailed description of a two-storied house, complete with a twin peak roof, a large kitchen, and a library. As Gary read, a surge of electricity ran down his spine. The passage described Bob's house in eerie detail.

"So," Gary said after he finished reading. "You wanted this house, got the money, and had it built to your specifications?"

"I didn't build anything," Bob said shaking his head. "I saw it listed, and bought it, as is." Gary stared blankly into his friend's face. "Did you read the square footage I asked for?"

"Yes," Gary said flipping back to the page. "It says here, twenty–seven hundred square feet."

"Guess how big this house is."

"No way."

"On the nose," Bob said with a broad grin. "The basement makes it closer to four thousand square feet, but that isn't counted in the total square footage. Did you read how many bedrooms I asked for?"

"I believe it was four."

"It was six and guess how many bedrooms this place has."

Gary's face broke into a grin. "You're kidding me?"

"I kid you not."

"Wow, that's remarkable. It's a little spooky even."

Bob took a seat and then waved a hand in front of his face. "Oh that's nothing," he said. "I could tell you stories that would make your head spin and your hair stand on end."

"But still, I can't help thinking this is somehow wrong."

"Wrong?" Bob said. "What's wrong with having nice things, that I pay my bills, and have few bucks left over at the end of the day? No, there's nothing wrong with that. We're good men my friend. We deserve it, and much more if truth be told."

"But if it's that simple, why doesn't everyone do it?"

"See, that's where the experiments come in. Everyone can and does manifest on one level or another; we visualize the house we want, the job, the relationship and we get some parts of what we saw. Problem is most people lack the faith or the visualization skills needed to master this technique. Did you see my sketches?"

"I'm sorry. Your sketches?"

"Yes. Keep turning the pages."

Gary flipped the page until he came to the first illustration. It was a pen and ink drawing of the Harris estate from the outside. He immediately recognized the perimeter brick fence, and its black, wrought iron–gate.

On its roof sat two brick chimneys, which gave the mansion its unique silhouette against the Western New York sky.

As Gary studied the drawing, he ran his hands over the dark lines and crosshatch that gave the illustration depth and dimension. This was no amateurish drawing, he thought. This was a remarkable illustration crafted by the hand of a polished artist.

"You drew this?" Gary asked. Bob nodded. "I didn't know you could draw like that."

"As scientists, we often have to detail our findings with illustrations. I do my best."

"I'm impressed."

"Turn the page."

Gary leafed through the pages, and a wave of expert drawings, floor plans, and detailed studies of the home's interior started to emerge. They were remarkably accurate to the house in which he sat.

Gary came to a drawing of the library, the very library in which the two men now sat. He moved in for a closer look and squinted. Then his eyes scanned the room, before returning them to the journal. He did this several more times to compare Bob's depiction of the library to the actual room. The resemblance was uncanny; the library's books, artwork, and furniture were clearly depicted in the drawing, right down to the position of each chair, table and artifact. In fact, it was a perfect match. Gary studied the picture for several minutes making frequent comparisons to the illustration and real life while shaking his head in disbelief.

"Surely, you drew this after you got the house," Gary said.

"Look at the date," Bob replied. Gary read the date silently in his head. "See? A full year before I knew this place even existed. Now, what do you have to say?"

Gary shook his head from side–to–side. "I don't know what to say."

Gary turned the page and saw another depiction of the library. This one was drawn from a bird's eye view looking down. He recognized the two leather chairs facing each other and the big oak coffee table separating them. Gary placed his nose a scant inch away from the page; he squinted hard, and his heart pounded beneath his chest. He made out two dark figures sitting and facing each other; in one chair sat a man with a beard. The man resembled Dr. Harris. In the other chair, sat another man who appeared to look very much like himself. Both men postured towards each other as if engaged in a serious talk. Gary gasped and then allowed the journal to slide off his lap where it landed with a thud on the hardwood.

"What's wrong?" said Bob.

Gary took a moment to regain his breath and wipe the perspiration from his forehead. "Nothing," he said. "I just got—"

"Gary, can I confide in you?" Bob interrupted.

"Of course."

"You know my lung cancer? I healed myself."

Gary bent down and retrieved the journal from the floor. "You did what?"

"Using the seven experiments, I healed myself of Cancer. In another journal are drawings of my lungs. I used colored pencils, and drew gorgeous, pink, and healthy lung tissue—over-and-over—and those are the lungs that are inside me now."

Gary's head spun. He could hardly believe what he was hearing or seeing. Either his friend had gone mad, he had, or they both lost their minds. He wasn't sure which it was.

"Yes, but you had surgery," Gary argued. "You took medicine. That's what cured you."

"The tumors, they came back, with a vengeance. The doctors told me six months."

"Six months?"

"Six months before I left this earth, but I wouldn't allow it." Bob balled his hand into a fist and held it to his face as if he were picking a fight. "I grabbed that fuckin' Cancer by the nuts, and I squeezed tight," he said in a shaky voice. "I squeezed the shit out of it. Do you understand me?"

"That's a remarkable story, Bob."

"Remarkable, and true."

"And you think this will work for me too? Do you think I can have what you have?"

"In time, yes. But we have to start out small and then build from there." Bob winked and smiled at his friend. "Green cars and yellow butterflies, Gary."

"Green cars and yellow butterflies," Gary repeated. "Got it."

"I'll get us our coffee."

CHAPTER SIX

The trees were barren, and the ground covered with a thick layer of white ice and blue snow. Winter seemed to last forever in Western New York, but on this day, however, temperatures hovered at a balmy forty degrees—quite nice for February.

It was Saturday; Gary and Sarah were driving on a desolate country road that led to their destination, the Chautauqua Institution. The Institution was a hotspot, their playground of sorts, a four-and-a-half-acre gated community populated with Victorian homes, quaint shops and expensive restaurants, which they could rarely afford. During the summer, it hosted live popular entertainment, the ballet, the opera, theatrical plays and acclaimed speakers. It was an art and cultural mecca, which catered to wealthy visitors from around the world. Guests lived and played here for three months out of the year, but it would be quiet today and nearly empty, the summer season long past.

Gary hardly ever whistled, but today he was lighthearted, free of the classroom and its accompanying cares. The song was badly out of tune and he knew it, but he didn't care, and Sarah had no complaints. Gary had hope. Tomorrow, he would deliver a sermon at the first Baptist church, but for now, he was content, relaxed and happy as he watched the scenery race past his car window.

"Chautauqua will be lovely today," Sarah said. "Don't you think?"

Gary's eyes darted from left-to-right as he studied the road. Traffic was light, but every passing car seized his attention, and caused his heart to beat faster. He heard his wife plainly enough, but he was preoccupied.

"Ah, there's another one," Gary announced while pointing to an oncoming car. "That's five, no, six—the sixth green car we've seen today. Don't forget, Sarah, six so far."

Sarah leaned back in her seat and took a deep breath that swelled her chest like a robin's breast. She glanced out the passenger window before replying in a monotone voice. "It's the seventh green car we've seen, and who cares? They're all over the place. Detroit must have manufactured a million green cars this year alone."

"Japan."

"Japan, Detroit, whatever."

Gary glanced at his wife and smiled. "Oh, I know It's silly, but it's kind of fun. Don't you think?"

Sarah rolled her eyes. "I'm glad it's warm. It will make for a pleasant walk. Do you think the lake ice will be melted?"

"Oh, no. It's much too early for that. It's only February."

"I'm glad you suggested this. It's getting so stuffy in the house. The fresh air will do us good."

Gary's eyes turned dark and intense. "It's the butterflies that will be the challenge," he said in a low voice. "Yellow butterflies."

"And where do you suppose butterflies will be at this time of the year? There are none. They're all dead, or hibernating, or whatever butterflies do in the winter."

"Yeah, well that's the challenge, isn't it? I think they migrate."

"What?"

"The butterflies—they move south for the winter just like birds."

"They do?"

"Well, I'm no expert, but that would make sense."

"Yes, that would make sense," Sarah said laying her head back and melting her eyes shut.

"The way I see it," Gary continued. "We won't see actual, real-live butterflies."

"No?"

"No. It will probably be a glass ornament in a shop window, shaped and colored to look like a butterfly."

Sarah turned her head sharply towards Gary. Her eyes were wide and piercing straight through her husband. "Is this why you suggested we go to Chautauqua today?" she said in an accusing tone. "To look for your butterflies?"

"Well no," Gary answered. "I just thought it would be nice to get out of the house."

"Yes, nice to get out and look for your butterflies."

"Oh, what difference does it make? We'll have so much fun. We'll walk the grounds and then go to Stedman Corners afterward, for some coffee or even dinner. Would you like that?"

"Yes," Sarah agreed. "That would be nice."

Gary spotted several more green cars in the next twenty minutes. He had turned it into a game, a fun diversion from the ordinary. He was ordinary, and he couldn't think of anything worse.

"Are we up to nine?" Gary said.

"That's ten," Sarah replied. "And honestly, who cares?"

Par for the course, Gary thought. Sarah was never for anything that smacked of silliness. She was the practical one, the one with the even keel. Gary, on the other hand, wanted to be that boy again, free from bills and worry and responsibility. The butterflies—well, they were his hope.

"I care," Gary said. "Bob explained it all to me."

"Did he?"

"Yes, yes he did. He said we attract things into our lives, good things and bad things too, with our thoughts, and that by commanding our thoughts we can better command our lives."

"Isn't that the law of attraction?"

"Yes, that's it," Gary said enthusiastically. "Bob explained it's not actually a scientific law, but that it does work. Problem is most people don't have the right mindset. They don't fully believe in their ability to manifest, and so they fail. To make it work, one must have perfect faith."

"Faith in seeing green cars?"

"Yes, and yellow butterflies, and pennies. I believed I would see green cars, and well, I've seen them. Lots of them. I was looking and, there they were all around us."

Sarah stared silently out of her passenger-side window. She took in the passing scenery as it flashed by in stretches of black and white broken up by an occasional pastel-colored farmhouse. Gary noticed his wife had fallen flat, her energy drained.

"You think its nonsense?" Gary said.

Sarah sighed. "Well, it's nothing new. You can call it the law of attraction or the power of positive thinking. I don't disagree with it. It's good to have positive thoughts I suppose."

"I hear a but in your voice."

"I don't know, Gary. Whatever happened to prayer?"

"Nothing's happened to it. I still pray."

"Do you? I don't see you pray anymore."

"I pray at church," he insisted. "I lead prayers even. I don't know; I've been praying my whole life it seems."

"And?"

Gary took his eyes from the road momentarily and smiled sadly at Sarah. "Exactly. And what?"

"It's done you no harm. You have your health, and we have each other." Sarah placed her hand on Gary's thigh and rubbed it reassuringly.

"Existing is more like it, while others around us flourish."

"Well, you certainly didn't choose to be a minister or a teacher to become rich, did you?"

"I picked the ministry to serve God, and I like to think teaching serves him as well. I would like to get paid for my efforts that's all."

"You do get paid."

"Yes," Gary smirked. "A pauper's sum. You deserve better; we deserve better."

"We pay our bills, we own our house—oh that reminds me, the village taxes are due at the end of the month."

Gary took his hands off the steering wheel and clasped his head in mock anguish. "Ah," he said. "See? That's what I mean. Every time I think we're doing fine, that we're finally caught up, finally ahead of the game, the village taxes are due, or the school taxes, or the town tax, or something. And for what? Why do we even pay taxes? Remember last fall, those teenager hooligans were messing around in our backyard? Instead of going out there with a baseball bat like I had a right mind to, I decide to do the right thing and call the police. When did the cops show up?"

"They never showed up."

Gary threw his hands in the air. "Exactly. They never showed up. I have no idea why I'm paying taxes, and don't get me started on the schools."

"Put your hands back on the steering wheel and believe me, I won't."

"I mean, what are they teaching kids nowadays? I get them as freshman in college, and they can't write the most basic sentence."

"Are you done?"

"Yes," Gary sighed. "I'm quite done."

"I think you need to focus on other things, Gary."

"Like?"

"Like me."

Gary realized he was ranting and patted Sarah's hand. "How much was it? Eight hundred?"

"No," Sarah replied, her face contorting into a forced smile. "This was the big one. Twelve hundred."

Gary bit his lower lip and nodded his head. "Twelve hundred," he repeated.

"I would get a job; you know, just to help out, but with my volunteer work at the church there isn't enough hours in the day."

"Yes, we need to talk about that, Sarah."

"Perhaps I could do some—"

"Ah look," Gary said, pointing to an oncoming truck. "That's green. Well, sort of green. Perhaps bluish green? I'm counting it. How many is that? Seven?"

"Eleven," Sarah answered stoically. "It's eleven."

. . . . . .

The Millers arrived at the Institution gate at ten a.m. Gary drove down one of the narrow veins that led to the center of town and parked the car in front of the Smith Memorial library. The grounds were deserted except for a few walkers enjoying the nice weather.

Gary stepped out of the car and took a deep breath. He smiled and turned toward the sun allowing its warm rays to spread across his face.

"I feel like I can breathe again," he said. "There's something about this place. It does something for my soul, revitalizes it, re-energizes me. I feel whole."

Sarah had stepped out of the car and joined her husband by his side. "I know," she said. "Me too."

Gary smiled at Sarah. Her cheeks were plump and red, and tufts of blonde hair flowed from her black winter hat and framed her face in a manner that pleased him. She is pretty, Gary thought.

"Come here," Gary said extending his hand. She grabbed it and Gary pulled her in close and kissed Sarah on her mouth. After a long, warm kiss that left Sarah breathless, she looked into Gary's eyes and whispered, "Jesus."

The next words spilled from Gary's mouth. They were spontaneous and heartfelt and made him feel good. "I love you, Sarah Miller."

Sarah's eyes were moist. "I love you too, Gary. And If this is what Chautauqua does to you, we should plan more trips here."

"Yes. I think we should."

The Millers strolled arm-in-arm through Chautauqua, past small shops, gingerbread-trimmed houses and quaint cafes. It was nearly a ghost town, but the couple derived pleasure from their walk and their imaginations. Whenever they passed a window display, Gary cocked his head and strained his eyes for a telltale yellow wisp, or a butterfly's shape. He saw lots of ornamental birds, frogs, mushrooms, angels, and even a few bats—one house proclaimed to be the residence of the bat lady and had a bunch of silhouetted bats to prove it—but no butterflies, yellow or otherwise.

Gary grew more glum with each passing minute. Sarah, on the other hand, well, she chattered away like a bird. He tried to smile and feign interest—he did try for Sarah's sake, but his once happy mood had soured.

"You're distracted," Sarah said.

Gary shook his head in disgust. "I'm not seeing them, Sarah."

"Why don't you forget about that and focus on me, on us?"

"I am focused," he snapped. "I can walk and chew gum at the same time ya know."

"You're not going to find any. It's February. I've already told you; they're in hiding."

Gary gave Sarah a dirty look. "Try and be positive, will you? Will you at least try?"

"I'm being honest."

Gary wasn't in the mood for candor. "Yeah, honesty is bad."

"Where are you going to see butterflies this time of year?

"Well, I wasn't expecting to see live creatures."

"You're not?"

"Of course not. I haven't taken leave of my senses."

"You haven't?"

"No. I already told you, I thought we'd see a picture or a glass figurine or something."

"Maybe a butterfly specimen display?"

"Yes, maybe a—" Gary saw Sarah grinning at him. "Oh," he said. "You're making fun of me?"

"No, I'm not."

"Yes, you are."

"Okay, yes I am."

"So you don't believe in this?"

"Do you?"

Gary shrugged. "I don't know. I'm willing to give it a try."

"That's funny. I knew a Gary who was conservative, unwilling to try new things. You always believed in what you believed and were seldom moved to think otherwise."

Gary agreed with Sarah. He had always followed the natural order: grow up, go to college, get a job, a wife, a church, love God and that sort of thing. It wasn't a bad life. Sure, there were problems, but they were the first-world kind, nothing life-threatening, nothing unbearable. Still, there was something eating at him; something was missing; he couldn't say what, but the ever-present emptiness gnawing inside of him served as a constant reminder.

"Yeah, I remember him too," Gary lamented. "It's just that being conservative and following the rules didn't get me far. Not as far as I hoped. I don't think you can pray for things and get them."

"No?"

"It use to make sense to me. God is good, and if you asked him for something, especially if it were good and reasonable, he would give it to you."

"Isn't that what you're doing with the green cars and butterflies?"

"No. Bob explained that when you pray for something, you're asking for it. Attraction means you believe something will come into your life, and it will manifest itself. You're not asking for that thing, you believe it's already there."

"And then its there?"

"Exactly. In fact, it's been there all along; it's your belief that helps you see it."

Sarah shook her head. "Hmm," she said in disgust. "And you can bypass God altogether?"

"Yes—I mean no."

"No?"

"Well, Bob called it the gallon milk theory."

"The gallon milk theory?"

"Yeah. He said you would have as much success praying to a gallon of milk as you would praying to God and that prayers are answered by the probability of the event happening in the first place with or without prayer."

"Gary, that's an awful thing to say."

"Well, I didn't say it. Bob—"

"And why would you take theological advise from him in the first place? For God's sake."

"I'm not taking—"

"You're an ordained minister. Not him."

Gary was frustrated. "I'm not taking advice from anyone," he argued. "I just think he has some interesting ideas, and I want to listen to them. That's all."

"Pagan-hedonistic ideas, if you ask me."

Gary stopped walking and turned to face his wife. "I should tell you something, Sarah. Last night, at his house, he showed me his journal."

"Yes?"

"Well, the journal entry was dated a full year before he bought the house he and Belle are living in now. It described his dream home, the number of rooms, the size right down to the square footage. Sarah, he journaled the exact house he's living in now, and he did this a full year before he even saw the house, and there's more."

"What?"

"Drawings. He drew pictures of what the house would look like too. I tell you it was uncanny."

Sarah's eyes grew wide. "For real?"

Gary leaned in close. "And there's more," he said in a hushed voice. "One of those pictures depicted two men sitting in the library engaged in conversation. Sarah—those two men were Bob and me. He had drawn the two of us talking in his library, a full year before it happened. Now, what do you think of that?"

Sarah began walking. "I think it's demonic and it frightens me."

"Demonic?" Gary laughed. "What on earth?"

"You don't find this strange?"

"Well, I have to admit, at first, I was a little freaked out."

"And now?"

Gary paused a moment to reflect. "I'm curious."

Sarah grabbed her husband's hand and squeezed it. "Curiosity killed the cat, you know."

"I want to learn."

"I'm just afraid you're chasing a bunch of half-baked ideas that don't align with your Christian beliefs."

"It's harmless enough."

"Is it?"

"Yes," Gary answered after a thoughtful pause. "Of course it is."

"Let's keep walking. I want to see the Packard Mansion. It's so beautiful."

The Miller's stepped into their car for the long trek home. It was late afternoon and what began as a sunny day had now turned ominous with threatening skies. The dark clouds, along with the falling temperature, reminded Gary that winter was far from over. He sat slumped over at the steering wheel for several seconds before turning the key.

"Is it supposed to snow?" Sarah said.

"Dunno," replied Gary.

Gary made a right hand turn out of the Institution and headed toward Route 394 where he would catch the onramp to the highway. He had forgotten about green cars and was no longer looking for them; he wasn't seeing them either. His thoughts were on butterflies or more accurately, their absence. Sarah's words haunted him. Where are you going to find butterflies this time of year? Where, indeed?

Sarah patted Gary's thigh. "Sorry about the butterflies," she said.

Gary turned to his wife and smiled. "Ah, the butterflies. I had forgotten all about them," he lied.

"Well, I guess it was kind of silly I suppose."

Gary said nothing. Instead, he watched the countryside stream past his window. His face was sullen. Saturday had come and was nearly gone; tomorrow, he would take the pulpit and deliver yet another sermon, and Monday, he would be back to teaching a classroom of disinterested students. Where does the time go, he thought?

"Do you have your sermon prepared for tomorrow?" Sarah said.

"No."

"No?"

"I'll wing it, or come up with something. Jesus good, Satan bad, that type of thing."

Sarah chuckled. "I see," she said. "It's so beautiful here in the country."

"Serene," replied Gary. "And peaceful. I could see myself living here."

"Just yourself?"

"Oh, and you, of course."

Gary eased the car to the stop sign at the four corners. The area was desolate farmland, save for a century-old general store, which had been converted into a restaurant. The interior was dark and the dirt patch, which served as its parking lot was empty.

"It looks like Stedman's Corners is closed," Gary said.

"I'm afraid we stayed too long at the Institution," replied Sarah. "That's okay. Let's head home. I'll make us something to eat."

Gary lingered at the stop sign for several seconds, carefully looking both ways for traffic even though the country road was clearly empty. Sarah helped her husband by checking too, turning her head left and then right before announcing the coast clear. With her final look, Sarah stopped and fixed her gaze on the side of the restaurant, leaning forward and squinting hard as she did so. Her heart beat faster and she wore a look of disbelief. Sarah opened her mouth as if to say something but stopped short, and Gary accelerated through the intersection.

"Stop the car," Sarah said.

"What is it?" Gary said.

Sarah put her hand on Gary's elbow. "Forgive me," she said. "I thought I saw something, on the side of Stedman's Corners. Would you mind if we turned around?"

There was something in Sarah's tone, an urgency that told him to keep his mouth shut and obey; he dutifully spun the wheel and executed a U-turn.

"What did you see?" Gary said.

"I don't know. Something."

"Oh well," Gary said laughing. "That narrows it down."

Gary pulled the car into the empty parking lot. As he approached the building, painted pastel figures came into his view.

As if in a trance, the Millers exited the car, and ambled toward the dark green wall. Gary's mouth hung open, inhaling the frosty air and blowing out clouds of white smoke while his eyes fixated on the pale, yellow shapes in front of him. There was no doubt. Standing a few feet away, he saw them for what they were, not shapeless blobs, but definitive forms made to resemble living creatures.

Sarah placed a hand on Gary's shoulder. "Look," she said. "Do you see them?"

Gary covered his mouth and whispered, "Oh, Jesus."

CHAPTER SEVEN

Bob's laugh was deep, and loud, and exploded from his chest like a lion's roar. His voice seemed to arrive from all directions at once as it bounced from the library's hardwood floor, off its walls and then back to Gary's ear in the form of staccato notes.

Bob thrust the cellphone towards Belle. "Look, look," he said. "Look at that."

Belle took the phone and her face grew taut as she studied the image. "And what am I looking at?" Belle said.

"Butterflies, my Dear. Yellow ones."

Belle looked at Gary and with her eyes, pleaded for help. Gary only offered a sympathetic smile.

"Someone remind me what the big deal is," Belle said.

Bob pointed at his wife. "It's experiment two, green cars and yellow butterflies. Remember?"

"Oh," Belle replied dragging the vowel out in exaggerated sarcasm. "I remember what a madman I'm married to. That much I remember."

Bob winced. "No, no, no. It's part of the second experiment. I told you about it. Gary was to look for green cars and yellow butterflies. He saw fourteen green cars—was it fourteen?"

"Fifteen," Gary corrected. "The final count was fifteen."

"Fifteen green cars, and there in your hand my dear are the yellow butterflies."

"And they are yellow, too," Gary added. "You can see the paint had faded to a near-white, but if you zoom in, you can see the yellow hue. It's very pale, but it's there."

"And in February," said Bob. "Yellow butterflies in February in Western New York. See, it works. There's your evidence."

Belle shook her head. "What works?"

"The experiment. The idea that you can manifest something just by looking for it. Think it, believe it and see it come to pass."

Belle paused as if in deep thought. "So," she finally replied. "If I think about a husband who will help with the dishes, I'll get one?"

Gary laughed and clapped his hands in a manner meant to antagonize his friend. Belle joined him, and Bob, being the good-natured type, joined in. They were all cracking up at Bob's expense.

"Well, you can always try," Bob said after he settled down.

Belle handed Gary's cell phone back to him. "Actually," she said. "That is really cool."

"That's what I thought," Gary said.

"It's kind of spooky."

"Why do you say that?" said Bob.

"I don't know. Getting what you ask for. It's just weird." Belle turned to Gary and said, "Sometimes, you have to be careful what you ask for."

Gary and Belle locked eyes. Though he didn't agree with her, he played along. "Yes," he said. "I believe you're right."

"I should be going," Belle said. "I'll let you two talk about the next experiment."

"Must you go?" replied Gary. "Stay. I hardly see you."

"Yeah, I know. But I promised a friend we'd go shopping."

Belle said goodbye and walked toward the double-doors.

"Shopping, shopping," Bob called after her in a mocking tone.

Belle—without turning around—flipped her husband off before exiting. Both men laughed. Gary loved her spirit; that fuck-you attitude missing from his own wife, well, Belle had it in spades.

"Well," Bob said turning to Gary. "Are you ready for experiment three?"

Gary's face grew stern and his eyes narrowed. He adjusted himself in his seat and leaned forward. "Ready," he said.

"I have a present for you."

"A present?"

"Yes, sort of." Bob reached down the side of his chair and retrieved two metal rods. They were each about two feet long with one end bent to form a makeshift handle. The contraptions resembled long-barreled dueling pistols. "Do you recognize these?" Bob said.

"Dowsing rods?"

"Some people call them dowsing rods or divining rods. I made them for you."

"You made them?"

"Yes, in my workshop in the basement. It wasn't hard, some metal, a little heat, a jig. You can simply bend a wire coat hanger if you like but I decided to make something nicer."

"Well, they look nice. And these are mine you say, to keep?"

"All yours. You can take them home with you."

Gary was humbled by his friend's generosity. "Thank you," he said. "Uh, what do I do with them?"

"You control them."

"Control them?"

"Yes, with your mind. Here, I'll demonstrate." Bob held the rods by their handles with the tips pointing straight at Gary. "You hold them like this and think of something."

"Think of what?"

"It doesn't matter. Anything you want. I'll think of the globe over there."

Bob trained his eyes on the dowsing rods. A moment passed before they moved. It was a simple twitch—almost imperceptible at first—then more definite as the tips slowly swung to Bob's left, away from the globe. Bob bore down; his eyes were wide and unblinking, and the rods came to a standstill. He took a deep breath before trying again. This time, the rods turned slowly as if an unseen force pushed them towards their target. The tips moved past the globe, then stopped and began a very slow return until they took dead aim at the sphere.

A satisfied smile waxed over Bob's face. "See that?"

Gary watched in stunned silence but was not convinced. "You're making them move," he said.

"With my mind, yes."

"With your mind?"

"Yes. It takes some trial and error, Gary. But with a little practice, they'll move by your will and your will alone."

"May I?"

Bob handed Gary the rods. He took them and held them in the set position pointing straight out in front of him just as Bob demonstrated. Then he stared at the rods for what seemed like a long time.

"Okay," Bob coaxed. "Make them move."

"But how?"

"Think of something in the room and they'll move towards that thing."

Gary concentrated, and thought about the fireplace. Sure enough, the rods moved of their own accord. Only instead of moving in controlled unison, the tips splayed wide in opposite directions. When he tried to correct them, they both turned the other way and passed over each other to form a big X.

Gary looked up and smiled nervously at Bob. "I don't seem to have the hang of this."

"That's okay," Bob encouraged. "It takes practice. Keep trying."

"What's the purpose of this anyway?"

"It will focus your mind, to strengthen it so that you can manifest things."

Gary was doubtful, and he felt silly. "How do you know all of this?" he said.

"Well, I read a lot, I studied, and then I applied my hypothesis and tested them using the scientific method. And then I personally conduct tests, or experiments to prove their veracity."

"Like a regular mad scientist?"

"Well, you can say that."

"Let me try again."

Gary brought the rods to the ready position. He focused his thoughts and placed every ounce of his mental energy behind the task. It was a game to him, sort of fun, but serious too, and he wanted to win very badly.

Again, the rods twitched with an invisible force that splayed the ends apart in opposite directions. This time, Gary was prepared. He squinted hard and knitted his brow. The strain on his face was palpable, beads of sweat formed on his brow, but after a few seconds, he returned the rods back to parallel. Frustrated but undaunted, he continued. This time, the rods moved slowly, in parallel and in unison to his left before stopping in the general direction of the fireplace.

"I've got it," Gary said with excitement. "Did you see that, Bob?"

Bob's chest swelled like a proud father's. "I see," he said. "Now try something else."

Gary once again positioned the rods at the ready, and once again, focused hard. "I'll make it go the other way, towards the lamp," he announced.

As before, the rod tips flared outward, but Gary was able to quickly regain control, and make them move in unison towards the lamp. Just then, the double doors to the library swung open. Gary looked up and saw Belle standing in the doorway. It broke his concentration, but the rods continued to move slowly past the lamp. They seemed to glide of their own accord as if they had a mind all their own. When they finally stopped, they pointed squarely at Belle.

Gary's cheeks grew flush, and he tried to put the rods down before anyone had noticed, but it was too late. The library was already resonating with Bob's laughter and thunderous hand clapping.

"Ah, ah, ah," Bob said in a loud, cackling voice. "I see what's happening you little Devil."

"Oh, please," Gary said. He hoped Bob would keep his mouth shut, but Gary wasn't that fortunate.

"I see what's going on," Bob said. "Your heart's desire—revealed, bared for all to see."

By this time, Belle had joined the two men in the center of the room. "Is my husband harassing you again?" Belle said to Gary.

Gary covered his face with his hand in order to hide his discomfort. "Yes," he said. "I'm afraid I'm once again the butt of your husband's joke."

"Should I tell her?" Bob said.

"Oh stop," Gary snapped. "You're embarrassing all of us. Yourself mostly."

"Tell me what?" Belle asked.

"Oh it's nothing, dear," Bob said. "I've been showing Gary how to use the divining rods, but he seems to have trouble keeping his, uh, rod under control."

"Is that so?" Belle said.

Gary shot Bob a nasty look, then turned to Belle and said, "What do you think of these experiments?"

"Quite frankly," Belle said. "I don't know much about them; nothing much at all."

"Well, I told you about them," Bob said.

"Yes, you told me, but I didn't understand it all. If it makes you happy, Bob, that's all that matters."

"Yes," said Gary. "But do you believe in them? Do you think they have any basis in fact? Have you noticed a difference since your husband has implemented the experiments into his own life?"

Belle thought carefully. "Yes, well, Bob had been working on the experiments even before he met me. Isn't that right, Bob?"

"Yes," Bob confirmed. "Right before we met as a matter of fact."

"I see," Gary said.

"I can tell you they work," Bob said. "They do work."

"Yes," Belle agreed. "They work well enough."

"So, you believe there's something to it?" Gary said.

"Yes. If you believe in something strongly enough…" Belle paused momentarily before concluding her statement. "…it will happen."

"So, this thing your husband concocted is actually quite amazing." Gary turned to Bob and said, "We should write a book."

"Yeah," Bob agreed. "That's what I plan to do. In fact, I've already started. Maybe I could write half the book from my perspective and you write the other half from yours."

"That would be great," Gary said. "We will tell the whole world about our genius—I mean your genius. What do you think about that, Belle? Should we write a book?"

Belle pursed her lips into a crooked smile and cocked her head to one side. "Yea, whatever makes you guys happy."

"You don't seem very enthused, honey," said Bob.

Gary sensed something off in Belle's demeanor. "You don't like the experiments," Gary said.

Belle forced a smile. "It's not that," she said. "I think the experiments are fine. It's just the motives behind them are questionable."

"What do you mean by that?" Gary asked.

"Yeah, what do you mean?" Bob echoed.

"I don't know," said Belle. "It's just that people want things, or they think they want things and when they get them, they find they don't really want them at all. Instead of making them happy, their possessions make them more sad and depressed. It's like they're a victim of their own success."

Gary bristled at her comment. "Wow. If you think having possessions and enough money to live makes you depressed, you should try struggling, living paycheck-to-paycheck or not even that well."

"Oh, I've done plenty of that too," Belle said.

"It's not all about wealth and possessions," Bob said. "My experiments can be used to heal the body both mentally and physically."

"Would you join us Belle?" Gary said. "I'd like to learn more about your thoughts."

"Actually," Belle said. "I came down for the credit card, Bob. Carnahan's is having a sale."

Gary crept from the breezeway and into his kitchen, being careful not to make a sound. It was no use, however. The metal rods made a dreadful clank that broke the silence.

"Is that you, Honey?" said Sarah.

Gary winced, then made his way through the kitchen and into the living room where Sarah was reclining on the sofa; her eyes were glued to a book she was reading, and she never bothered to look up.

Sarah's face and torso were lit by the soft light of a 60-Watt bulb. It gave a glow to her cheeks and made her round features look rounder. Gary saw something motherly and seductive in Sarah; her full figure and soft bosom caught his eye and standing over his wife, looking down at her cleavage, he felt a twinge, a small pull in the groin he had not felt in a long time—at least not towards Sarah.

"What do you have there?" Sarah asked, her nose still buried in the book.

Gary was taken aback. "What?" he said.

Sarah turned away from her book for the first time and looked into her husband's eyes. "In your hand, behind your back? What are those metal things?"

"Oh, oh. Yes. Well, they are divining rods."

Sarah looked amused. "Divining rods?" she said with a smile. "And what are you going to do with them?"

"Divine with them I should think." Sarah didn't respond. Instead she continued to smile and waited for a more reasoned response. "Okay, they're part of the third experiment. Bob gave them to me."

"And what do you do with them?"

Gary held the metal rods out, pushing them towards Sarah and said, "You're supposed to control them—with your mind. I'm supposed to practice with them."

"I see," Sarah said returning to her book. "And did Dr. Harris give you anything else, perhaps a potion, or magic beans? How about a Pentagram? Maybe we can draw a Pentagram on the floor and activate it, and then call forth the Devil and his minions. Wouldn't that be lovely?"

Gary rolled his eyes. He should have left the rods in the car, he thought, and take them out after Sarah went to bed.

"Oh stop," Gary said. "It's not like that at all."

"Isn't it?"

"No, of course not. I wouldn't have any part of that. It's just, well, you know."

Sarah set her book down and sat up straight. "Okay, show me how they work."

Gary sat next to Sarah. "Okay," he said. "I'm not an expert at this, but Bob told me you can control their movement with your mind. You hold them out like this." Gary held the rods by their pistol grip. "Now, what you do is make them move with your thoughts. See, I'll try to make them move to my right toward the TV."

Gary gazed at the rods like a snake charmer trying to summon a Cobra from its basket. At first, there was nothing, but after a few seconds there was a slight but noticeable twitch. Gary continued to concentrate, and after a few more seconds there was a definite movement as the two tips pointed inward and then overlapped into the shape of a cross.

Gary began to perspire. "Damn it," he said wiping the sweat from his brow. "Okay, let me try again."

Gary focused and made the rods straighten momentarily before the tips flailed outwardly in the opposite direction. Then, they suddenly changed direction and formed the cross once again. This back–and–forth pattern happened several more times before Gary finally gave up in frustration.

"Well," he laughed. "I haven't quite got the hang of it. At Bob's house, I was getting good at it."

"May I try?" Sarah asked.

Gary thought for a moment and decided there was no harm in it. "Go ahead," he said, handing the rods over to his wife.

Sarah took the rods in her hands and held them out in the ready position.

"Okay, now what?" she said.

"Concentrate. Think of something in the room and use your mind to make the rods point to it."

Sarah squinted, and her eyes became two black slits.

Gary shook his head and said, "I find it's best when—"

But before he had a chance to finish, the rods snapped to attention as if a current of electricity had suddenly passed through them. Though they barely moved, Gary saw they were vibrating slightly, and he sensed an energy that wasn't there previously. Then the rods made a controlled turn in perfect unison towards the corner of the living room. The tips pointed at Sarah's knitting basket, and there they remained as if waiting for their next command.

"Ah," Sarah said. "Like that?"

Gary's jaw dropped. He shook his head hard and said, "No, no, no. You can't use your hands. You can only use your mind."

"But I didn't use my hands."

"Sarah, I could see you were moving your entire upper body in the direction you wanted the rods to go. That's not how it works."

"I was simply moving my body in the direction the rods were pointing. I swear they were moving on their own."

"Yeah?"

"Yes. It was kind of odd, actually."

"Well, try again. Bob said they work best when you think of something that's personal to you, your true heart's desire."

"Well, my knitting is personal to me."

"Yes, maybe that's why it worked so well for you, and not so much for me."

"Perhaps. Let me try again."

Once again, Sarah held the rods at the ready, but this time, she closed her eyes. Just as before, the metal appeared energized. The tips then tracked slowly to Sarah's right and stopped. Gary was now staring down the barrel of both rods.

Sarah smiled. "Oh my gosh, Gary. Would you look at that?"

Gary tugged at his collar and chuckled. "Yes. I see that. Are you sure you're not making them move with your hands?"

"Yes, quite sure. I feel them get warm, and they turn as if they had a mind all their own."

"They get warm?"

"Yes. I can feel the warmth travel from the sticks into my hands and through my body. Did you feel anything like that when you tried?"

Gary scratched his head and wrinkled his forehead. "No, not exactly."

"Oh well," Sarah said as she set the rods aside. "I'm not sure I like any of this anyway."

"Any of what?" Gary said.

"You know, yellow butterflies, divining rods. It has an air of—"

"Go ahead."

"I don't know. I'm just conflicted that's all."

"Yes, I know what you mean."

"You feel the same?"

"Sort of, but then I tell myself there's nothing wrong with it. Look at Bob. He does this—he invented it—and he has an amazing life. Why shouldn't I have as much, more come to think of it?"

"Gary," Sarah said, winking at him. "You know I think you should get everything you deserve."

"Come, sit closer to me Sarah." Sarah nestled up to her husband and placed her head on his chest. Their knees and thighs touched. "You say you felt a warmth in your body?" Gary said.

"Yes, I did."

"Tell me where."

"Like I said, I felt it flow through the rods and into my arms, and eventually my entire body."

Gary planted a kiss on Sarah's forehead. "Your entire body, you say?"

"Yes."

"Did you feel it here?" Gary said while grabbing hold of Sarah's left breast.

"Ah, yes, I believe so."

Gary massaged Sarah's breast in a slow, circular motion, and despite the layers between hand and flesh, he could clearly feel the acorn-sized, lump swell beneath his touch. He placed his free hand on her right breast and was able to produce a similar result there.

"How about here?" Gary said.

"Oh, yes," Sara gasped. "Only it wasn't as hot as it is now."

Gary slid his hand between her knees. Then like a snake, his fingers slithered up her thigh. "And here?" he said. "What about here?"

"Oh dear," Sarah whispered. "I think you better take me upstairs. Then I'll be able to show you exactly where I felt it."

"Gladly," Gary said grabbing Sarah's hand and standing her to her feet. "Don't forget the black stockings."

CHAPTER EIGHT

Gary developed into a virtuoso with the divining rods, a regular Paganini and his Stradivarius, and he did it with the power of his mind. When he held the rods, they pulsated with a white-hot glow that remained cool to his touch. He was excited by his progress, and his confidence grew just as Bob said it would.

Gary practiced often; he would sit on the couch watching television and absentmindedly play with them, or at work, during office hours when he should have been grading papers. He could make them turn in unison in either direction with a deft maestro's touch. He could splay the tips apart in opposite directions and then return them to parallel, or form the cross or stop them on a dime. He could even spin them in different directions at once, the left counterclockwise, the right clockwise before stopping and reversing their field. He moved them quickly in sudden jerks or nudged them slowly in micro movements measured in millimeters as his mind commanded.

"Stop playing with your sticks," Sarah called from the kitchen. "The Harris will be here soon, and I need your help."

"I'm not playing with my sticks," Gary protested. "I'm practicing, and they're called dowsing rods."

"Can you make those dowsing sticks peel potatoes, I wonder? Because that would actually be useful."

Oh, shut up you fucking cow, Gary thought as he stood up and joined his wife in the kitchen. "They're called rods," he said. "Dowsing rods, and yes, I almost think I can get them to peel potatoes."

"The potatoes are by the sink. Wash and peel them. Thanks. Does Belle like chicken, I hope? We should have asked beforehand. Too late now I suppose."

"She likes pot," Gary said with a smile. "If we had pot, that would make her happy; I'm sure."

"Oh for God's sake. You're kidding?"

"Nope, she reeks of the stuff every time I go over there."

"And have you developed a habit of sniffing Belle?"

Actually, Gary was in the habit of sniffing Belle, every chance he got. It was the thing he looked forward to most when he visited Bob. However, he wasn't about to admit as much to Sarah. Gary shrugged her off and said, "Oh, my God. There's no need to sniff her per se. The scent follows her as she enters the room. She even offered me some on my last visit."

"And you refused her of course."

"I didn't actually," Gary said trying to stifle a smile. "I wanted to see what it was like, so we both got high, Bob too." Sarah glared at her husband. "Kidding," Gary said releasing the tension.

"For God's sake, Gary. I should hope you're kidding. Sometimes you worry me."

Gary nodded his head. "Yes. I must say I worry myself sometimes too."

The doorbell rang with a harsh, clatter that startled both Gary and Sarah. "Oh, God," Sarah said clutching her chest. "They're early. What are they doing here so soon?"

"It's ten past," Gary explained. "They're ten minutes fashionably late. We're the ones that are behind."

"Oh, God."

"Don't worry. I'll get the door. It's just the Harrises. No need to panic."

Gary ran down the stairs, and into the entryway. He opened the door and was greeted by Bob's smiling face; a step behind, stood Belle. She was dressed in a black winter coat, and her prominent bosom peaked through an opening. Gary saw white flesh; that's all it took. He shut his eyes and took a deep breath. What a thoroughbred, he thought.

"Well, hello," Bob said in a loud voice that woke Gary from his daydream. "We come bearing gifts."

Bob thrust a bottle-shaped bag toward Gary. "Hello," Gary said. "I'll take that, and welcome to our humble abode."

"It's so nice to see you," said Belle. Gary placed his lips aside Belle's cheek and gave it a light peck.

"Follow me to the kitchen," Gary said.

Bob led the charge and made a beeline straight for Sarah. He wore a broad smile and held his arms wide open.

"Sarah," Bob gushed. "It's nice to see you."

It was as if Bob and Sarah were long-lost friends whom hadn't seen each other in years. Sarah's face lit up. She spread her arms like wings and accepted the hug and a peck on her right cheek. With Dr. Harris pressed tight against her torso, Sarah closed her eyes, and took a deep breath. Gary didn't notice the big smile on her face.

"Oh, Bob," Sarah said. "I'm so glad you could come."

"We're so glad you invited us," said Belle.

"Belle," Sarah said. "I'm glad to see you." The two women exchanged a pleasant if rather cold and awkward hug.

"Look," said Gary enthusiastically. "They brought us wine."

"Thank God," Sarah said. "From the sound of it, I was afraid they brought something else."

Gary shot his wife a confused look. "Shall we eat?"

"Well," Sarah replied. "I'm afraid we're not ready to eat. The potatoes aren't even done yet. My husband was too busy playing with his, uh, rods earlier and I fell behind."

There was an awkward silence while the room tried to decipher what Sarah had just said. Then, a knowing look came over Bob's face. "Oh, the divining rods," he said. "How's that going?"

"It's going great," said Gary. "I have them obeying like trained dogs."

"Yes," said Sarah. "I can attest to that. He plays with his rods all day and all night it seems."

There was another awkward silence before Belle spoke up. "What do you need done?" she said. "I'll help."

"That's okay," Sarah said. "I can't ask you to help. You're guests."

"Nonsense. Give me an apron and tell me what needs to be done."

Sarah's face turned red. "I—I don't have an apron."

"Who needs an apron? Did you say you needed help with the potatoes?" Sarah nodded her head. "Okay, I'm on potatoes. Bob, find something to do. Cut the bread or something. Gary, break out the wine." Belle clapped her hands twice in quick succession. "Chop, chop. We have work to do."

Sarah stood awestruck at the flurry of activity now taking place in her kitchen. There was a whirlwind of bodies in motion where there had been inert statues seconds prior. Belle peeled potatoes. Gary opened the bottle and was pouring overflowing glasses of red wine; Bob found a pitcher and for some reason, filled it with water.

•   •   •   •   •

The guests ate, the wine flowed, and the clamor of voices and tinkling of glasses filled the Miller's kitchen. As usual, Gary and Bob dominated the conversation, talking about everything from religion to global warming. The two friends bickered intently but civilly, directing well aimed but good-natured barbs at each other to their wives' amusement.

"You and Gary should get married," Belle said to Bob.

"And why is that?" Bob said.

"Because you sound like an old married couple already."

Bob looked at Gary, and his friend shrugged. Then Bob turned to Sarah for help. "Do you believe that," he said, jerking a thumb towards Belle.

Sarah laughed. "Tis true," Sarah replied. "You do sound like an old married couple."

Bob turned back to his friend, and the two men looked into each other's eyes. "Will you marry me?" Bob asked with a stone-cold expression.

Gary did his best to maintain a straight face, but couldn't. The wine was working too well.

When everyone settled down, Bob turned to Sarah and said, "The meal was wonderful. Everything was delicious. Thank you so much for inviting us."

Sarah blushed. "Oh, the pleasure was ours, right Gary?"

Gary nodded. "Yes, the food, the wine, the conversation—It was the least we could do for all you have given me."

"Okay," Belle said. "We need to clear the table, and get these dishes cleaned." In unison, the Millers waved them off and insisted they sit down, but Belle was having none of it. "I have an idea. Why don't the men go into the living room and do—well, you know, whatever men do. Sarah and I got this."

"Really," Sarah replied. "It's not necessary. I can take care of it."

Belle stood up with a handful of dirty dishes and headed towards the sink. "C'mon, it will go quick, and besides, we'll get a chance to talk."

"Yes," Bob agreed. "You two do that. Gary and I will be in the living room. C'mon, man, bring your wine."

.   .   .   .   .

Belle and Sarah stood side-by-side at the kitchen sink. Belle washed, and Sarah dried.

"You have a lovely home," Belle said.

Sarah shrugged; she had never been to Belle's house, but Gary had told her stories. "It's small," Sarah said apologetically.

Belle placed her hand on Sarah's elbow. "Yes, but it's perfect for two people. Cozy ya know?"

Sarah smiled. "It is cozy to be sure."

"Living in a large home isn't what it's cracked up to be."

"It isn't?"

Belle shook her head, sending a wave through her dark curls. "I thought I would like it more than I do. I just feel—I feel so lost in it sometimes. It's like Bob, and I live in separate houses."

"I heard it's lovely."

"We'll have you and Gary over next time. I would love to cook for you. How long have you and Gary been married?"

"Twenty-seven years."

"Oh wow. That's a long time. Bob and I will celebrate our third anniversary in July."

Sarah was envious. She remembered her early days with Gary. Things were simpler then, better. "Where did you two meet?"

"College."

Sarah looked at Belle with raised eyebrows. "Oh?"

Belle laughed "It wasn't like that," she said. "I was his student, but he only asked me out after graduation."

"Well, that's good. You know St. Mary's frowns upon that sort of thing."

"Yes, I know. That's why we waited."

"That's so romantic," Sarah gushed. "You two seem to live a charmed life."

Belle stopped washing and turned to face Sarah. "Really?" she said. "And why do you say that?"

"Oh, I don't know for sure, but you live in a big house, and you and Bob seem very happy together. You have an ease about each other."

"Yeah, Bob and I get along well. He's very irreverent you know, but so am I; it all works I suppose."

"I can tell you love each other very much."

"You can?"

"Yes. The way he looks at you. I see him stealing glances. He'll be arguing politics or religion with my husband, but every once in a while he'll sneak a peek at you. He looks at you with a glint in his eye. It's adorable, actually."

Belle worked in silence for several moments, furiously scrubbing a stubborn stain that was not actually there. "You know," she finally said. "Bob is a very brilliant man. That's one of the things I admire about him." The two women worked in silence until Belle spoke again. "I can see the same thing in Gary—his love for you."

Belle had seen no such thing, Sarah thought. The glint in Gary's eye had long passed. Sarah was smart and sensitive, and she knew it as well as anyone. It was easier for her to pretend it wasn't so than to admit as much to a practical stranger.

"Uh, huh," Sarah replied after a long delay.

Belle placed a hand on Sarah's shoulder. "I don't want to pry," she said. "But is everything okay?"

Sarah took extra care with a dish she had been drying; making sure every speck of water was removed before placing it in the dish rack. "Everything is okay," she finally replied. Another long stretch of silence ensued. "I don't know, Belle, some of the spark has been lost. It just seems like after twenty-seven years of marriage—"

Belle quickly dried her hands and then placed her arm around Sarah. "It's okay," Belle said softly.

Sarah didn't know why, but she was on the verge of blubbering to her house guest. She was angry with herself for getting emotional. "I—I shouldn't be talking like this. We barely know each other."

"Sometimes, you have to talk about these things, right?" Sarah smiled and nodded her head. "If you don't you'll burst."

"Can I ask you something personal, Belle?"

"Of course."

"Is Bob still passionate—I mean for you?"

Belle pursed her lips and nodded her head rhythmically. "Bob is quite a bit older than me," she said. "And the cancer drugs he takes—"

Sarah sensed she had pressed too far and abruptly cut Belle off. "Oh, I see."

"We do a lot of snuggling."

"Yes, I understand. I—I didn't mean to pry."

"You know what helps, Sarah?"

"No. What?"

"Pot."

"Marijuana?"

"Cannabis. It's called Cannabis or pot. Don't call it Marijuana. That's a racist, derogatory term."

Sarah could hardly believe she was having this conversation. "Oh dear."

"Yeah, it's like natural Viagra."

"Well, Gary and I are Christians. That sort of thing goes against our religious beliefs."

"Oh yes, of course, I didn't mean to—"

"What's it like?"

"You mean smoking pot? You've never tried it?"

"No. Never."

"Weren't you ever curious?"

"I was always too afraid."

"What about Gary?"

"No, not to my knowledge."

"I have some if you ever want to smoke. I could even make edibles if you prefer that."

Sarah paused and considered Belle's offer, but the image of her and Gary getting stoned on the sofa, while intriguing, was a bit frightening. "No, but thanks anyway, Belle."

"Well," Belle replied. "You let me know if you change your mind."

"You know something, Belle?"

"No, what's that?"

"I like you. I'm so glad you and Bob came over."

Belle's face lit up. "Me too. We'll do this again at my home."

•　　•　　•　　•　　•

After the Harrises left, Gary turned to his wife and said, "What did you and Belle talk about?"

Sarah cocked her head to the side and replied, "Well, your usual girl—"

"Guess what Bob and I talked about?" Gary interrupted.

"Uh, I don't know. World—"

"Experiment four."

"Oh, God. I should have known."

Gary stared at his wife with an expectant smile. "Well, aren't you going to ask me what it is?"

"I wasn't, but I'm afraid you're going to tell me anyway."

"We're supposed to grow plants."

"Plants? Oh, dear God, no."

Gary was so excited, he didn't even notice the pained expression on his wife's face. "Yes. I knew you'd like it."

"Marijuana? I mean, pot?"

"What on earth?"

"I mean Cannabis."

Gary was confused. "Sarah, have you taken leave of your senses?"

"Well, one of us has. I'm sure of that much."

"I'm talking about bean sprouts."

"Bean sprouts?" Sarah said clutching her chest. "Oh, bean sprouts."

"Yes, beans sprouts. Why on earth would you think it was marijuana?"

"It's called cannabis, or pot, not marijuana. Marijuana is a racist, derogatory term."

"Just what did you and Belle talk about?"

"Oh, never mind, Gary. Tell me about the bean sprouts."

"Okay. We're to get an empty egg carton, and fill it with potting soil. Then we plant the bean sprouts in each of the little receptacles. Got it?"

"Okay?"

"Then we're to concentrate on the little seeds, send them positive thoughts, but only for one side of the carton, let's say the right side."

"Just the right side?"

"Yes. The idea is that the right side—the side that receives our positive thoughts and prayers—will grow and blossom. The other side, well, not so much."

"I see."

"Do you?"

"Yes, I think so."

"Bob explained that our thoughts release energy out to the universe, and these thoughts can change the world around us. Send positive thoughts to the bean sprouts, and you will be rewarded with healthy, vibrant plants. He called it something... the collective consciousness—that's it."

"It sounds like new-age stuff."

"So what if it does?"

"Tell me something, Gary. Six months ago, if someone told you to pray for plants, or play with divining rods, or this collective consciousness, what would you have told them?"

"I would have laughed."

Sarah placed her hand on Gary's chest. "Exactly. And now look at you. You're practically giddy about this whole experience. I can feel your heart racing."

Gary grabbed hold of Sarah's hand. "And so what if it is? I'm excited about something. What's wrong with that?"

"Nothing. But when that something pulls you further-and-further from your roots, then it worries me. What if in six months you find out these experiments were a bunch of hocus pocus nonsense that really have no merit?"

"Well, then I would have learned something. I would have tried it, and learned that it was nonsense, instead of just taking something on faith without proof either way."

Sarah drew a deep audible breath. "There's something else, Gary."

"What?"

"It's your ministry."

Gary felt a chill. His mind raced, and he wanted to know what Sarah knew without giving too much away. "What about it?" he said coldly.

"I don't know if its related to the experiments or what it is. Maybe you're having a crisis of faith."

"Well, what is it?"

"Your last couple of sermons."

"What about them?"

Sarah shook her head from side-to-side. "They weren't very good," she replied in a hushed voice. "I mean, you were rambling a bit, and I couldn't tell what your point was."

Gary listened intently and was actually relieved to hear her explanation. "Oh, is that all?"

"I mean, you always had a message that was based on biblical teachings. For God's sake, Gary, last Sunday you told the parishioners to trust not in God, but to trust in themselves."

"Oh, I did not," Gary laughed. "And if I did, all I meant was that God gave us the ability to help ourselves and that we should make good use of this ability. We don't need to beg God to do every last thing for us when we're perfectly capable of doing it for ourselves."

"See? That's what I mean. You would have never said that before."

"Yes, and that's a good thing, Sarah. My faith is evolving, it's growing to be more in line with reality rather than being driven by the Christian platitudes that have been force-fed down my throat ever since I can remember."

"There's more," Sarah quickly added.

Gary picked up a half-full glass of wine, and despite not knowing whom it belonged to, drank the contents in a single gulp. "Yes," he said. "What's that?"

"It's Chuck. He has concerns too."

Gary shot his wife a hard glance. "You've been talking to my deacon?"

"He's worried about you too, Gary."

Gary felt the back of his ears burn. A single step separated him from complete control and absolute panic. Gary caught himself, however, and took a breath before he spoke. "Did he not like my sermon either?"

"He just wanted to know—"

"You know," Gary interrupted. "If Chuck has something to say to me, he can say it to my face like a man. That Asshole."

"Gary, for God's sake, he just wanted to know what was going on."

"Nothing is going on. Did you tell him that? I hope you did." Gary picked up another half-empty wine glass and downed its contents. He was done with this conversation. "Are you going to the store tomorrow?"

"If you want me to, I can. Soybeans, you said?"

"It's bean sprouts, Sarah. I told you bean sprouts. Weren't you listening?"

"Sorry. Bean sprouts?"

"Yes, please."

CHAPTER NINE

Belle bent forward at the waist and poured Gary's coffee. Her blouse separated from her chest and placed her bosom at eye-level, giving Gary a titillating albeit abbreviated glimpse of her breasts. "Do you take sugar?" she said.

Gary quickly lifted his eyes to avoid detection, but he was too late. Belle noticed, and it made her cheeks burn.

"Uh," Gary said.

"One spoon?"

Gary nodded his head. "Honestly," he said after regaining his breath. "Bob and I are perfectly capable of pouring our own coffee. Where's the kitchen? We'll serve ourselves."

"What are you talking about?" Bob said. "She's already brought our coffee. Besides, you'd get lost if you went looking for the kitchen. I live here, and I still don't know where the damn thing is."

"I just feel bad having Belle do all this work."

Belle smiled warmly at Gary. "It's okay," she said. "I'm happy to do it."

Belle stood straight up. Her cleavage now paved the way down her low-cut V-neck. Gary tried to focus on her face, but as pleasant as it was, it was impossible to keep his eyes from wandering down her neck where they feasted before quickly looking up. He repeated these sneak attacks several more times all while trying to look nonchalant. He came off as anything but. Instead, he looked like a man with a maniacal, nervous twitch. Damn it, he thought. It was like showing raw meat to a savage wolf and expecting him to sit still. Unfair.

"Doesn't Sarah bring you coffee?" Bob said.

Gary turned quickly towards Bob. "Sarah?" he said in disbelief. "Ha. You ask Sarah to get you something, and she'll as likely tell you to jump in the Chadakoin as much as anything else."

Belle and Bob responded with a chuckle. "I'm sure that's not true," Bob said.

"Oh don't let her fool you," warned Gary. "She's not the angel she appears to be."

"Maybe you should start by bringing her coffee," Bob suggested. "That's what Belle and I do. We take turns."

Gary scoffed and turned his head away from Bob and towards Belle.

"She seemed very nice when I talked to her," Belle said.

"Eh," Gary shrugged. "Nice enough I suppose."

"We'll have to have the two of you over for dinner soon."

"Yes," Bob added. "I quite enjoyed our get-together. We'll do it again at our house."

Gary smiled and nodded. "Belle, won't you have a seat and join us?"

"I wish I could, but I have shopping to do."

"Again?" Bob said in disgust. "It seems like all you do is shop."

"You want your wife looking nice," said Belle. "Don't you?"

"My wife already looks nice."

Belle chuckled. "I won't be long. I'm taking the T."

"Okay."

Gary's eyes were glued to Belle's backside as she exited the library. He carefully studied her swaying hips as she made her way across the hardwood floor until she disappeared behind the double doors.

Gary turned to Bob and said, "What's the T?"

"It's the Tesla," Bob replied.

Of course it is, Gary thought. "Oh, you got one of those?" he said knowing full well he did. "How nice."

"You should feel the acceleration on that thing. It will pin your balls back in your seat."

"You're a lucky man my friend."

"Luck had nothing to do with it."

Gary smiled. "Is that so?"

"That is so," Bob confirmed. "How are you doing, my friend?"

"I'm doing well."

"Have you completed experiment four?"

"Yes. Sarah and I planted the little buggers two weeks ago."

"You've been praying for the right side?"

"I have."

"And?"

"Yes, well, they're sprouting all over the damn place, like an overgrown jungle. And the funny thing is, I never gave them any food or water."

"You didn't?"

"Nope. I've just been sending positive thoughts their way."

"And that's the right side of the carton? What about the left side?"

"Nothing."

"Nothing?"

"Not a blessed thing, maybe a bud or two, even the soil looks unhealthy, dry and cracked."

Bob pointed at Gary and smiled. "See?" he said. "It works. It really does work."

"Yes," Gary agreed. "It works."

"Are you amazed?"

Gary was more than amazed, actually. Before now, he never understood the well of untapped potential trapped in the recesses of his mind. He was like a baby discovering his first steps, unsteady as they were. But those small steps were leading him somewhere, guiding him forward, and forward was better than standing still, he thought.

"Yes," Gary answered. "These experiments—I doubted them at first."

"And now?"

"There's something at work here to be sure. I don't know quite what it is."

"That's ok," Bob explained. "Science, math, physics, energy, the cosmos, the collective mind—they hold all the answers we will ever need. For now, just know that it does work and there is a shift taking place within you. Can you feel it?"

Gary nodded his head. He felt something to be sure; there was a change, a shift in thought or consciousness, or both. It was palpable too. He felt lighter and walked with a straight back and a renewed sense of purpose. Others noticed too. "Have you lost weight?" they asked. Though he hadn't changed his diet or exercise routine, he thought he had lost weight. He never bothered to step on a scale, but he looked trimmer and even a bit taller.

"I do feel different," Gary confirmed.

"Good. Think of experiment four as a test—your thoughts against the inertia of inanimate objects."

"But the bean sprouts are not inanimate," Gary reasoned. "They're alive."

"True enough, Gary, but that's an even greater test. You can control living organisms, to use the power of your mind to bend the energy contained in living cells."

Gary sat at the edge of his seat. "Bend the energy in a living cell," he repeated. "Yes, that's it, Bob. The right side looks like a bean sprout infestation. We eat those damned plants every night. Sarah puts them in salads, and no matter how much she takes, there's always more the next day."

"It doesn't surprise me, my friend. It worked for me and now it's working for you. It will work for the entire human race. Imagine the possibilities, what it could mean for mankind?"

Gary thought about the possibilities. If he made rods move, or influenced plants to grow, what else could he do? What couldn't he do? Anything and everything—in time—were his for the taking. He was close now, so close, he could see the future and the future looked good.

"I am ready for experiment number five," Gary said. "Tell me; tell me what it is."

"Before I tell you, I have something for you, a present."

"A present? For me?"

Bob opened the drawer to the end table. He reached in and emerged with a book, which he offered to his friend. Gary eagerly took it and turned it over several times. He recognized this was no ordinary book. It was small, just slightly bigger than Gary's hand. The chocolate brown cover was soft and was made of a pliable swath of brushed leather that flexed easily beneath his grip. The skin wrapped the book like an embrace and a large bowknot, tied with a sinewy leather string, secured the cover. There were no letters or distinguishing marks to indicate what the contents might hold, but nonetheless, it oozed with the character of a 17th-century hand-bound text. Gary held the book to his nose and inhaled its dark, earthy scent. He stared at it for several seconds and then looked up at Bob with questioning eyes.

"It's a journal," Bob explained.

"A journal? Oh yes, like your journal, only this one is brown."

"Yes. Remember when I told you to get a journal? You never got one, did you?"

"I meant to."

"Well, now you have one."

"What do I do with it?"

"You write down your thoughts, your feelings, your wants, your desires."

"Like you did with the house?"

"Exactly."

"So, I should journal a new house?"

Bob held up his hand. "Uh, no. Not just yet. In time."

"Does this have anything to do with experiment five?"

Bob cocked his head to the side. "Yeah, sort of. What you're going to do is journal something, whatever it is you want, and then watch it come to fruition within twenty-four hours."

Gary's mind immediately went to work. He thought of all sorts of things he had wanted: money, a new house, a new car, more money. His eagerness was clearly written in his eyes and made Bob speak up.

"Eh," Bob said holding up a hand. "Keep it small at first. Baby steps for now."

"But why can't I just do what you did, and journal a new house, or at least a new car. Lord knows I could use a new car—my piece of crap—"

"When you have finished experiment seven, then you can manifest big things. For now, we're still trying to build your faith. Remember, that's the key to manifestation; it's the belief that anything is possible that indeed makes it possible. We have to start slowly and build up your belief."

Gary slunk back in his chair and let out an exasperated breath. "Yes, but my faith is through the roof, Bob. I'm ready for bigger things don't you think?"

"Take it slow," Bob warned. "Baby steps."

"Baby steps," Gary echoed.

Gary looked down at the journal and then pulled slowly at its leather string. The knot unfurled allowing the cover to spill open and expose its milky white pages. Gary ran his fingers over the paper's rough surface and imagined filling them with words and pictures.

"Imagine the possibilities," Bob said in a soft, deliberate tone. "All that pristine paper, just waiting to soak up your ink like a sponge." Gary looked up at Bob and the two locked eyes. "All your dreams, your wants, your desires, Gary—they will be written on the pages. You just have to fill them like a grocery list."

"A grocery list?"

Bob nodded. "Yes—a grocery list to the Universe. Soon, nothing will be beyond your grasp, Gary. What is it you want?"

Gary smiled and shook his head. He was about ready to tell Bob what he truly wanted but caught himself. "I'm afraid I can't tell you what I truly want, my friend."

"That's okay," Bob assured him. "Write it in the journal. Tell the Universe."

"The Universe? Not God?"

"You can call it God if you want. Many of us call it the Universe. Whatever you call it. It's same thing either way."

"And what about pictures? I remember you illustrated your journal."

"It's just another technique I used. The spoken word is powerful. The written word is more so. Writing has a permanence and a physical component that speech does not. A picture—well, pictures add a visual component that make them more potent."

"But I cannot draw," Gary protested.

"That doesn't matter. You can make stick figures, right?" Gary nodded his head. "Then make stick figures. The Universe, God, is smart enough to know what you mean. Besides, once you start, you will relax, and you'll be surprised by the images that appear."

Gary looked at the journal and felt guilty. He hadn't been a good friend. When Bob was sick, he had never bothered to visit. Instead, he daydreamed of fucking Belle. And now, Bob was kind enough to gift him this journal. Sure, it didn't cost much, perhaps a few dollars, but to Gary it was the world.

Gary carefully tied his journal with the leather lace, then wiped a tear from his eye. "Bob, I don't know what to say—thank you my friend."

"Oh, it was nothing. It only cost a few bucks. I got it at—"

"I'm not talking about the journal," Gary interrupted. He sat quietly for a few seconds trying to compose himself. "You know," he continued. "I was reluctant to get mixed up in any of this."

"Yes, I remember, Gary."

"But you know something? I'm glad I did. I must tell you, I wasn't doing well before. Still not. But these experiments…" Gary paused and caught his breath. "…these experiments have made a difference—they gave me hope. Things are still tough but—"

"It's all right, Gary. I know what you mean. A little hope is sometimes all we need. That's why I've developed the experiments, to give hope to you and others like you."

"Well, thank you again, my friend."

CHAPTER TEN

The sound of rubber grinding against loose stones signaled Gary's arrival. Snowball stood on his haunches, his back slightly arched as he wiggled his ass from side-to-side. Snowball waited until he saw the black leather shoes walking towards the porch before springing forth in full attack mode. When he reached his prey, he rose on two back legs, then pawed frantically at the bouncing laces as they swung past him in a blur. His tactic was futile, so he tried another. This time, he chased after Gary and leaped high into the air before landing with a thud on his instep. Gary shook his leg wildly in an unsuccessful attempt to buck the cat off its perch. Snowball was having none of it. He clutched tightly with his teeth and claws and held on for dear life. Snowball appeared to enjoy himself—Gary, well, not so much.

"Sarah," Gary yelled up to the house. "Sarah, come get this rodent off of me." Sarah was nowhere to be seen. A final mule kick, however, caused Snowball to fly through the air where he landed unceremoniously but unscathed into a snow bank.

"Sarah," Gary called out as he walked into the kitchen. "Have you been feeding the cat again?" The words were no sooner out of his mouth when he remembered. Today was Tuesday. Sarah was grocery shopping.

Gary grabbed a pen; he made his way to the living room but stopped short when he noticed something odd—it was the beansprouts, or more specifically, the left-side sprouts. They looked wild, untamed like a bird's nest that bourgeoned into an unsightly mess. The left now rivaled their right-side counterpart in both height and volume. Gary ran his hands over the sprouts in a sweeping gesture meant to compare the two sides. While the right side still maintained a slight advantage, the gap had narrowed, and the demarcation line between left and right had been nearly erased.

"That's strange," Gary whispered to himself. "I reckon I better concentrate harder."

Gary took a seat in the living room sofa and began writing in his journal.

From the Journal of Gary Miller: March 6th

Well, it's been an eventful day I suppose. Went to see Bob, and he gave me the journal in which I now write. I never had a journal before, never been much for writing except for scholarly papers and sermons. So this ought to be interesting. Bob said I should use the journal to write down my feelings, my wants, and desires, and that by doing this, I will manifest them into the real world. Fascinating, eh?

It makes me laugh for I still don't know about any of this. I sometimes question the experiments, their validity and their rightful place in my life. Sarah questions them too. She thinks it some sort of crazy mishmash of new age pseudo-religion gibberish that diverts me from my real relationship with Christ. She may be right, but since talking to Bob and performing these experiments, I've been more energized about—well, about everything to be honest. Before, I lived as a man who's reached the pinnacle of his life and who is now on the downward slope heading towards his inevitable decline (death as it were). But I'm not ready for that. What happened to me? Where did my life go? Is it enough that I was born, married, worked and died without really leaving a mark behind, not even a child, an heir? Sarah blames me for that too. Oh, well, add that to the list I suppose.

I worshiped and prayed to an unseen God, and assumed I was living the good Christian life because I followed the same prescription that other Christians had followed and muttered the same Christian platitudes as they. And if they were good Christians, then I must be a good Christian too. Only, I hardly feel that way, not any more. I question everything, now. What is a good Christian? The term seems unnatural to me. Are there bad Christians out there, and are they destined to burn in the fires of Hell, or is any one of us doomed to spend eternity in Hell? Somehow, I don't think so. I doubt Hell even exists, or Heaven for that matter. I never use to have these doubts. One time I believed they were real places with physical form replete with gatekeepers and a populace who justly belonged to one or the other. Now, I am skeptical to say the least. When I think about such things (and I think of them often these days). It doesn't make sense to me. How can a God, so loving and benevolent, a God whom I've worshipped freely, and wholly ever condemn anyone to Hell, even the worst among us? And what about Heaven; our eternal reward for our faithfulness? What is so great about Heaven that it would make an eternity palatable? An eternity after all is a long time.

Furthermore, how does doctrine determine our fate? What we believe in is more a product of where we were born and whom our parents were than any absolute truth. Why am I a Christian? If I'm being honest, I'm a Christian because I was born in the United States to Christian parents. It makes me sad to think this, but its true. If I were born in India, I'd be a Hindu. If I were born in Japan, I'd be a Buddhist. My entire spiritual life has been based more on a genetic accident than on anything else.

This doesn't make sense. The luck of birth should have no determination of where you should spend the afterlife, and yet so many of us accept this idea as freely as we accept the nose on our face. When I ask myself these questions—the hard questions, the questions I was too afraid to ask for fear of tossing an anvil into everything I once held dear—the answers don't add up. Do they?

I must say it feels good to ask questions and not just blindly follow what others say and do for no other reason than it's the status quo. For my entire life, I've merely accepted the company line as it were. God is this and God is that, and here are a bunch of rules we need to follow even though the rules were framed by a time and culture that no longer exists; you need to follow them anyway, Gary, and this is how you get to heaven, Gary and all of this and that… How can anyone pretend to know about such lofty matters as God, heaven, and hell? They cannot; I certainly can't. I'm not going to pretend anymore either. I was good at pretending and it's only served to hurt me, to dig myself deeper into a hole of darkness. For the first time in a long time (maybe forever) I'm beginning to think for myself, and not rely on a book to tell me right from wrong.

I don't know; perhaps Sarah's right. Maybe these experiments have pulled me away, and I have lost my faith in traditional Judeo-Christian beliefs, but I don't think that's such a bad thing. Maybe all Christians should think about what they believe in and more importantly why they believe in them. Do we believe in the truth or do we merely accept what we were told to avoid eternal damnation? Fear seems to be the central theme in religion, in ALL religions… fear of Hell, of doing and saying the wrong things. Is this what religion is for? Is this why it was invented? Perhaps it was to keep the masses in check, to keep them obedient, subservient and easily controlled. I'm tired.

Look at me. I'm supposed to be writing about what I want to manifest into my life, but I've been babbling instead. Perhaps the problem is I don't know what I want. That's not true. I do know, but I'm too afraid to ask (see there's the fear again). Yes, that's the real problem. I have time still. Let me think on it. I'm new to this journaling thing. Give it some time, Gary. You will get there.

I best go now. I'm hungry, and Sarah will be home soon.

Gary put down his pen and carefully folded the cover shut. Then he secured it with a knot that had two large loops dangling from the center. He held the cover up to his nose and inhaled the earthy brushed leather. It smelled like a well-worn baseball mitt. He remembered the scent from his boyhood and it made him smile.

A sound from the kitchen brought Gary back to the present. It was Sarah.

"Hey, Gary," she said. "Help me put away the groceries?"

Gary walked into the kitchen, journal in hand. He extended it toward his wife and said, "Look. It was a present from Bob."

"What is it?"

"It's a journal. It's experiment five. I am to write down what I want to manifest into my—"

"Ridiculous," Sarah said cutting him off.

Gary's smile quickly disappeared. "Now, why would you say that?" he said.

Sarah reached out and pinched the journal between her thumb and forefinger. "Because," she said. "You don't write things down and get what you want. That's not how the world works."

Gary yanked the journal from her grasp and said, "Oh, and just how does the world work? Tell me since you seem to know so much about it."

Sarah turned her back on her husband and began putting away the groceries. "I don't want to argue about this now."

"No, no. I'm not arguing. I'm just asking. How does the world work? When you want something, do you not pray to an unseen God in hopes he'll grant you your wish?"

"Stop it, Gary."

"Like a genie in a bottle?"

"Grow up."

"I am fucking grown up," Gary spat. "At least the experiments have some basis in fact, in science."

Sarah wheeled around to face Gary. "Ha. What science?" she said. "This is nothing more than pseudoscience dressed up to sound important."

"Oh, and how would you know? You're not a scientist. Bob is. You—you're nothing more than a bible school dropout."

Sarah's lips quivered, then she turned her back on Gary. He could tell his arrow had penetrated deep, a little deeper than he had intended, but it was too late to take it back. He had opened a wound and Gary saw it stung like a hornet's nest. Sarah said nothing, but her sobs and the slamming cabinets spoke volumes. *Fuck her,* he thought.

Gary slowly walked over to the sink to pour a glass of water. Then he looked up and nearly let the glass slip from his hand. It was the beansprouts again. The left side had a growth spurt in the past hour and was now taller and denser than its right twin.

"Sarah," Gary bellowed. "What have you done?" Sarah ignored her husband. "Sarah."

"What?" she said. "What is it? I haven't done anything."

"Like hell, you didn't. The bean sprouts."

"What about them? I haven't touched them."

"You've done something to them." Sarah walked over to the sink and saw the egg carton sitting on the windowsill. "Look," Gary fumed pointing at the carton.

"What am I looking at?"

"The left side has surpassed the right. They're bigger than they ever were."

Sarah hesitated before replying. "And what does this have to do with me?"

"You've done something to make this happen."

"What? Have you lost your mind?"

"Fed them miracle grow or something."

"Oh my God. Like I care enough about those stupid plants to do as much. This is your foolish deal, Gary. Not mine."

Sarah went back to putting away groceries and left her husband still fuming at the sink.

"You've done something," he muttered to himself.

CHAPTER ELEVEN

Gary was in his office early the next morning. He kept the door closed, and ignored the knocks that occasionally sought entry. Undoubtedly, they were from students looking for help. He had no time for them. His class was at ten, and he was eager to journal before babysitting the brats.

Gary sat at his desk and carefully undid the bow; he opened the cover, and slowly flipped through the inked pages until he arrived at the first blank page. He closed his eyes, took a deep breath through his nose and then exhaled forcefully through his mouth as he began to write. His hand was slow and unsure at first, but as he warmed to the task, the words flowed, and the pages filled effortlessly.

From the Journal of Gary Miller – March 16th

Bob's right. I spent my entire life praying with mixed results; the probability of success always in proportion with achieving success with or without prayer. I might as well have been praying to a half gallon of milk. I hate to say that cause it makes me sound like an atheist and God knows I am not. But I'm sick of spitting out the same, tired platitudes, the same one's I've spewed over the past twenty years, parroting other Christians because I thought I should.

I want to be honest with myself and with God. I want to know the truth. The truth is Godly. The truth is righteous. The truth is good. I must remember and keep that thought at the center of my journey.

I've learned this much over the course of these experiments: prayer is not enough. Real prayer is manifesting what you want through thought. It's science. It's math. The laws of physics explain it. It can be measured, and examined, and studied. And most importantly it works. I know it does.

Okay, experiment 5 then. I've decided to ask for something simple, a $20 bill. It's not earth-shattering or groundbreaking, but Bob did say to keep it simple (though I'm tempted not to). My faith is still a speck, however. It's a graduation of sorts from pennies to twenties, and very doable I think—a $20 bill within 24 hours. In fact, it's more than doable. It's done. It's already happened I just haven't reached that moment in time yet. Bob explained this to me. It has something to do with one of Einstein's theories on time and space. That everything that will be done has already been done; we just haven't reached that slice of time. He said that all of time can be viewed as a single sheet of paper and that time is linked to space and that if you bend space, you consequently bend time so that both ends of the paper (the beginning of time and the end of time) can be joined, and we can travel anywhere on the sheet of paper, either backward or forward (like going backward or forward in time, hence, time-travel). I don't pretend to understand it all. It is fascinating. I asked Bob how far he had gotten. Could he use his mind to time travel or to defy gravity? He said he could not, but has no doubt it's possible, that the experiments showed him as much. One just needs to erase all doubt, like Jesus stepping from the boat. Christ was a practitioner of mind-over-matter. I'm convinced. He didn't have the experiments—or did he? Perhaps Christ did have his own version of the experiments, and maybe this was his greatest talent. He was simply a man ahead of his time, and Bob has only caught up to him now. I wonder how far I will get with all this. I CAN'T WAIT TO SEE.

Gary Miller, you will find a 20-dollar bill in the next 24 hours. Believe it. See it. Achieve it. It's already done. You are on a collision course with your fate, Gary. Believe that.

I know she did something to those plants. She must have. Maybe she's been feeding and watering the left side, and allowing the right to starve? I thought about this a lot. It's not in Sarah's character to fuck with plants (me maybe, but not plants). She takes in strays for God's sake and nurtures them back to health. Maybe she's trying to teach me a lesson. She doesn't like the experiments. She's told me as much. She indulged me at first, but maybe this is her way of discouraging me or trying out some major mind fuck. That could be. She's trying to fuck with my mind. I'll not be dissuaded. I'm going to see it through for my sake and hers. Well, for my sake at any rate. I feel like I'm a train, a locomotive and I'm barreling down the track and if she wants to jump on board, she can jump on board. Otherwise, fuck her.

I don't know, Gary. It's not all her fault I suppose. It's yours mostly if I'm being honest. It hasn't been easy for her and God knows, it wasn't easy *for me. I think she knows me too well, and my true feelings. I've tried to suppress them, but that's nearly impossible for me. Still I try. I've come a long way I think.*

The money worries don't help. It's getting old. I could deal with it before, but it's starting to get to me. I'm forty-seven, not young anymore. It was okay to struggle in my twenties, but now it's just a pain in the ass. The other day, I had to choose between getting a sandwich or a drink in the cafeteria, but not both. For God's sake, I have a Ph.D. I'm a professor. Okay, it's a two-year Catholic school, but shouldn't I still be able to afford both a drink and some food in the school's cafeteria? What's the use? My life has become a joke. Only I'm not...

A gentle knock interrupted Gary. He was willing to ignore it, but it persisted, and grated on him.

"Come in," Gary answered sharply.

The door slowly swung open, and one of Gary's students, Amber, gingerly stepped into the office. She wore a short skirt that showed off a pair of shapely and tan legs. Gary's mood softened; Amber had his full attention.

"Hello," Amber said. "I was wondering if you had a few minutes to discuss my grade in World Religions."

Gary looked down at his journal and then closed it. "It's okay, Amber. Have a seat."

Amber took the empty chair next to Gary and crossed her legs at the knee. Gary's gaze traveled the length of her bare thigh and eventually came to rest on the opening in her blouse. Gary strained to catch a glimpse of her small breasts. His heart raced, and a warm, wet mass formed on his upper mouth. He slowly licked his lips. Gary became aware of what he was doing and quickly raised his eye level.

"Um, what can I do for you, Amber?"

"It's about my grade, Dr. Miller. I did bad on the last exam."

"What's your class grade right now?"

"I think I have a D right now, maybe a borderline C."

"I see. And why do you think you did so poorly on my exam?"

"I don't know," Amber said wringing her hands. "I like your class, and I like you a lot, but I get so confused, on all the different religions."

"I see. And did you study for the exam?"

Amber scrunched her face. "I did, but maybe not as much as I should have."

"Well, Amber, we still have a long way to go. Midterm grades are two weeks away, and you still have your paper. How is that coming along?"

Amber shrugged. "I just started it."

"Okay then, work hard on the paper, do the research and make sure it relates to the major discussion points we covered in class. Plus we'll have at least two major tests before the end of the semester. I suggest you get a study partner for those. Find someone in the class who looks like they know what they're doing and make friends with them. Okay?"

"Okay," Amber replied with a giggle. "I was wondering."

"Yes, Amber."

"I was wondering if there's anything else I can do to raise my grade?"

Gary closed his eyes and formed an image of him and Amber. This wasn't the first time he pictured Amber and himself, naked and intertwined. However, this picture was more vivid than it had ever been, and it produced a reaction that was both pleasant and uncomfortable at the same time. He saw Amber on top of his desk, her legs spread-eagled, and her panties wrapped like a silk restraint around her thin ankles. *How easy it would be*, he thought. No one would know. I'm sure lots of male professors had done the same thing, and some women too.

When he opened his eyes, he saw Amber sitting across from him smiling. He rubbed his fingers together. How easy would it be to reach out, just one touch, a squeeze, to feel that pliable skin in his hand or better still, his mouth. It was all he could do to keep his hand still and by his side.

Gary shook his head. "No, Amber," he finally said with a smile. "I'm afraid there's nothing else you can do other than study and work harder."

Amber uncrossed her legs and rose from her chair. "Okay, Dr. Miller."

"Amber, can you close the door on your way out?"

After the door shut, Gary's heart rate returned to normal.

"Oh, dear God," Gary whispered to himself before opening the journal to where he had left off. This time, instead of writing, he sketched. He illustrated a dollar sign with a thick cartoon-like font that gave the symbol both weight and dimension. Then he drew the number twenty in a similar style. He made these symbols repetitively—absent-mindedly, varying the stroke for variety and flavor. He was lost in thought and nearly hypnotized by the rhythmic nature of what he was doing. Over-and-over his hand moved without thought and without effort. When his mind came back, he became aware of what he was doing and stopped—but not after two entire pages had been completely filled with ink and the paper almost completely black.

Gary stared at the page. His eyes were wide, and his mouth hung open. Did I do this, he thought? Gary turned to the next page and started writing.

...laughing. I'm sick of it and ready to end my long spiral down. Sure, it hasn't been horrible—first world problems they're called—but I've fallen well short of my expectations. I've always thought by doing the right thing, it would get me far, but unfortunately, life isn't about doing the right thing. It's about taking care of business. Sure, morals and ethics are important, but they don't pay the bills. Banks don't want to hear how godly you are, they want to know when you'll make your next car payment.

Then I look around at the treachery around me, and it makes me sick to my stomach. So many of our so-called leaders misusing their power to our detriments, not theirs, but ours, the little guys struggling to survive. If they don't get a raise, so what? They're pulling in 10k per month after taxes (I did the math). They won't miss a cost of living raise. But for us meager wage earners, we are the ones that suffer for their crimes—yes, crimes, for they're no better than common thieves—thieves without guns as Mommy called them. And all the rhetoric I spewed in Sunday sermons. Our leaders are put in power by God. What utter nonsense. I can't believe I was so stupid. God had nothing to do with this motley crew of politicians and managers that I'm forced to cower to. They arrived at their power through cunning and deceit, through nepotism and cronyism.

Why do I complain? Why? It doesn't help. Action is what I need. Take the bull by the horns, and make things happen as I please—AS I SEE FIT. What's wrong with me? Why did it take this long to figure it out?

People don't care. They say they do, but at the end of the day, people care about themselves. The administration claims wage increases are a top priority, and another year goes by and still nothing. Yet, I see another building go up, a new field house, renovations to the student union, at what cost, millions? Oh and get this, they hired a compensation consultant. I try to bite my lip, but I wonder how much they paid him to tell us we need to be compensated fairly? Yet, without sufficient funds to do so, we won't be. I wonder what kind of genius you need to be to figure that out? Hell, I could have told them that. That's where are raises went to, paying some asshole 100k to tell you that no one will get a raise without the necessary funds to do so. What a fucking joke. My God...

Twenty dollars, that's all I ask. Even this meager sum would make me so happy, like a human being; what it would mean to feel human again?

Besides its face value, it would mean so much more than that. What it will do to my confidence, my faith, my belief in this system Bob devised. Bob remains the shining example. If I keep going, I can have what he has.

Twenty dollars, a twenty-dollar bill, a twenty.

Gary put down his pen and checked his computer. It was ten o'clock. His class was starting at that very moment and without him. Where had the time gone, he wondered? It seemed to disappear when he wrote. He reluctantly closed his journal, gathered his briefcase and hurried out of his office, and down the hallway. He walked past Ryan's office, and though he was in a rush, he couldn't resist popping his head in.

"Ryan?" Gary said. "I'm trying to plan for the summer. Do you know how many overloads I have?"

Ryan averted his eyes. "Oh," he said. "I was going to send you an email."

Gary was alarmed. "An e-mail?" he said. "An e-mail about what?"

"Do you have a minute? Have a seat."

"No, no," Gary said forcefully shaking his head. "I don't have time. I'm late for my class as it is. Just tell me."

Ryan shook his head. "I'm sorry, but there are no overloads for the summer. There just weren't enough students to justify the extra classes."

Gary was stunned. His first thought was to hold his tongue, but despite this resolution, he could not. "But—but I was counting on that extra money."

"I know you were, Gary, but there simply weren't enough students to fill the classes."

"Oh. What about fall of next year?"

"Maybe. I haven't looked at fall yet, but I'll do what I can to find you an overload."

"Fine."

"Gary, I'm sorry. I did my best."

"Sure," Gary said as he marched off. "Of course you did."

• • • • • •

Gary watched the cat bounding toward him like a deer, ready to pounce on his shoelaces in the prescribed manner; but a well-timed kick caught Snowball squarely on the jaw and sent him flying in the direction from which he came. The cat landed with an acrobatic tumble before scrambling back to its paws, then scurried to the relative safety beneath the porch.

"Stupid cat," Gary snarled in a barely audible voice. Gary mounted the steps with heavy footfalls. He opened the door and slammed it shut as he entered his home.

"Sarah," he yelled. "I've told you not to feed that cat."

Sarah's voice bellowed back from the kitchen. "I've told you, Gary. I don't feed the cat."

"Yes, I know," Gary said while plopping his briefcase down on the kitchen table. "It feeds itself, right?"

"That's right."

"That's right, my ass."

Sarah turned to her husband and shot him a disapproving look. "And why are you in such a good mood?"

"I had a bad day at work."

"Another one?"

"What do you mean, another one? What do you mean by that?"

"Seems like you've had a lot of bad days lately."

"There are no overloads for the summer."

"Oh no," Sarah said.

"Yes. I found out today. Not enough students."

"What are we going to do?"

"Same thing we've always done. Tighten our belt, scramble, rob from Peter to pay Paul. Bounce checks and pay overdraft fees."

Sarah walked over to Gary and placed a hand on his shoulder. "And pray?"

"Yes, yes, of course. And pray." Then he added beneath his breath, "Like that does any good."

Sarah rested her cheek on Gary's shoulder. "It will be alright," she said.

Gary produced a weak smile and then placed his hand on top of Sarah's. He felt sad and lonely and some remorse had crept into his heart. "I'm sorry," he said. "You know—about the bean sprouts."

"I kind of wish we had never planted the bean sprouts for all the trouble they've caused."

"I just don't understand. Every other experiment has worked so well, but this one, well, not so much. I mean it started working."

"We're having meatloaf for dinner. Oh, and I almost forgot. Chuck called."

"Chuck?" Gary said with some alarm. "What did he want?"

"He didn't say, but he wants to meet with you at your earliest convenience. At the church."

"Did he say what it was about?"

"He did not."

. . . . . .

A bead of perspiration formed on Gary's upper lip. His knee bounced uncontrollably, so much so that he used his hand to steady it. The clock on the rectory wall read ten past nine in the morning. *Where is he*, Gary thought?

Gary racked his brain for a reason. In the nine years he worked for the church as an associate pastor, he had never been called into the office, at least not formally. There could be a thousand reasons why he was asked in, and some of those reasons could be related to good news, like a raise, or a new title. His thoughts were dark, however. His logical mind told him it was nothing. His intuition told him something else.

When Chuck finally arrived, Gary's trepidation only grew. Chuck didn't say anything right away. He didn't have to. The consternation was evident on his face. Gone was the jovial smile, which Gary had grown accustomed. Instead, Chuck wore a forced smile, like someone trying to keep up a pleasant appearance under troubling circumstances.

"Gary," Chuck said. "Thank you for coming in on short notice."

"Yes, of course," Gary responded in a weak voice. "What—what did you want to see me about?"

Chuck took in a deep breath of air and then blew it out in a long, sustained gust. He did not look Gary in the eyes. And with that simple gesture, Gary knew his fate was sealed—even before a single word had been uttered.

"Gary, I want to talk to you about the collections."

CHAPTER TWELVE

Gary went into work despite canceling his classes for the day. He wanted to be alone, and he knew his office would be the only place he would find peace and solitude before having to face Sarah again. The inevitable confrontation filled him with a sense of dread the likes of which he had never experienced before. His stomach churned at the thought. Gary closed the door behind him. There would be no office hours today.

After taking his seat, he carefully produced the journal from his briefcase and gingerly laid it on his desk. Then he undid the leather bow, flipped to the first blank page and began to write. He wrote quickly, with a frantic hand that seemed to glide across the page while leaving a trail of black ink in its wake.

*From the Journal of Gary Miller: April 19*th*, 2017*

Shit. SHIT. SHIT. SHIT. I fucked up this time. Royally. When I was a child, I stole some cheap candy from Hebner Heights grocery when the owner wasn't looking. I thought that was bad, like going to Hell bad. This is worse. Much worse.

I explained to Chuck that I had merely borrowed the money and that taxes were due, and I was in a pinch. I even tried to appeal to his Christian nature (supposed Christian nature that is) and asked for his forgiveness. There I was practically groveling and near tears. The tears were fake, but the groveling was real enough. He told me he had already forgiven me but that he had no choice but to relieve me of my duties (fire me). What a crock of shit. Before I left, I gave him one parting shot. I told him while he was at it, he should trace the money pastor Meyers had borrowed during his tenure. Where did he think I learned that little trick from? I nearly cracked myself up watching the blood drain from his face.

I almost don't even care. A part of me is relieved I won't have to come up with the same tired bullshit sermon again-and-again. Let me think; Jesus good. Satan bad. Oh yes, I've think I got it now. I don't believe it anymore. Satan and Jesus and heaven and hell. What's my reward for obeying the rules and following Jesus? Oh yes, heaven, for an eternity no less. My god, the thought of spending eternity somewhere / anywhere is unimaginable. I don't care how nice it is. I'm sure I'd be bored out of my skull.

I'll miss the extra money. As meager as it was, it helped. I don't know; if this goddamned school would pay us what we're worth, maybe I wouldn't have to dip my hand into the coffers. Sometimes, I wonder who the real thieves are in society. Is it the people carrying guns, and robbing up the place, or is it the respectable businessmen and politicians who live off the backs and toil of the common man? My dear Mommy, God rest her soul, she told me real criminals don't need a gun to steal. How right you were, Mommy, though I never believed you at the time. I should have listened. I was not a good son, a good son, not a good son.

God, what will Sarah think? She's already a bitch, bitches at me every five seconds. She always has been a bitch, since the day we were married, always wanting more than what I could provide, always dissatisfied, unhappy; never that bright, cheerful…. I can't say I blame her. I suppose it hasn't been easy for her. She knows. She must know—ever since the day we were married, on our wedding night. Jesus, our wedding night. Funny what I think about, what pops into my head. It's tormented me for the past however-many years. God, I can't believe I'm saying this, but perhaps it's about time to release these thoughts into the universe; let them be known. It's the truth, and maybe it's about time to stop running from the truth. The truth is Godly.

Gary put down his pen and buried his face in his hands. The pain in his belly reminded him he hadn't eaten in the past twelve hours; he stood up, checked inside his wallet, and was grateful to see a dollar bill, just enough for coffee and maybe he could swipe a cookie; all he needed to wake up.

Gary left his office and returned fifteen minutes with a cup of coffee and a Styrofoam foam container. He opened the container and inhaled the aroma of bacon, eggs, and sausage; it was intoxicating and brought a much-needed smile to his face. Gary reached in and hurriedly placed a piece of bacon into his mouth. Then he opened his journal and began writing furiously, his pen dug into the paper and left deep canals filled with ink.

It worked. I got my $20 bill. I had almost forgotten about it, but it came, nonetheless. Get this; it was spit from the ass of a pretty, dark–haired cod-ed. She was walking in front of me about five paces. Okay, yes, I was admiring her ass stuffed into a tight pair of Levis. Why shouldn't I? It was there for all to see. She wanted people to look at her ass and, well, I obliged. It was plump and quite lovely I must say. Well then, I saw her reach back into her pocket and pull something out. I don't know what it was, a comb or something, but along with it came a bill. It must have caught a draft because it floated up and hung in the air just long enough for me to pluck it in midflight and without breaking stride. I swear it would have struck me in the face if I hadn't grabbed it (the kismet). I stole a quick glance before I stuffed it into my coat pocket. It was a twenty.

Yes, I kept it. Why shouldn't I? I had asked for it, and the universe came through just as I knew it would. I could have given it back, but I'm sure I need it more than she. I didn't recognize her. Probably a rich bitch, here on her daddy's dime. Perhaps she was a government welfare case or on the GI bill. I could have returned it, and that would have satisfied the experiment, but that's not the point. The Universe wanted me to have it and now it's mine. At any rate, I'm $20 richer, and I bought real food with it.

I'm so happy. The experiments work. What else can it be? I can tap into the universal power and make it do my will. Well, we all have this power evidently; I've learned to harness it with Bob's help. God, that man must be a genius. No, he's not a genius. He's just a smart man, who has studied science and religion and philosophy and who has stumbled on a way to manipulate the law of attraction through practice and experimentation. It's like a golfer learning to shape his golf ball around the course, to have the ball do his bidding through hours of training and repetition. Practice. Practice. Practice. That's it. Train the brain, Gary. Train the brain. It's a powerful weapon.

I've come to realize I've spent my entire life waiting for someone—a woman, a parent, or God himself—to believe in me. As if this external belief was permission to achieve success. I was wrong. I need to believe in me. That's all. I'm the only one who needs to believe in me. To Hell with everyone else. To Hell with the church. I see now losing my job was actually a blessing in disguise. At the end of the day, the extra money I made delivering sermons, went back to the church through tithing. Ten percent of my gross income went towards tithes. I felt like I was working for the church simply to pay the church. Why? Because the Bible tells us so? That's a joke, a fucking joke. I now realize the church wrote that part *into the Bible. And the part that says wives should obey their husbands. Yes, someone's husband wrote that. And where it says slaves should obey their master's, and their master's will have to answer to God in the end? A Master wrote that.*

I've learned this much: the biblical authors were scoundrels just like the rest of us. God didn't inspire them. They were inspired by their own greed and selfish causes and power-hungry motives. Now I know.

So there will be no extra income from the church, but the government will get less tax from me, and the church will lose my tithe. No great loss. Far better for it as I see it.

Okay, what is next? What can't I ask for? What can't I achieve? What remains beyond my reach? Nothing. I am sure of this. NOTHING. I can't wait to tell Bob. He will be so thrilled. It's funny, I consider Bob my mentor; he's the architect of these experiments after all. But I feel he's missed some greater point. I see now that everything he has, his beautiful wife, his house, and even his health are the result of manifestation, mind over matter. He's tapped into the power that surrounds us all. And yet, he had not gone far enough. What he's achieved are mere toys, trinkets, and a trophy wife (a gorgeous trophy, I'll grant you). They are nice to have, I'll admit, but I wonder if there's not a greater cause that is lost amongst the superficial, something that is not possessed but resides within one's soul.

Gary stopped writing and placed his pen down. He felt a presence walking down the hall towards his office. It was a young male, and though he could not see or hear this person, he knew he was there nonetheless; Gary anticipated the knock before it happened. This phenomenon was nothing new to Gary. He sensed things with increasing regularity. It was odd, but Gary was accustomed to it.

"Come in," Gary said in a loud voice.

The door swung open, and Brandon slowly shuffled into the office. "Dr. Miller. I didn't think you'd be here since class was canceled."

"It's okay, Brandon. Come in and have a seat."

Brandon carefully closed the door behind him and took a seat in the chair across from Gary. "Is your paper finished?" Gary said.

Brandon's eyes grew wide. "No," he answered. "I thought we had another week."

"Oh, yes you do but don't wait till the last minute."

"Oh, no Dr. Miller. I have the paper outlined. I got a good start on it."

Brandon stared at Gary as if he were about to ask a question, but never did. After a few awkward moments of silence, Gary said, "Is there something I can help you with?"

"You—you're a pastor?"

Gary lowered his eyes and let out a long breath. "More accurately, young man, I was a pastor."

"Oh? What happened?"

"My church and I had an amicable parting of the ways, just this morning."

"Oh, I'm sorry."

"Don't be. It was for the best. Let us just say, for our purposes, I'm still a pastor. Are you in need of one? Did you get your girlfriend pregnant?"

"What?" Brandon answered quickly. "No. I have some questions."

"About?"

"Like religious questions."

"Well, I have degrees in both religion and philosophy, and I teach these disciplines, so I can probably help you. Right?"

"Oh, yes of course."

A long silence ensued before Gary spoke again. "Brandon?"

"Yes, Dr. Miller?"

"I'm a busy man. I have a lot of grading to do. What is your question?"

"Do you think homosexuality is an abomination to God?"

Gary had to cover his mouth to hide a smile. He searched Brandon's stoic face, but the young man gave nothing away. "No," Gary finally said. "Of course not. Why would you even consider such a thing?"

"No?"

"People believe it's an abomination, Brandon, simple-minded people who cannot grasp the world beyond the tiny hemisphere in which they live, breathe and die. That is to say their tiny brains. And what these people believe, their beliefs suddenly become God's will. Funny how that works, isn't it?"

"But the Bible verse that says it's an abomination—"

"Which verse would that be?" Gary interrupted.

"I don't know which one."

"Brandon, if you're going to reference the bible, then please know the book and the verse, and you should know the entire passage, not just bits and pieces. The reference you're looking for is Leviticus 18:22 and 20:13, or perhaps its Romans 1:26–27 of the New Testament?"

"Yeah—yeah, I guess," Brandon stuttered.

"Listen to me. People twist what the Bible says, or they simply don't have the knowledge to understand the context in which it was written."

"Yeah?"

"Yes. I should know. I was as guilty as any, I'm ashamed to say."

"You were?"

Gary averted his eyes. "Yes, but I'm not doing that anymore."

"So the Bible doesn't say homosexuality is an abomination?"

"Brandon—" Gary stopped abruptly. He was about to admonish the boy but saw the fear in Brandon's eyes. It reminded Gary of his own youth and so he softened his tone. "Brandon, the Bible says a lot of things, many of which would land you in prison if you tried to practice them in today's society, and rightfully so. The problem stems from selective reading and attempting to make scripture fit society's stupid prejudices and ignorance. The Bible does not say homosexuality is an abomination. If it did, then you and I and everyone we know would be total abominations for reasons completely unrelated to our sexuality."

"Oh, okay. But I talked to my pastor—"

"I don't know who your pastor is, but if he told you homosexuality is a sin, then he's an idiot. I'm sorry, Brandon, I don't know any other way of telling you this."

Brandon loosened his grip on the armrest and then let his body slink back into his chair. "You're sure about this?"

Gary nodded his head. "Brandon, I'm surer of this than anything else in my life."

"Oh good," Brandon replied. "I hope you don't think… I'm not gay or anything."

Gary knew different. He could see through Brandon's thinly veiled disguise, but he wasn't about to shatter the boy's delusion.

"Of course you're not," Gary said. "And if you were, I could hardly give a rat's ass."

"It's for a friend. He wanted to know if he was going to Hell. You won't tell anyone about this conversation, will you, Dr. Miller?"

"Why would I do that?"

"Oh, I don't know. Can we just keep this conversation between the two of us?"

"Of course, Brandon. I'll not tell a soul. I promise."

"Thanks." Brandon stood up and made his way towards the door but paused just before leaving. "Why was class canceled today?"

"Because I felt like canceling," Gary responded in a matter of fact tone. "Class will resume Friday."

"Oh, okay, and thank you again for helping me, Doctor Miller."

"Of course, Brandon."

After Brandon left, Gary once again wrote in his journal. Only this time he had lost control of the pen. An outside force seemed to push the instrument forth, and ink spilled in a conscious stream of thought. His hand moved, but he had no say in how it moved. Gary thought it was fascinating if not a bit alarming. But after several deep breaths, he resigned himself to the phenomenon. Gary sat back, relaxed his grip and allowed the pen to move unencumbered by his mind nor his body.

From Gary Miller's Journal:

We have become slaves to a great corporate wheel that churns mindlessly, and endlessly to keep itself going. We the people are mere cogs in this machine; we're worn and ground until we are broke and useless only to be replaced by a shiny new part when we wear out, and eventually die. And then what? We are supposed to believe that our reward lies in heaven. What if it doesn't? What if there is no heaven? What if heaven is an invention of the fools that run our society? Heaven (and God for that matter) was likely invented by the church to keep the masses silent and working towards a common goal. Shut up and do your job. Your reward awaits you in heaven. Yeah right. It sounds more-and-more to me like bullshit to appease the lower classes, to keep them bound in slavery to serve society, the wealthy, the powerful and the church.

Speaking of slavery, I feel more-and-more like a slave every day. The school hired a compensation consultant to help compensate the faculty more equitably. More fairly? Yeah right. I wonder how much they paid this so-called expert. 100k? Take that money and split it amongst the faculty, and that will be the most significant raise we'll see or ever will see. I don't need an expert to tell me that if there is no money, THERE WILL BE NO RAISE. End of story. I've seen this type of thing before. Companies / organizations legitimately fall on hard times and stop giving cost of living raises. A year passes, then two, then three, and no one makes a stink, or if they do, if they speak their mind, they're dismissed. It becomes easier-and-easier to not give raises even when there is plenty of money to do so. Soon, the people who remember a time where raises were the norm will be gone. They'll be replaced by the gullible fools who only knew hardship and have become accustomed to it. It's George Orwell's

Animal Farm all over again. I didn't understand it much when I first read it, but now I do. Fuck it, I say. I don't need a raise. I'll give myself one. I've found the way. Pennies turn into twenty-dollar-bills and so on. There's a map drawn for me. I only need to follow it.

But enough with butterflies and green cars and pennies and all sorts of useless things. If the law of attraction works, I mean really works, the universe will bring me anything I want, bigger things, and greater wealth still. Harris said it was a matter of confidence, to believe that it has already happened. Well, something has happened. I feel it—maybe it's the twenty-dollar bill I manifested, or the hot meal sitting in my belly—but I'm flush with confidence and well-being as if I were high or drunk or something. My entire body tingles. I could put my fist through a brick wall if I so wished. I am sure of this.

Well now, it's time to make a grocery list, a grocery list to the Universe:
$200
A new watch (one of the fancy digital ones)
A new home. Big and spacious with a big-ass library (like Harris).
Clothes, some decent clothes for once.
A new car (Tesla or a T as Belle calls it?)
A new...

Gary stopped writing. He placed the end of the pen into his mouth and then bit down hard on the plastic. He thought twice about completing his last request but decided better of it. There was time, he thought. Then he ended his journal entry for the day.

Keep the faith, Gary and keep practicing. As Bob said, when your mind changes, everything around you will change.

CHAPTER THIRTEEN

Snowball rushed to greet Gary but stopped short when he saw the black-cloaked legs approach him. There was something different in Gary's step this evening; he moved with rhythm, an elongated stride, and a new sense of purpose that could only be sensed by an animal's heightened awareness. Snowball looked up and saw a scowling face staring back at him. It was his friend, perhaps a bit off, but it was Gary all the same. Snowball continued down the walkway in his usual playful manner, bounding like a whitetail until he was within striking distance of Gary's right foot. Then with the timing of an Olympic athlete, the cat executed a perfect swan dive that landed him squarely on Gary's instep. Once there, Snowball bear-hugged Gary's right ankle and sunk his claws into the fabric to maintain his hold. Snowball rode Gary's foot for several hurried steps before a mule kick to his head punctuated his departure; it left the kitten dazed as he watched a pair of blurry legs disappear inside the house.

.   .   .   .   .

Gary saw his wife sitting at the kitchen table. She was writing something in a book. He strained to see what it was, but Sarah put down her pen and closed it quickly before he could get a closer look.

Gary raised a single eyebrow. "What's that you're writing?" he asked.

"Recipes," Sarah answered quickly while closing the book shut. "I'm writing down my recipes."

Though Sarah held the book in her hands, Gary was quick and used his superior strength to rip it from her.

"Hey," Sarah yelled. "Give it here. It's mine."

Gary looked at the cover, and smirked. "You're writing recipes in a diary?" he said.

"Well, yes."

"Since when did you start keeping a diary, Sarah?"

"Well, you have your journal. What's wrong with me keeping a diary?"

"Nothing. Nothing at all, but your diary has a lock on it. Are you afraid I'll steal your recipes?"

Sarah appeared nervous. She smiled, held out her hand and said, "May I?"

Gary tossed the book on the kitchen table and walked to the sink. He saw the egg carton sitting on the windowsill and shook his head in disbelief. "What's for dinner, Sarah?"

"You're home early. I wasn't expecting you so soon. How was work today?"

Gary did not want to be grilled. He bit down hard on his lower lip and said, "It was fine."

Sarah sat silent for several moments before responding. "Work was fine?"

"Yes," Gary said trying to remain calm. "It was okay. You know, it's work."

"What did Chuck want to see you about?"

"Chuck?"

"Yes. Didn't you meet with Chuck this morning at the church?"

"Oh yes—just some church business. I'm going to go upstairs and lie down before dinner if that's okay with you."

"Yeah, sure."

"Are you sure? I could stay and help if you need me."

"It's okay, Gary. Go upstairs. I've got this."

"Thanks. I've been feeling a bit under the weather as of late. I hope I'm not coming down with anything."

"Yes," Sarah said after a pause. "It must have been a hard day."

CHAPTER FOURTEEN

Gary opened his wallet and pulled out a ten-dollar bill. He held it up between his thumb and forefinger and then released it. The bill floated like a lame bird before landing next to the Bourbon-filled glass. Gary picked up the glass and swallowed the contents in a single gulp.

"Ah," Gary said. "That is some fuckin' good Bourbon, my friend."

Bob stared at the bill for a moment, then he looked up at Gary's smiling face.

"It worked," Gary said. "Experiment five. It worked."

Bob clapped his hands together loudly and his baritone laugh filled the library. "This is what you asked for?" Bob said. "Ten dollars?"

Gary nodded his head. "A twenty-dollar bill, actually. This is the change after I bought lunch. You'll never guess where it came from."

"Where?"

"From a student's ass."

Bob's confused expression begged for an explanation, so Gary explained how he came to possess the cash.

"She had a nice ass?" Bob said after Gary had finished his story.

Gary smiled and nodded his head slowly. "A very nice ass. I would even say a fuckin' nice arse."

This sent Bob into another explosion of laughter and hand clapping, which pulled Gary in. The two were a spectacle, cutting up like teenaged boys at a sleepover.

"Oh, Boy. Oh, Boy," Bob said. He stopped suddenly and took on a more serious tone. "Do you see now?"

"Yes, but before it had been pennies, and butterflies, and metal rods." Gary picked up the bill and crushed it in his hand. He held his fist to his face and said, "This—this is real." Gary leaned in close, and in a staccato beat repeated, "This—is—real."

Bob leaned in and whispered, "I know."

"This is how you did it, man, your house, your wife, your money. You manifested these things, right?"

"I told you as much, way back when I first introduced you to the experiments."

"Yes, I know. Well, you tried to tell me, but I was blind then. My eyes are open now, my friend. At first, I thought you were mad, and then I became hopeful, and now—"

"And now?"

"And now, I can have anything I want, everything you have. Isn't that so?" Bob nodded his head. "Yes. I can have anything," Gary continued. "And Bob—I don't know how to say this, but—"

Bob held his hand up to stop Gary. "You're welcome," he said. "But you know I didn't do anything special. I simply stood on the shoulders of giants who came before—the great philosophers and spiritual leaders, and yogis and gods—and I took what they knew and mixed it with what I knew and well, here we are."

"Yes, but that's what any of us do. We all stand on the shoulders of giants don't we?"

"Perhaps."

"Yes, I think we do, and now I stand on your shoulders. Bob, I want to have everything you have, more if you don't mind me saying."

"Not at all. I don't mind. I want this for you too. I want it for all mankind. Why should a few people live in luxury, while the rest struggle? It doesn't make sense to me. We live in a land of plenty. There's enough to go around. This is why I chose you."

"Chose me?"

"Yes. It's because you're a decent human being, Gary. I trust you will use this knowledge for the betterment of mankind, regardless of their religion, or race, or whatever. I can count on you?"

Gary's reply was quick and certain. His friend had asked for help, and Gary was eager to repay his friend. "You can count on me."

"Good."

Gary picked up the decanter, refilled his glass and immediately took a sip. "I'm afraid I've grown impatient," he said. "I've journaled other things I want to manifest."

"That's okay, Gary. Journal your heart's desire. That's what its there for."

"But am I ready for that? You told me I had to go step-by-step."

"And you have. You've completed five experiments. You're ready for experiment six, and soon after, the final experiment—experiment seven. I can just look at you and see you've changed. Your vibrational frequency is on another level; it's more in congress with the rest of the universe."

Gary's face went blank. Once again, Bob—with his scientific jargon—had made him feel inadequate. "My vibrational frequency?"

"Yes. Everything in the universe is vibrating, both living and dead. Even inanimate objects emit this frequency. In fact, every atom in the universe is in constant motion."

Gary took another sip. He wasn't sure he fully understood, but the topic fascinated him. "Continue."

"Well, my experiments are designed to raise your frequency, and thus your ability to manipulate your world as you see fit."

"And my frequency is higher than what it was before?"

"Yes."

"And you can tell just by looking at me?"

Bob's voice rose with excitement. "Yes," he answered. "I can see it has. Your eyes, in fact, your entire countenance is more alive. You almost look like a different person."

"I feel like a different person."

"See? That's it. You've now reached a higher state of consciousness. Your frequency has risen, and you can feel it can't you?"

Gary touched his hand to his chin and ran his fingers against his rough, three-day growth. "Yes. I feel something. It's like I have this—this energy or power like I've never known before. It's quite strange, actually."

"Do you remember how you were when I first told you about the experiments? Gary, you were depressed as Hell. Defeat was written across your face, and now look at you."

"How do I look?" Gary said pressing a hand to his face.

"There's a fire in your eyes, man, and that fire will grow, and it will get stronger and never be doused."

"Explain it to me. How does it work from a scientific standpoint? What does raising one's frequency have to do with creating the life I want?"

"It has <u>everything</u> to do with creating the life you want. See, frequency is just another term for energy, and everything in this universe is made up of this thing we call energy. Understand?" Gary nodded his head. "Okay, then. So when you increase your frequency, you have a more positive state of energy, and since like things attract, you will attract more positive things into your life. When your energy is low, then you will attract more negative things into your life. Make sense?"

Gary's face lit up. He didn't know if it was the Bourbon or if some of Bob was finally rubbing off, but for the first time he was actually able to follow along. "Why, yes," he said. "That actually does make sense. And this is all scientific? It's not some pseudoscience you made up?"

"Of course not. It's physics. Laws explain our universe, and how it works. I just applied these laws to solve practical, real-world problems. You see, Gary. Everything is connected; all of us are attached, so that what you put out into the universe comes back to you. What you do to one man, Gary, you do to yourself."

Gary understood the concept well. It was biblical in nature. "For whatsoever a man soweth, that shall he also reap?"

Bob pointed his index finger at Gary. "Exactly. It's the same thing our spiritual leaders have been telling us all along." Bob paused, sat back in his chair and gazed at the ceiling. "What you have done unto the least of my brethren, you have done unto me."

Gary recognized the quote. "Matthew?"

"Yes. Matthew. Twenty-five, forty. Have you heard of the butterfly effect?"

"I've heard of it."

"It's part of chaos theory. It simply means that minute changes in one state could have sweeping changes in a later state of a non-linear system. A small disturbance such as a butterfly flapping its wings in one part of the world can cause tsunamis to occur in another part of the world."

Gary pressed his middle fingers to his temple and said, "You're blowing my mind, Bob."

Bob sat up straight and punched the air with his fist. "Good," he said in a loud voice that echoed throughout the library. "I want to blow your fucking mind. That's the whole point, to raise your level of awareness, to make you understand that everything you think becomes your reality. Our world is defined by our thoughts. The world doesn't exist out there..." Bob pointed to his temple. "...it exists in here."

Gary was both fascinated and bewildered by the lesson. He was familiar with religious dogma—Jesus, Satan, Heaven, Hell, good and evil—but Bob's ideas were strange and wonderful. The experiments were a different way, he thought, a way based on both faith and spirituality and still backed by science. More importantly, they worked. Gary saw they worked.

"I think I understand," Gary said. "Your experiments develop more positive thoughts, and thus a more positive world?"

"Yes."

"You are brilliant, Bob."

"Yes, I am, but that's beside the point."

Gary smiled. "So, am I to understand that since my world is defined by my thoughts, that I am limited only by these thoughts and nothing more?"

"That's right. You've got it."

"So what's not possible? That is the real question."

"Exactly, Gary. Now you understand. Ask that question, and keep asking it. What's not possible? This is so much more than obtaining material wealth, trinkets and toys. It's about changing your world, our world for the better. Think about it. What is it you want? I don't mean possessions that end up broken and relegated to the garbage heap. I'm talking about the things that last forever. You're journaling every day?"

"Yes. I've grown to love it. I wasn't sure at first, but now I see how beneficial it is."

"See? Journaling, or writing down your thoughts helps you manifest. By writing things down, you give shape and form to your ideas, and this will help raise your frequency and bend the universe to your will."

Gary smiled as he thought about his journal. He considered it a secret weapon of sorts, a way of controlling his life by writing down his thoughts, needs and desires. He was unaware of the phenomenon before, but now he understood. He knew something very few people did, and this filled him with a sense of pride.

Gary stared into his glass as he swirled the Bourbon. "One thing is peculiar," he said. "Sometimes, when I'm writing, it's like I'm not even writing. It's like the pen has a mind of its own. I'm holding it, but I'm not actually writing the words down. It's frightening actually, but I've learned to accept it."

Bob laughed and clapped his hands together. "That's called automatic writing," Bob explained. "It's nothing to be frightened of. It happens to me all the time."

"What's this automatic writing?"

"It's just like it sounds. It's when the words come automatically instead of you consciously producing them."

"But who is doing the writing?"

"You are, Gary, or rather your soul is."

"My soul?"

"Yes. Remember I said you're reaching a higher plane of consciousness? Well, your conscious mind is simply getting out of the way, so that your unconscious mind, the part that holds your deepest desires, can come forth."

Gary was aware of these conscious and unconscious states. He was in the habit of slipping from one and into the other without so much as a thought. The line between dream and awake states became blurred and sometimes he couldn't tell which he was in or remember how he had gotten there. That was one matter, but other things happened too, strange things that Gary could not explain and made him question his own mental state.

"There's something else," Gary said.

"What is it?"

Gary hesitated. He wasn't sure if he should say anything for fear of sounding weird. Then he remembered who he was talking to and pressed on. "I–I'm seeing things, Bob."

"Seeing things? What kind of things?"

"It's silly," Gary laughed. "Maybe seeing is the wrong word. I mean, I know things before they happen. The phone will ring, and I'll know who it is before looking at caller ID. Someone will knock on a closed door and I'll know who it is before they enter."

"For real, Gary? That's fantastic."

"What do you mean? You mean that's normal?"

"Yes, quite normal, but these phenomena usually occur after experiment seven, and here you are on five."

Gary felt relieved. The supernatural things were sometimes frightful and brought to mind his own evangelical warnings. Do not mess with soothsayers, psychics or the dead, he preached out of ignorance or habit or both. However, Bob had set his mind at ease. These were normal events, and he was normal for experiencing them. Bob said so. There was nothing to be afraid of, he thought.

Gary ran his hand across his thinning hair. "All this is still quite strange to me. Like my drawings. You should see them. I've made all kinds; fantastic drawings I never knew I was capable of."

"Yes, yes. Like automatic writing, your soul has taken over the pen; the God within is taking over and he is a master artist. Keep it up good man."

"Yes. I'll draw every day and write too."

"So, are you ready for six?"

Gary smiled and said, "I am."

CHAPTER FIFTEEN

Gary arrived home and was immediately accosted on the porch by Snowball and his wife. Both appeared to lie in wait for his arrival—Snowball with his usual youthful enthusiasm, and Sarah with a fierce energy that belied her chubby but diminutive stature. She didn't have to say anything. Her emotions were palpable; her body trembled, and her face contorted into a menacing sneer.

Gary was proactive, launching into his rhetoric before Sarah could speak. "Hello, my Dear," he chirped. "What's for dinner?"

"And when were you going to tell me?" Sarah said.

Snowball threw his body onto Gary's instep and sunk his teeth into the loose lace dangling from his shoe. He ripped and tore into the cotton string as if he were slaying a mouse.

"Tell you what?" Gary replied while trying to shake the pesky cat free of his shoe.

Sarah's face was beet red. "Do you think I'm stupid, Gary?"

"No. No, I don't think that."

"I spoke to Chuck's wife."

"Oh, so she told you?"

"She was concerned. She was reaching out to me."

"What did she say?"

"Everything."

Gary laughed. "Oh well, that must have been an awkward conversation. Oh, would you fucking please get away from me?" Gary shouted at Snowball. He shook his foot hard sending the cat flying into the hedge.

Gary stormed past Sarah, brushing hard against her as he made his way into the house and some needed refuge. Sarah followed closely behind and caught up to him in the kitchen.

"When Gary, when were you going to tell me?" she said.

Gary turned quickly and placed his nose a mere inch from hers. He took a deep breath and composed himself before answering. "I was ashamed," he said in a soft voice. "Okay? I was too embarrassed to tell you."

Sarah's eyes grew moist. "Ashamed of what? There's no shame in losing your job."

Gary's eyes widened. "Oh. So, you don't know?" he said. Gary headed straight to the cupboard where he kept the wine. He poured himself a glass and stared into the red liquid before taking a sip.

"Gary? Tell me what happened?"

Gary took another sip, and then another. "Chuck accused me of stealing money from the church," he said.

"What?"

Gary let out a chuckle. "Yes. Can you believe that?"

"Why would he do that?" Gary emptied his glass. Then he poured himself another. "Gary?" Sarah repeated. "Why would he do that?"

Gary looked at his wife and pleaded his case with open arms. "Taxes were due."

Sarah covered her mouth with her hand. "Oh, God. Then it's true?" she said in a muffled voice. "Gary?"

"No. Of course, it's not true. I simply borrowed the money. I was going to put it back. In fact, I did already—some of it—I was going to put the rest back out of my next paycheck."

"Oh God," Sarah said grasping her stomach and taking a seat at the kitchen table. "I think I'm going to be sick."

"Please, Sarah. Don't be so dramatic."

"Oh? I'm dramatic? You steal money, from the church no less, and I'm being dramatic?"

Gary's face turned red. "I did not steal it."

"What will people think? I won't be able to show my face."

"Who the hell cares what people think?"

"I do," Sarah shot back. "And what about church? We'll have to find a new place to worship."

Gary grabbed Sarah by her shoulders, and spoke to her in a calm, deliberate voice. "Look at me," he said. "It's going to be fine."

"Fine? How's it going to be fine? We've lost face, our church, not to mention the extra income."

Gary shook his head. "No, no. I have that figured out. Working for the church was actually costing us money."

"Costing us money? How?"

"Well, it raised our tax liability, so we end up paying more income tax. It's like government was telling us we don't need the extra income so give it here. And, and, and, the tithing. I was making more money, so I was required to tithe more, right? It was like I was working extra to pay the government and the church off, not to actually get ahead. No more of that."

"Gary, why didn't you say something? I could have gotten a job."

Gary walked back to the counter to retrieve his wine glass. He emptied it in one gulp. "Well, then why didn't you?" he said. "We had talked about you getting an extra job. Did you ever look?"

"No. I guess I didn't realize how bad things had gotten."

"Look, Sarah. It's okay. That's what I'm trying to say. I'll have more time to pursue other ventures. I can write more, and make extra money that way, plus we won't have to tithe to the church anymore."

"What?"

"You heard me."

"We're not going to tithe?"

"No," Gary said. "Hell, no. We can't go back to that church."

"Then we'll find another."

"Well, you find another then, but I'm telling you this much. No church is getting my money. That's my money. I worked hard for it, and I'm keeping it. All of it."

"Gary?"

"What? There's nothing wrong with that. See? I figured it all out."

"Figured what out?"

Gary rapidly paced the kitchen floor as he spoke. "The scam, the lies we were led to believe, the brainwashing that's taken place since we were children. God doesn't care about what's in my wallet. He cares about what's in my heart. Its people, Sarah, people care about my money. The church cares about my money, the government cares about money, the banks and mortgage companies care about my money. When the bible says tithe ten percent of your gross income to the church—do you know who wrote that part?" Sarah stared into space and shook her head. "The church wrote that. Of course they did. What a joke." Gary pointed to the microwave. "How can we follow an antiquated, two-thousand-year-old text when we now have magic?"

Sarah rose quickly to her feet, and then made her way to the door.

"Where are you going?" Gary demanded.

"Out."

"What about dinner?"

"Get your own damn dinner."

Gary listened carefully. When he heard the car engine, he hurried outside to see if he could catch her, but when he reached the porch, it was too late. She had already left. That went well, he mused.

A loud meow came from beneath the porch. "Oh shut up," Gary said. Then he returned to his house.

. . . . . .

Gary sat in the living room and let out a long sigh. He picked up the wine bottle and drank directly from it. Then he opened his journal and started writing with a slow, methodical hand. Within seconds, however, the automatic writer appeared and took control of his pen; now that he knew what it was, he freely stepped aside and allowed his soul to take over; it did not disappoint. Words poured from his inner-self and onto the pages without a thought on Gary's part. Even long swigs from the bottle did not interrupt the flow of ink as the pages filled. He was amazed at how quickly the words appeared as if conjured forth by a magic trick. It was odd to look at but very amusing as well. He was able to play games too. He would get himself aroused thinking of naked co-workers while the pen did its work. This is wonderful, Gary thought.

Soon, there were more than words appearing. Sketches seemed to materialize from thin air. He watched in amazement as a house exterior, came alive in a three-dimensional shaded drawing. And though it was his hand that moved the pen, the words and pictures were not his own. Gary could make nothing more than stick figures on his best day. A master draftsman was clearly at work here.

Gary closed his eyes, confident that he was no longer needed in the process, He detached, and fell into a deep trance, unaware of his surroundings and what appeared on the paper in front of him. An hour later, his hand stopped suddenly. He woke from his trance and began flipping through the pages darkened by ink.

What he saw was miraculous to him. He marveled at the illustrations, and the detail and the precision with which they were drawn. Both the exterior and the interior of the house were clearly represented. In addition, there were detailed images of the library. Then, he realized something. His lips quivered. This wasn't just any house. He knew this place. He had been in it many times before.

Gary continued to flip through the pages; more drawings appeared. There must have been fifty in all. Gary recognized the outline of Bob's house; other images showed the interior; drawings of the library emerged. Inside the library, were two dark figures sitting across from each other— one tall and robust, the other, frail and hunched over. Then, on the last page, a portrait of a woman appeared. Her hair was black, and her eyes were seductive.

CHAPTER SIXTEEN

Gary fidgeted in his chair as he waited for the meeting to begin. He wondered out loud what lies he and his co-workers would endure this morning. A quick glance from side-to-side confirmed that his comment went unheard and for this, he was grateful.

A few more anxious moments passed before Ryan joined him. "How's it going Gary," he said. "Is this seat taken?"

Gary extended his hand towards the empty seat. "Be my guest," he said.

"So I guess we find out what the compensation consultant had to say."

"I already know what the compensation consultant said."

"Oh yeah?"

"Yes. He said without the necessary funds, there will be no raises."

Though Gary was deadpan in his delivery, Ryan laughed. "I guess we'll see."

"Oh honestly, Ryan. Do you really think—" Gary stopped abruptly, leaving Ryan to wonder about the rest.

"Well," Ryan continued. "I'm hopeful."

"You are, are you?"

"Yes."

More professors entered the conference room and filled the chairs around Gary; three suits lingered near the podium, awaiting the start time. Gary squirmed in his seat, crossing and re-crossing his legs in a futile attempt to find a comfortable position. He was anxious to get back to his office where a growing pile of term papers sat on his desk, waiting to be graded. He wondered why he had even bothered to assign the mid-term papers. After ten years, it was mostly an exercise in futility—students would regurgitate a bunch of facts to impress him and perhaps earn a passing grade. Worse still, were the students who never made that much of an effort, choosing instead to plagiarize their paper by lifting entire passages from the Internet.

Rarely—perhaps twice in his ten years at St. Mary's—would a student truly impress him with a thoughtful comment or an astute observation, or any small spark that would indicate a truly imaginative mind was at work. For the most part, students turned in useless drivel that not only increased his workload but also did little to enhance their learning experience.

Gary looked at the imaginary watch strapped to his wrist. Then he checked his cell phone and saw it was 8:59. If the meeting goes for an hour, he thought, he could be journaling by 10:00, perhaps no later than 10:15. A wave of panic overtook him as he wondered about the journal's whereabouts. Yes, he thought. I brought it. It's in my briefcase in the office. Satisfied, he smiled and slunk back in his chair.

"If everyone will take their seat we can get the meeting underway." The voice belonged to Dr. Campbell, the provost of St. Mary's college.

The meeting dragged on for an hour just as Gary predicted. Each suit took a turn at the microphone and gave his account of the school's financials and the possibility of future cost-of- living raises. Much to Gary's dismay, the meeting digressed into a rah, rah session in which the sad state of financial affairs was presented in the best possible light, and the promise of impending raises was dangled like a carrot.

During the speeches, Gary shook his head in disgust and made subconscious clicking sounds with his tongue and his mouth to voice his opinion.

When each speaker had their turn at the podium, the floor was opened for questions. Gary usually sat quietly during these question and answer sessions, preferring to keep in the background rather than making himself conspicuous, but on this occasion, his hand shot in the air along with a half dozen others. However, Gary didn't wait to be called on. Instead, he heard his own voice rise above the din as his words came spewing forth.

"Dr. Campbell," he said in a mannered voice. "It's been five years since I've gotten a raise, since anyone has gotten a raise, even a two percent cost of living raise. For five years, there's always a promise of better times with the prospect of raises just around the corner." Gary paused, swallowed hard and caught his breath.

"Yes," Dr. Campbell started. "As you know, enrollment—"

"And yet, every time I turn around a new building is going up, or a new student union, or equipment for this or that…"

Gary found himself on his feet, though he didn't remember making a conscious effort to stand. The room's murmur and the blood rushing in his ears sounded like a raging river. He felt every eye on him like the glow of a white-hot pin prick. He took a deep breath and cleared his throat before continuing.

"…why don't you tell us the truth? There aren't going to be any raises this year or the year after that or the year after that. In fact, all of us will be long gone before any raises are given out—if then."

The room went silent; Gary heard his heart beating, and he felt it too. He turned to face his colleagues and continued his appeal to the crowded room.

"I've seen it before," he announced. "In other schools, I've worked at. One year, they stop giving raises because of hard times. Then the next year, and the year after that, still no raises. After a while, it becomes easier-and-easier to not give raises. People forget a time when they ever got them and those that don't forget and make a stink about it—well, they're simply dismissed or just leave of their own accord. Soon there's a new policy in place. No raises, ever. The topic is never broached again."

When Gary had finished, every eye turned towards the three suits standing uncomfortably at the podium. Doctor Campbell shifted his eyes to the left and then the right before speaking. "Doctor?" he said.

"Miller," Gary said in a pissed off tone. "It's Doctor Gary Miller. I've been a professor here for ten years. I would think you would know my name by now."

"Yes, well, Doctor Miller, I can assure—"

"I don't mean to say you're a bad person, Doctor Campbell. I'm sure you have good intentions; all of us do. But the fact of the matter is, without the necessary students, the school can't afford to give us raises. Isn't that right?"

"Well, yes that's true, but—"

"So why not just tell us that? Instead of filling us with false hope and dangling carrots in front of our noses like we were donkeys pulling a cart?"

The room bubbled with excited voices. It filled the air like the chatter of wild animals at feeding time. When the voices finally quieted down, Gary stood alone with the weight of silence balanced firmly on his shoulder. Gary felt every eyeball; his fear worsened by the response from the suits, which is to say there was no response at all, only stunned, stupid faces staring back at Gary in disbelief.

Oh God, he thought. What have I done? Seconds passed like hours. Gary couldn't stand it any longer. Anything, even a tongue-lashing would have been preferred to the silence. He looked off to his right and saw the bright red exit sign calling like a beacon. It was his escape, but he didn't take it just yet.

"Look," Gary said. "Tell us the truth, as harsh as it may be. We're all big boys and girls here. We can handle the truth; it's false hope that causes more problems." Gary stopped and glanced at the exit sign again. "You people believe what you want. I've said my peace. I've said too much."

Gary walked quickly towards the exit. He felt every eye in the room follow him out.

When Gary reached his office, he closed the door sharply behind him. He was near–panic. His breathing was labored and sweat had formed on the back of his neck. Then, as suddenly as the fear set in, it went away. Gary had come to a realization; he no longer needed his job, so why care? What he needed and what he truly wanted was at his fingertips at a moment's notice and no costlier than the air he breathed. He was calm now and filled with a sense of well–being that bordered on manic and caused him to laugh out loud.

A knock at the door disturbed his celebration. "Go away," Gary snapped.

"I'm Lucas," the voice at the other side of the door happily announced. "I'm the book reseller. I was coming to see if you have any used textbooks you may want to sell."

"No. I haven't got any."

"Are you sure? It could be worth some money to you. Open the door."

Gary focused and tried to sense who it was but could not; all he saw was blackness. He walked to the door, swung it open with a violent motion and then spat at the stranger. "I told you, I haven't—"

The man's face stopped Gary in mid-sentence. Lucas was ordinary in one matter, but he was quite extraordinary in another. He was tall and thin and stood with a slight stoop. His face was long, white, doughy, and he was completely bald except for a few grey tufts above each ear. Gary thought he was possibly the ugliest person he had ever seen. But when he looked into the man's eyes, he thought he recognized something familiar in them.

"I'm sorry," Gary said. "Have we met before?"

The book salesman slowly nodded his head. "Yes," he said softly. "Many times before."

"We have?" Gary asked suspiciously. "Where?"

"My name is Lucas," he said extending his hand forward. Gary and Lucas shook hands. Lucas' hand was clammy and unpleasant to touch, so Gary immediately broke the hold. "I'm the book reseller," Lucas continued. "I buy books from the professors and then resell them. I'm sure I've come to this office before."

"Really? I don't remember. Perhaps it was one of my colleagues?"

Lucas extended a long spindly finger and waved it in the air in front of Gary's face. "No, no. I remember you. I never forget a face."

"Indeed."

"Miller, right? Doctor Gary Miller?"

Gary was shocked. He was sure he had not seen Lucas before today. A face like his was hard to forget. "Why, yes. That's right."

"I was wondering if you have any books you want to sell? It could be worth some money to you."

"Well, I doubt I have any books that are worth much. I teach religion and philosophy, and I'm afraid there's not much of a market for that discipline."

"Ah," Lucas replied. "I wouldn't be so sure about that. Many people are interested in religion."

"Well," Gary relented. "I have a bookshelf full of used books I no longer need. If you'll be quick about it, you can have a look."

Lucas smiled, stepped into the office and brushed past Gary on his way to the bookshelf. As he did so, Gary wrinkled his nose at the unpleasant odor.

"It's over there," Gary said trying to hold his breath.

"I know where it is; thank you."

Lucas went to work, and Gary sat at his desk. He thought about grading papers, but decided he wasn't in the mood. Instead, he took the journal from his briefcase and held it to his nose. After taking a deep breath, he slowly flipped through the pages while marveling at the worn pages. The words and doodles made for a pleasing aesthetic. This was a work of Art, he thought.

Happy with the progress he had made, Gary picked up his pen and was about to write when he glanced over at Lucas. To his alarm, Lucas was staring back at him with large, dark eyes and upturned lips shaped into a macabre grin. After holding Gary's gaze for a moment, Lucas turned his attention to the books. What an odd human being, Gary thought.

Gary tried to write, but the stranger's presence threw him off, and the words came in fits and starts. The automatic writer did not appear. Lucas' occasional comments didn't help matters.

"Ah," Lucas would say holding a book in the air. "*The International Directory of Philosophy and Philosophers 1995–1996*. This will fetch a sum." Then he'd carefully set the book aside along with the rest of his finds before resuming his search.

"Are you almost done?" Gary said. "I have quite a bit of work to do."

Lucas raised a bony index finger in the air and said, "Almost. I have a few more stacks to check, and then I'll be on my way. You have quite the collection here, Gary. Lots of texts on all the major religions."

"Yes, well, teaching religion for ten years does that. You should see my friend's book collection."

"And who is your friend?"

"Oh, his name is Dr. Harris, but he no longer works here. He's retired."

"Robert? Dr. Robert Harris?"

"Yes, that's him. Do you know him?"

"Yes. I've checked his books many times."

"I bet you got a lot from him."

Lucas shook his head. "No," he said. "Your books are far more interesting; like this one, for example, Christian and moral ethics. This should fetch a nice sum."

Gary smiled, shook his head and then turned his attention back to the journal. This time, instead of writing he focused on doodling. The first lines he made were stiff and forced, but after few seconds, he had found a groove, the automatic writer had returned, and he was happy to see familiar artistic shapes appear on the page. Gary was engrossed in his task but was startled back to reality by Lucas who now stood next to him.

"I'll take these," Lucas said holding a stack of books. "I'll pay you two hundred dollars."

Gary jerked his head back. "Did you say two hundred?"

Lucas slowly nodded his head. "If this is copacetic, I have cash."

Gary grinned. "Yes, yes that's fine. I could use the money since I might be losing my job."

"Oh? I'm sorry to hear that."

"Well, I don't know for sure. But I said some stupid things to the president of the college in front of a room full of people."

"Well, perhaps they weren't so stupid. Perhaps they were things needed to be said."

"Perhaps," Gary agreed. "But my mom told me something once. She said its better to keep your mouth shut and let people think you're an idiot than to open your mouth and confirm their suspicions."

Lucas laughed. "It sounds like your mom was very wise."

"Yeah, she was. More than I gave her credit for at the time."

Lucas set the books down on Gary's desk and then produced a wad of cash from his coat pocket. He carefully parsed the tens and twenties from the roll and handed them to Gary. "Well," Lucas said. "Thank you very much. It was a pleasure doing business with you."

"Come back again. I typically get sample textbooks from the publisher that I don't need."

Lucas smiled, bowed his head and made his way towards the door. "Would you like this closed?" he said before stepping out.

"Please."

The door shut, and immediately there was a knock.

"Did you forget something?" Gary said.

To his astonishment, Ryan opened the door and stepped in.

"Oh, it's you," Gary said.

"I'm sorry," Ryan replied. "Were you expecting someone?"

"No, I thought you were Lucas."

Ryan looked confused. "Who's Lucas?"

"Lucas, the book salesman that just stepped out before you knocked. Surely you saw him leave."

"There's no one out here."

Gary sprang from his chair, walked past Ryan and then looked down an empty hallway. "That's odd," Gary whispered.

"I wonder if you had a minute to talk, Gary?"

Gary returned to his seat. "Yes, come on in, Ryan. I suppose you want to give me my walking papers."

Ryan smiled as he took a seat opposite Gary. "No, not at all."

"Well, maybe you'd like to berate me for making an ass out of myself during the meeting?"

"No."

"What are my colleagues saying about me? Dr. Campbell? I'm sure I'm the talk of the campus right about now."

"Well, most are shocked."

"Shocked?"

"Yeah, Gary. I mean you're a quiet, soft-spoken man and then you stand up during a campus–wide meeting with guns blazing. I mean it came as a surprise."

"You didn't know I had it in me?"

"Quite frankly, no."

"Yes, perhaps I should have kept it in me."

"Gary, I know how you feel. None of us have gotten raises."

Gary closed his eyes and shook his head. "Forgive me, Ryan, but you don't know how I feel. Most people have spouses that work. Mine chooses to volunteer her time for worthy or not-so-worthy causes. So when you're struggling to get by on two incomes, I'm struggling to survive on one—one meager salary I might add."

Ryan nodded his head. "Yeah, I can imagine."

"Do you know my checking account is in the red this month? And did you know it's been in the red for the past five months?"

"No. I didn't."

"And every month I pile up NSF charge after NSF charge on top of all my other bills."

"I'm sorry. I didn't realize—"

"And my wife has no marketable skills. None whatsoever. It's up to me to keep us afloat, and all she can do is…" Gary pursed his lips and drew a deep audible breath through his nose. "…It's an embarrassment, Ryan. It's an embarrassment to me, and it's an embarrassment to this school that one of its professors should struggle like a pauper."

"Gary, if it's any consolation, I've talked to Dr. Campbell. He really is a good guy, and he is concerned about our situation. He's confident we'll have a balanced budget soon, and the raises will resume."

Gary laughed. He heard the same promises for years and was worn out by them. Perhaps there really was a good reason for the hardship. He just didn't care to hear them.

"What difference does it make?" Gary said. "I probably just blew my career after that little stunt I pulled."

"Don't worry about that," said Ryan. "I talked to Campbell after the meeting."

"And?"

"I told him that you were under a lot of pressure and you were blowing off steam and you said what many were thinking. He understands."

"Does he?"

"Yes."

"Well, look, I have to get going," Ryan said while rising from his seat. "If you need to talk, my door is always open to you."

After Ryan left, Gary sat quietly in his chair for several moments, and then he remembered the two hundred dollars in his pocket. He felt for the lump to make sure it was still there. It was. Then, another thought popped into his head. He opened his journal and began fumbling through the pages until he found what he was looking for, the entry he made several days earlier. When he arrived at the page, his eyes widened, then he slowly mouthed the top line of the bulleted list: *Two hundred dollars*.

Gary reached down with a trembling hand and felt the wad bulging from his pocket. It gave him a sense of calm.

CHAPTER SEVENTEEN

Amber crossed her leg at the knee. One could perceive it as an act of modesty, but to Gary, it was provocative. He stared at her long, smooth legs—the highway to her genitals, he thought. Gary made no attempt to hide his lustful gaze. Instead, he fixated on her fleshy thighs like a wolf eyeing its next meal. He looked up and smiled at her, and she returned his confident smile with one of her own.

"You wanted to see me?" Amber said.

Gary did not immediately reply. Instead, he got up and walked past Amber, deliberately brushing against her thigh as he did so. Then, he pushed his office door shut before returning to his seat.

"Amber," Gary said cheerfully. "A week ago, you asked me if there was anything you could do to raise your grade in my Religion class."

Amber's eyes grew wide. "Yes, Dr. Miller?"

"Well, I thought about it and decided to give you a chance to raise your grade if you still want."

"Oh, yes. I'd like that Dr. Miller."

"Good."

A silent and awkward moment passed before Amber spoke up. "What will I have to do?"

"A paper."

"A paper?"

"A research paper. Sex in the Bible." Amber smiled tentatively. "Is that okay with you?"

"All I have to do is write this paper?"

"It's a research paper, so you'll have to work hard. It's not going to be easy."

"And what kind of grade will I get for this paper, if I do a good job?"

"Well, you have a C in my class? I suppose I could bump it to a B."

"How about an A?" Amber quickly added.

Gary laughed when he thought about Amber getting an A in his class. God, he thought. What would she have to do to get an A? The possibilities intrigued him.

"Well," Gary said. "For an A you would need to do a really good job. Are you up for it?"

"Sure. When do I begin?"

"Well, you can begin right now if you'd like. I made up an outline of what you should include. Pull your chair up, and I'll show you."

Amber uncrossed her legs and pulled her chair alongside Gary's. Then she leaned in close to get a good look. As she did so, Gary took in her scent; he closed his eyes and admired the fresh, young aroma that stood in contrast to his wife's perfume—old woman perfume as he referred to it. Amber was intoxicating and conjured images, which he didn't even try to suppress. He rather enjoyed the visuals floating in his brain.

"It's about sex," Gary began. "In the Bible."

"Okay?" Amber said with a smile.

"Amber, I'm going to ask you a personal question. Please don't take offense."

"Okay."

"Have you had sex?"

Amber smiled and nodded her head. "Yes, of course," she replied while grabbing a strand of her long blond locks and twisting it between her fingers.

"Ah, I see."

"Why do you ask?"

"Well, just as a curiosity. The Bible is pretty salacious you know."

"What?"

"Salacious," Gary repeated. "You know it gets hot and heavy with the sex."

"Oh," Amber laughed and waved her hand dismissively. "Yeah, you don't have to worry about that."

"Good."

Amber leaned in closer; the air was thick with perfume and caused Gary's nostrils to flare. "What are you looking at?" Amber asked.

"What? Nothing. I wasn't looking at anything."

"Dr. Miller," Amber giggled. "I think you were." Gary's jaw hung open, and he could feel his face grow warm and flush. "Its okay," Amber said softly. She lifted her blouse away from her chest and gave Gary a better view at her pink bra.

Gary smiled as he delivered his half-hearted rebuke. "Jesus Christ, Amber, you shouldn't be doing that."

"Oh, do you want me to stop?"

"No, no."

"Do you like what you see?"

"Of course I do. Who wouldn't?"

"Here," she said unbuttoning her blouse. "I'll make it easy for you." With her blouse undone, she held it open and took a deep breath. Her pink bra pressed tightly against her light brown skin and pushed a mound of seductive flesh above the cotton seam. Gary was transfixed by the sight. He subconsciously held out a hand only to stop a mere inch away from her breast.

"May I?" he said.

Amber nodded her head. Gary grabbed her left breast and gave it a firm squeeze. Amber closed her eyes and offered a soft moan between her parted lips. Gary continued to massage her flesh as he leaned forward and kissed her mouth.

"I've wanted to do that for a long time," he said.

"Don't stop."

Gary left her chest alone and grabbed Amber by both cheeks. He pulled her in close and rained kisses on her face. "Have you done this before?" Gary said between breaths.

"Done what?"

"Have sex with a professor?"

"Yes."

Her admission surprised Gary. With his curiosity peaked, he paused and said, "Who?"

"Doctor Harris." An eternity seemed to pass as Gary stared into Amber's eyes. "Is there something wrong?" she said.

"Dr. Harris is retired," Gary said with a suspicious tone.

"Last year, when I was a freshman."

"Yes," he said nodding his head. "I should have guessed as much."

"Kiss me."

Gary kissed Amber's face repeatedly, placing his lips on her cheeks, forehead, nose, and chin while taking an occasional taste with his tongue.

"Dr. Miller?" Amber said in a breathless voice.

"Yes?"

"Do I still have to do this fucking paper?"

Gary smiled at Amber. Then he reached into desk drawer and pulled out a pair of black, sheer stockings. "Here," he said tossing the stockings at Amber. "Forget the paper."

·　　·　　·　　·　　·　　·

The room was dark except for the faint moonlight that fell between the parted curtains. Gary pressed his mouth firmly against Belle's forehead. Belle looked up at him with her dark eyes and smiled. Then she rested her cheek against his shoulder, her head nodding to the rhythmic rise and fall of his chest.

"I love listening to the sound of your heartbeat," Belle said.

"What's it sound like?" Gary replied.

"It's a strong beat, definite and with purpose, like a man who knows what he wants."

Gary laughed. "Well, I do know what I want."

"Yeah, what's that?"

"I want a big house with you in it."

"Ah, you're drunk."

"I am not. I've had a glass of wine, maybe two."

"Then why do you say you want me? You barely know me."

"Because I love you, Belle."

Belle paused before answering. "You do?" she finally said.

"Yes, I do."

"Will you take care of me?"

"Of course I will."

"I'm not easy you know. I have expensive tastes."

"That won't be a problem anymore."

"I have other tastes too." Belle paused allowing her words to sink in. "Bob is able to satisfy me financially, but not in other ways."

"Oh?"

Belle ran her tongue up Gary's cheek leaving behind a wet swath on his skin. "I have a lot of needs."

"Tell me about them, Belle. I want to know what your needs are."

"I need a large cock," she said while reaching down between Gary's legs and stroking his inner thigh.

"Is that right? Doesn't Bob feed you his cock?"

"He tries to. The cancer meds you know?"

"Ah."

Belle placed her fingertips between Gary's crotch and stroked him slowly. Within seconds, her touch had produced a reaction. "Ah," she whispered in his ear. "But you apparently have no such problems."

Gary smiled nervously. He wanted nothing more than to roll Belle onto her backside and have his way but was too afraid. "We should stop."

"Why?"

"My wife—Sarah is downstairs."

"I'll be quiet. I promise."

"What if she walks in?"

"Then we'll give her a show, a glorious show. Or perhaps we'll ask her to join us. How would that be, Gary, two women at once?"

Gary had never had two women at once. He had thought about it—often—but until now, it had always been a farfetched fantasy. "Um, that sounds amazing."

"Let's call her."

"What?" Gary said in alarm. "Are you crazy?"

Belle giggled. "Look at you, so frightened like a child."

"I'm not frightened, and you're going to make me come if you continue to do that."

"Would you like me to stop?"

"Yes, I mean no. Hell, I don't know what I mean anymore."

"Just lie back and relax. I'll take care of you." Belle's face broke into a wide smile; her energy filled the room like a soft breeze.

Gary could hardly believe this was happening. It was like a dream, but more of a waking dream in which he was fully conscious, aware of his surrounding, his thoughts, and his emotions. Belle appeared to him as clear as a movie picture, but even more real than that. He could hear and feel her presence and smell her. The line between reality and imagination had become sufficiently blurred so he hardly knew the difference between the two.

"This is amazing," he said.

"What is," Belle replied.

"You, me—the here and now."

Belle did not say anything. She just smiled at Gary.

Suddenly, the bedroom door swung open; light from the hallway flooded the room, placing Gary directly into the spotlight. Startled, he sprang to an upright position, and then used his hand to shade his eyes against the harsh light while he studied Sarah's dark outline standing in the doorway.

"Who were you talking to?" Sarah asked.

"Talking to? I wasn't talking to anyone."

"I thought I heard you carrying on a conversation."

"Perhaps, I was sleeping?" Gary said in an unconvincing tone. "I may have been talking in my sleep."

"I thought I heard a female's voice."

Gary chuckled. "Well, obviously there's no one else here but me."

"Yes, of course. But it's funny."

"What is?"

Sarah sniffed the air. "I smell perfume."

Gary didn't know what to make of it. He felt guilty, but for what, he wasn't sure. Belle wasn't there; she hadn't been there except for in his mind, and yet Sarah sensed something. Gary thought this was strange, and wonderful and yet unnerving. He tried to appeal to Sarah's common sense.

"Well," Gary replied. "That must be your perfume. It's Jasmine, right? The one I like so well?" Sarah pursed her lips and nodded her head. Gary stretched out his arms and said, "Sarah, there's no one here but me."

"Yes, I see that. Are you coming down for dinner? I've made chicken."

"In a moment. I want to journal; I'll be down in a spell."

Sarah looked at the journal sitting on Gary's desk. It was tied in a fancy bow; next to it sat Gary's special pen, the one he used specifically for journaling. "What do you write about in that journal?" she said.

Gary ran his fingers through his new goatee. He liked how the facial hair enhanced his chin and gave a hard edge to his boyish, featureless face.

"Oh," he said, pointing a long, spindly index finger towards the journal. "It's just my thoughts; ideas, you know."

"And these thoughts and ideas, are they to become reality? Is that how this stuff works, Gary?"

Gary and Sarah were now engaged in a staring contest. Though neither one intended it as such, neither would back down. After several seconds passed, however, Gary finally averted his eyes. "Well, as you said countless times," he replied. "It's most likely a bunch of nonsense, mind games you know, and parlor tricks."

Sarah's face was taut and expressionless. "Don't be too long," she said before leaving.

As soon as the door closed, Gary jumped out of bed and hurriedly made his way to his desk. He fumbled nervously for the first blank page and began writing.

From Gary Miller's Journal:

EXPERIMENT 6: IT'S ALIVE! ITS ALIVE! LOL Oh my God. It works. My hand is trembling.

It's truly amazing. It's as though she were really there, with me, speaking to me. I could feel her soft skin, taste the coffee on her breath, and smell her perfume. Even Sarah said she could smell the perfume though I think Sarah is a bit daft, but still. I don't know how this is working, but there's no mistake. REMOTE VIEWING IS REAL.

I feel guilty, a little; I'm summoning this woman forth without her consent, without her knowing, as if I were raping her from a distance in the safety and privacy of my own bedroom. I know it's not real, but it is very real. I'm at once frightened by this power and excited by it. A part of me wants to stop. Yet another part of me wants to explore the depths of this phenomenon. What can't I do? I fear there are no limits—none. Bob indicated as much. I had my doubts, but those doubts are slowly being erased from my mind. I'm no longer a hapless twerp. This is me, the real me, filled with the knowledge of the ages. I can have anything I want, fuck anyone I want, or travel the world without stepping out of my house. Bob was right when he told me, your world is not out there, it's in here (inside your mind). Whatever happens in your mind is happening in real life. That is your life. Your mind is your life. Your mind is your life. Your mind is your life…

CHAPTER EIGHTEEN

Gary spotted the little cat from a distance, but he paid no attention to it. Instead, he plowed straight ahead, with a stride that was both solemn and deliberate. Snowball pounced at Gary's laces, whiffed badly and fell precariously between his hard heel strikes, which thundered against the cement walk in rapid succession. Snowball scrambled to his feet, then gracefully floated between steps as if he were performing a choreographed dance routine between Gary's feet and legs.

Gary did his best to ignore the annoying pest, but the streak of white maneuvering in an erratic pattern underfoot made it impossible to disregard the dancing fur ball. Gary delivered his famous mule kick, which barely missed Snowball's cranium. The near miss, however, did little to dissuade the cat. He persisted until Gary reached the front door.

Gary made his way to the kitchen and poured himself a glass of wine. He finished this glass in short order and then poured himself another. In between sips, he noticed the bean sprouts on the windowsill. The left side grew wild, overflowing their container like an Amazon rainforest. The right-side-plants were dead, non-existent would be more like it.

"Jesus Christ," Gary muttered under his breath. "What the fuck happened?"

Gary studied the plants for several moments trying to decipher the mystery behind their growth spurt. He was convinced Sarah had something to do with this, but he couldn't prove it. Gary placed his fingers in the soil, expecting to find the left-side moist and the right-side dry as a bone. He felt no such thing. Both sides were parched as if neither had a drink in days, nor weeks. He looked carefully for telltale signs of a soil enhancer. But there were none. Still, a nagging voice told him Sarah was at the root of this. She must be, he reasoned. He had been praying diligently every day for the right-hand plants. None of the other experiments had failed, so why should this one?

"That bitch," Gary whispered.

Gary reached into the kitchen drawer and pulled out a steak knife. Then he grabbed a handful of left-side sprouts and severed their heads. He held his trophy up for inspection, and with a satisfied smile, discarded the plants into the kitchen sink.

"Salad," he spat in a final parting shot.

Gary walked to the refrigerator and opened the door. "Is there anything to eat around here?"

"I haven't gone shopping," Sarah's voice said.

Gary turned and met Sarah's gaze head on. Her pale, emotionless expression startled him. "Oh, Sarah," he said trying to sound calm. "I didn't know you were home. I thought I was alone."

"I was upstairs. You're hungry?" Sarah said. Gary nodded his head. "How about some bean sprouts?"

Gary laughed nervously. "Ah, bean sprouts sound lovely," he replied cheerfully. "Do you know where we can get some, fresh cut that is?"

"Yes, that's very funny. I have a question for you?"

"A question? For Moi? By all means."

Sarah was deadpan in her delivery. "Who are you?"

Gary was confused. "Who am I?" he repeated. "Well, I'm Dr. Gary Miller, your husband at your service my dear." He bowed with the theatrics of a circus clown, bending deep at the waist and hanging his head low to the floor. He held this pose for several seconds before standing straight up.

Sarah shook her head from side-to-side. "No. You're not my husband. You've become something else, something I don't recognize. Look at you?"

Gary ran his fingers through his goatee in self-examination. "What's wrong with the way I look?"

Sarah closed her eyes and shook her head as if trying to recapture a memory of her husband.

"You're different, Gary."

"I grew some facial hair for crying out loud."

"It's not just that."

"Then what?"

Sarah looked her husband up and down and said, "You're thinner."

"So what? I've been watching what I eat, getting more exercise. You could stand a bit more exercise yourself, Sarah."

"I know this is impossible, maybe it's the weight loss, but you look taller too."

Gary was surprised. The thinner part was evident. He saw his leaner body in the mirror and in the shower. The taller part he had to guess at. He felt like he was seeing things from a new perspective but wasn't sure if it were a physical reality or just a manifestation of his new mindset. Now Sarah could see it too. It must be both, he reasoned.

"I'm probably not slouching," Gary said. "I'm walking around with my head high, my shoulders back, and my back straight, like a man, a real man, a proud man."

"There's something else—a hardness that was never there before. I miss my old Gary. He was a gentle, kind soul. He had his faults to be sure, and I know we didn't have the best marriage." Sarah stopped and swallowed hard. "I know he never loved me, but I thought we could at least make a go of it. And we did, Gary. We were making a go of it."

In twenty-two years of marriage, Gary had never admitted anything to Sarah. He was too afraid, so he kept his true feelings bound tight inside him; he tried—successfully—to suppress his inner voice. To say it out loud, to admit to a loveless marriage was a shameful guilt-ridden admission. And though Sarah's words made him feel, they also brought a sense of relief. He could be honest now and speak his mind.

"Oh, Sarah," he said softly. "It's just that I've grown up. I'm awake now."

"Awake? Is that what you call it?"

"Call it what you want, Sarah. But a veil has been lifted. Its like I see the world in color now. I no longer believe what I'm told. I demand proof. Without proof, everything is meaningless."

"And what about your faith?"

"Faith? What good is it? Just shut up and do what I'm told? Do you know what faith is? It's *not* knowing something but believing it anyway."

"Yes, exactly," Sarah said. "Blessed are those who believe."

"Blessed my ass." Sarah looked like she had taken a blow to her gut. "Sorry," Gary continued. "But you don't realize the power I have, and what I can do with my mind. When it's focused, there's nothing beyond my grasp. I realize this now. It's me, not God, not some invisible savior, but me. It's inside us all. We just have to tap into it."

"It's all this crazy business with the experiments. That's what's changed you?"

Gary nodded. "Yes, and I'm proud of that. I still have faith. It's stronger than it's ever been. Only it's faith in me, my abilities, my power to manifest the life I want, and not worry what some outside force can do for us when we're so capable of doing for ourselves."

"Oh, God."

"You should see what I can do, what I've been able to bring into my life. It's a small miracle, and it's only the beginning."

Sarah walked over to the sink, picked up the dead plants and waved them in front of Gary. "Like these?" she said in an agitated voice. "Are these your idea of a miracle?"

Gary's lips turned upward in a sinister smile. "I'm afraid you know more about them than I do."

"Really? And what if I did have something to do with fouling up your plant experiment? It's not much of a miracle if a simple woman as myself can interfere."

Gary reflected for a moment. It did seem strange to him, that someone, especially Sarah, could interfere with what his mind brought forth. "Yes, you're right," he concluded.

"Well, then how do you explain it?"

"I can't," Gary said shaking his head. "Look, I don't know everything yet. I'm in the middle of it. I'm learning everything as I go. Much of it is still a mystery."

"And what about me? Can I practice the experiments? Will I be able to perform these tiny miracles too?"

"Well, no. I mean yes you could, but you'd have to believe, and practice them. You have to focus your mind. Not everyone has that ability."

"But you do?"

Gary became agitated. "Yes, I do," he said. "I have a talent for it. I'm convinced of that. I'm more gifted than Bob, and he created the experiments. You have to have a gift, and for some reason, I have it—in spades."

"Hmm."

Gary pounded his fist repeatedly and rhythmically into his flat palm, and in a singsong voice said, "You… don't… understand. The plants are one thing, a small thing. There's so much more. Things you wouldn't understand, Sarah. Things I don't fully understand but suffice to say are real."

"If it works so well then where is everything?"

"What do you mean?"

"I mean where's my mink stole and our new car or Hell, how about some grocery money? I'd settle for that much at this point."

Gary reached into his back pocket and produced his wallet. He pulled out a wad of cash and placed the crumpled bills on the kitchen table under Sarah's watchful gaze.

"Grocery money you said? There's a hundred dollars there. Go buy some groceries."

"Where did you get that?"

"I asked for it, and someone gave it to me." Gary saw the disbelief etched on his wife's face. "I know. I know," he continued. "It sounds crazy, but it's true. And there's more."

"More?"

"Yes, Sarah," he said reaching out with his open palms. "I—I feel like I can bend brick with my bare hands. Do you know what I mean?"

"No. I don't understand a damn thing you mean anymore."

"It's just a way of saying I'm in control; like I can shape my world— bend it to my will."

"That's great, Gary."

"You don't sound happy."

"And what about us, our life, our marriage?"

"Marriage," Gary scoffed. "Do you know what marriage is?"

"Oh, Jesus. I'm afraid you're going to tell me."

"It's a business arrangement, okay? It was a way for men to spread our sperm and our wealth to the next generation to ensure our survival. During biblical times, women were virtually sold to the highest bidder, and if she bled on her wedding night, then her father got more money for the transaction. You know, all this bullshit about no sex before marriage? God doesn't care about any of that. It was all about the money. That's all it's ever about. Marriage, wars, laws, religion—it's all about keeping the rich, rich and the poor, poor. Our government is in on it, the church, all of society."

Sarah walked to the kitchen table, took a seat, and then rested her head in her hands. After a few moments of silence, she said, "You seem to know it all."

Gary took a seat next to Sarah and grabbed her arm. "Well, yes, I do. I've been reading, and well, a lot of this I figured out on my own. That's what I meant about having my eyes opened. Everything we've been taught as children—It's nothing more than brainwashing."

"Brainwashing?"

"Yes," Gary said with a sharp nod of his head. "Well, don't get me wrong; some of it's necessary to keep us alive, like don't run with scissors or wait an hour after eating before swimming, but much of it is a bunch of lies intended to keep the masses, the lower masses, in their place."

"What are you talking about?"

"It's all bullshit, Sarah. That's what I'm talking about."

"What is?"

Gary pounded his fist on the kitchen table. "Like America is the greatest country ever."

"It's not?" she answered.

Gary stood on his feet; spit flew from his mouth like sparks from a welder's torch as he launched into his tirade.

"Well, I don't know if it is or it isn't," he said. "I haven't been to every country, and neither have you. But that's not the point. The point is that if people believe it's the best country in the world, it's much easier to convince the young and poor to defend her in war, and these wars make people wealthy, especially the people who are already wealthy. In the meantime, the poor are killed off like lambs to the slaughter, just a bunch of hapless, gullible people whose blood covers our battlefields in ever-increasing frequency and for what? Every time I turn on the news, we're at war with a new country for some reason or another. A deranged young kid shoots up another school, and our government does nothing, not a goddamn thing. But some third world country does something we don't like, and we're dropping goddamn bombs like its raining gumdrops. I tell you, Sarah, it doesn't make any sense. Does it make sense to you? Is this the message of our God? Destroy thy enemy? Pick up thine sword and protect everything that is yours with the greatest amount of weaponry this planet has ever known? Well, is it?"

Sarah shook her head. "I don't know."

"It's all about the money, and it doesn't stop there. It's infiltrated every part of society, even law enforcement. You see law enforcement follows the money, not the crime."

"What? What are you talking about?"

"It's like this; the money allocated to the various police departments is determined by the amount of crime those departments have to deal with. So the more crime a district has, the more money they get."

"Well, that makes sense."

"Sure it does. Only the type of crime plays no factor in how the money is allocated; convicting one person on cannabis possession counts as much as a murder or rape conviction. And because it's so much easier to arrest someone—usually a young black man—on simple possession, our jails are filled with individuals who've committed these low-level, bullshit crimes. This does nothing to help society, Sarah. It just makes it far worse. Do you see, Sarah? Everything is a fucking scam built around money."

"I understand, Gary. But there's one thing you're forgetting."

"What's that?"

"I agree with you. Everything is a scam in its own way. But as Christians, we are called to rise above that. You became a minister, a teacher to help people, not to get caught up in the workings of the secular world."

"But that's just it. The church is in on it too. They're just as bad as secular society—worse even. Don't you see?"

Sarah grew quiet, and her face took on a tired, worrisome look. "I'm trying to understand," she said after a long delay. "Really, I am."

"Yes, well, try harder. Because everything I've been telling you is the truth."

"Okay, for argument's sake, let say it is the truth. Now what?"

"And now, we fix things."

"Fix things? How about we begin by fixing our marriage?

Gary shook his head. He was tired of their marriage, and of Sarah, but most of all he was tired of the lies.

"I know you don't want to hear this," Gary said. "But you as much said so yourself. Our marriage was a mistake. You're not the woman for me, and if I'm being honest, I'm not the right man for you. There's nothing to fix because we were never whole to begin with."

Sarah's lower lip quivered; she was on the verge of tears, but managed to sit up straight and in a calm voice say, "So you want a divorce?"

"Yes," Gary replied without hesitation and with no emotion. "Doesn't that make sense? At least this way, we still have a chance. We can find someone who is right for us while we're still young enough to do so."

"I see."

"Do you?"

Sarah shook her head back and forth. "What I see is a confused little man who thinks he's found all the answers through a series of misguided principles, pseudo-science, and spiritual mumbo-jumbo. I see a man who's lost his way, his faith, and his god. I see that much, Gary."

Gary sneered. "Yes, well, if you say so," he said. Then he stood up and marched out of the kitchen.

"Where are you going?" Sarah called after him.

"Upstairs," he shouted back. "I need to journal."

• • • • •

The bedroom was dark except for the glow of a pipe. The pipe burned dim, then bright and then dim again as Belle sucked smoke into her lungs and then back out again. Though Gary could not see the smoke, the pungent smell made his nose wrinkle.

"For God's sake," Gary whispered. "Put that out. Do you want Sarah smelling that?"

"She can't smell it," Belle's voice replied from the dark.

"If she can hear you, she can smell the smoke."

"She can't hear me."

"She said she heard a female voice that one time," Gary snarled.

"That was you she heard. She can't hear me."

"What are you talking about?" Gary scoffed. "How is that possible?"

"Come to the bed," Belle demanded. "You need to hit this bowl more than I do."

Gary's eyes had now adjusted to the light; he walked to the bed where Belle's nude silhouette sat upright, holding the pipe between her thumb and forefinger. He sat at the edge of his bed next to Belle and took the pipe from her. Then he held it to his lips and awkwardly took a deep breath, trying to mimic the way he had seen Belle do it. Immediately, he felt a burning sensation in the back of his throat as the hot gas torched his lungs. And though he tried to hold it in, he choked and coughed the burning fumes back into the air.

"Jesus Christ," Gary said in a raspy voice. "No wonder our government wants to make this stuff illegal."

Belle laughed. Gary was now close enough to see her face; he gently placed his hand aside her cheek and gently spoke to her. "Belle," he said.

"You're coming to me now. I don't have to call you."

"You did call me."

"No, I didn't. I've been downstairs, talking to my wife."

"Your heart was calling me, and your heart speaks louder than your mind."

"Oh sweet, Belle," Gary said stroking her face. "My sweet, sweet Belle."

"What troubles you, my love?"

"Nothing troubles me, not anymore. Except not having you."

"But you do have me."

"Not really. Not the way I want you."

"Soon, my love. Soon."

"Yes. I can't wait." Gary held Belle's hand and kissed it.

"Are you going to journal?" Belle said.

"I was going to, but I'd rather talk to you."

"I think you should take a look at your journal," Belle said nodding her head in the direction of the desk.

There was something odd in Belle's tone that caused Gary some alarm. "Why?" he said.

"Go and look for yourself," she said smiling.

Gary walked to the desk. He turned on the lamp and saw the journal laying where he last left it. Belle was now standing by his side and gently placed her hand on his shoulder.

"Notice anything different?" Belle said.

"No."

"Look at your bow?"

Gary wrinkled his forehead and then slowly reached out and touched the leather string, which secured the journal in a knot. He now saw what Belle alluded to.

"This isn't my bow?" Gary said. "Belle smiled and nodded her head in agreement. "I tie it very carefully with two large loops," he continued. "This was done in haste."

"Uh, huh."

"Well, perhaps I was in a hurry last time I used it. Maybe I just quickly tied it off. I don't remember."

Gary looked at Belle for confirmation. She shook her head from side-to-side and in slow motion. "Nope," she replied.

"Well, who, then?"

"Okay, think, Gary. It certainly wasn't me."

Gary's eyes grew wide, and his face melted into a gray, brooding mass of angry flesh.

CHAPTER NINETEEN

Gary rang the bell. After a brief wait, the door swung open and he was greeted by Belle's smiling face. Instantly, his mood lifted. A broad smile wrapped his face, and his knees trembled. "Belle," he gushed.

"Ah, Gary," said Belle. "It's been a while. Where have you been?"

"You know, been busy with work and other things."

"Come on in. Bob is looking forward to seeing you."

Gary stepped into the house and followed Belle as she led him down a long corridor leading towards the library.

"How have you been, Belle?"

"I'm fine, and yourself? How's Sarah?"

"Fine, fine," Gary replied.

"Bob misses you. He talks about you all the time."

"Does he?"

"How are the experiments working for you?"

Gary was smug. "Experiment six was brilliant," he answered. "But I guess you already knew that, huh Belle?"

Belle stopped walking and turned around to face Gary. The two spoke in hushed voices just outside the library doors. "You've been a naughty boy," Belle said.

"What do you mean?"

Belle tapped her index finger against Gary's chest. "You know exactly what I mean," she said. "Bob practiced on me before you did."

Gary leaned in close. "Who's better?" he whispered.

"You are," she replied. Bob was able to speak to me. With you…"

"Yes?"

Belle looked toward the ceiling. "I can see, and touch and feel—"

"And taste?" Gary added.

"You need to stop."

"Why? Don't you like it?"

"I like it very much, too much in fact. That's the problem. I'm married, and so are you."

Gary dismissed the notion for the nonsense it was. "Are you?" he said. "Am I?"

"Yes, of course."

Gary shook his head. "In name only. My marriage is a farce, and so is yours."

"Gary—"

"Oh Belle, I married the wrong woman. I mean Sarah is nice enough. She's quite a wonderful person, actually, but we're not compatible. She doesn't make me feel like you make me feel."

"And how do I make you feel?"

"I don't know—all tingly inside I suppose."

"That tingly feeling is lust."

"And what if it is?" Gary reached out and placed both hands on her breasts. Belle closed her eyes and let a moan slip past her slightly parted lips. "Belle, you don't know how I've felt. I've wanted to do this ever since I first met you."

Belle suddenly recoiled at Gary's touch. She grabbed his wrists and ripped his hands away. "Stop it," she said in a loud whisper.

"Tell me you don't feel the same way."

"I don't."

"Tell me you'd rather be with a broken-down old man."

"Shut the fuck up. He'll hear you."

Her rebuke had barely left her mouth when the library doors swung open; Bob stuck his head out and opened his mouth as if to say something but stopped short. "Gary?" he said after a pause.

"Of course it's me," Gary said putting on a happy face. "Who else would I be?"

Bob stared intently at Gary as if something were amiss. "Uh—nobody," Bob said after a moment of stunned silence. "I just heard a couple of hens cackling out here, and I thought I'd see what all the commotion was about."

"There's no commotion," Gary quickly answered. "Belle and I were just having a little chat. Right, Belle?"

"Come into the library," Bob said. "We have a lot to talk about."

Bob reached into his back pocket and produced his wallet. From it, he pulled out his credit card and extended it towards Belle.

"Go ahead and take it," Bob said. "Buy something nice and give me a private show tonight."

Belle smiled and took the card from her husband. "What experiment are you on?" she asked.

"Seven," Bob said grabbing Gary's elbow and leading him into the library. "Seven," he repeated. "The final experiment."

．　　　．　　　．　　　．　　　．

Gary fidgeted in his chair and shifted his eyes left-to-right while Bob filled his glass with an amber-colored liquid. Gary took a sip, and then stroked his mustache. In less than a week, his facial hair had grown into a robust growth of jet-black hair, which Gary proudly pruned and coaxed it into a makeshift handlebar that turned upwards at both ends.

"You look different," Bob said.

Gary nodded his head. "It's the goatee and mustache," he said smiling. "It defines my jawline better and gives me an edgier look. Do you like it?"

"Yes, but its more than that," Bob said shaking his head.

"Oh? How so?"

"It's your face—its—well, its more chiseled, or something. I don't know, sharper, more stern." Gary shrugged. "And you look thinner, more gaunt, long and lean."

"I've been eating right," Gary answered proudly.

"How does Sarah like the goatee?"

"Sarah? Sarah doesn't know what she likes. She seems to take exception to everything I do lately. I don't think she likes it, but I don't care about that. I'll be damned if I change for her or anyone else."

Bob bowed his head and stared at his clasped hands. "I—I'm sorry to hear that."

"Sorry?" Gary said his voice rising in pitch. "Sorry for what?"

"I don't know; it sounds like you and Sarah are not getting along so well."

"Is that so? And when did we ever get along?"

"Well," Bob said tentatively. "If there's anything I can do."

Gary saw the concern on Bob's face and was now aware of his own agitated state. He offered his friend a consolatory smile. "It's okay," he said gently. "It's just little squabbles and niggles, petty stuff. We're fine."

"Well, I hope so. You know you and Sarah mean a lot to me. It would make me sad to see either one of you unhappy."

Gary let out a small laugh and then took a sip of his drink. After a noisy swallow, he lifted the glass to the light and said, "This is damn fine Scotch. It is Scotch, right? You run a first class operation here." Gary pushed the glass toward Bob as if celebrating an imaginary toast. "No, Sarah and I are just fine," he continued. "It's just stuff. You and Belle must have your own stuff, things you have to work through; am I right?"

Bob offered a weak smile and nodded his head. "Of course."

"Yes, everyone has their stuff to work through."

"Well, I just want to let you know I'm here for you, Gary. Like I said, you and Sarah mean a lot to me."

Gary studied his half–filled glass before lifting his head and responding. "Yeah, I know, Bob. I feel the same about you." The two men sat silently for a few minutes before Gary spoke again. "You know, Bob. I do want to thank you. I mean for introducing the experiments to me."

"They've helped you?"

"Of course they've helped. Look at where I was six months ago. Okay, maybe I haven't reached the summit yet, but I'm doing better, financially, and I know I'll do better still. This—this is only the beginning. I've merely scratched the surface, and there's more to come. Much more."

Bob smiled. "Well, I'm glad to hear that, Gary. I'm a scientist, and so often people forget the true aim of science."

"And what is that?"

"To help society, to make this world a better place for all of us."

Gary laughed. Make the world a better place for all of us, he thought? It was too Tiny Tim for his taste: *God bless us, everyone.*

"Yes, of course," Gary said. "But something is missing from your vision."

"Yes?"

"Yeah, it's like you don't fully understand the power of what you've created."

Bob held his hands out, palms raised in resignation. "But I haven't created anything," he said. "I've merely stood on the shoulders of geniuses who came before me. I've merely discovered a practical methodology for implementing their ideas."

Gary looked into his glass and agitated the Scotch. "Yes of course, but you stopped short. Don't you realize what can be achieved?" Bob questioned him silently with a glance. "For God's sake," Gary continued. "A nice home and worldly trinkets are well and good, but there is so much more to be gained from this knowledge."

"Such as?"

Gary was agitated by his friend's ignorance. How could a man as smart as Doctor Robert Harris, have such little imagination? "Think," Gary said pointing a middle finger at his own temple. "I can visit any place in my mind, converse with anyone I wish. Perhaps, even with people who are no longer with us, or cultures that no longer exist. Man, that would change everything—How we act and think and feel. This will put an end to archaic religious practice. I'll create a new religion, or better still, get rid of all the religions…" Gary took another sip and then thrust his glass forward as if stabbing the air with a sword. "…including Christianity."

"Is that what you want?" Bob said.

"I want the truth," Gary said leaning forward. "That's all I ever wanted. That's what anyone wants. The truth is good, it's pure, and it's righteous. Lying to people and telling them they're damned to Hell, by an angry, vengeful God for the smallest slight, real or imagined—Well, that doesn't work for me."

"Did it ever work for you, Gary?" Gary bowed his head and stared into his glass. Several moments passed before the sound of Bob's voice brought him back. "Gary?"

"I don't know what worked for me or what didn't," Gary said softly. "To be honest, I'm ashamed of the things I said and did as a minister."

"Ashamed?"

"Because I never believed half the stuff I was saying. You know, you grow up; your parents tell you things, your teachers, your priest, or whomever, and you just believe them—maybe because I had no other choice, or perhaps I was too afraid of burning in Hell or not getting my Christmas presents. I don't know. But that became my world, my religion, my life or whatever."

"But that's okay, Gary. Millions of people go through that. It's just what we humans do. Religion probably did you some good, kept you out of trouble. Perhaps you helped some others along the way, performed some acts of kindness because of your beliefs."

"Listen to you," Gary said aiming the glass at Bob and squinting through the liquid as if peering through a rifle scope. "Defending organized religion, and I once accused you of being a heathen."

"Yes," Bob laughed. "I can't believe I'm saying any of this."

"Yes, and that's fine until your life becomes dissatisfying." Gary raised his glass and emptied it in one gulp before slamming it down on the coffee table. "More," he demanded.

Bob dutifully filled Gary's glass. "Tell me about six?" Bob said.

"Six?" Gary chuckled. "Well, it worked."

"It did?"

"Like magic. Like real magic."

"You were able to contact someone, send them a message?"

"More than just a message," Gary said his voice rising with excitement. "It was like I could feel their presence in the room, taste their perfume, talk to them like I had superpowers. I swear there were times I couldn't tell the difference between reality and fantasy. I was transported to another world and yet, I never left my bedroom. It was all in my mind, and it was so real." Gary took another sip of Scotch. "I'll say it worked."

"Holy fuck, Gary. I was never able to do all that. Who did you contact? You said you could taste their perfume?"

Gary shrunk in his chair and took another sip; this time he sucked the ice cube into his mouth and crushed it between his molars before swallowing. "Uh, just a friend," he answered.

"I see. Then you're ready for experiment seven?"

Gary had mixed emotions. He was happy to reach the final experiment, but it meant graduation was near. He would no longer be a student; he would no longer have a Master. The last several months had been remarkable, and he was excited for his future—he was also scared. He didn't want to go back to what he was. He never wanted to go back to that.

"I am," he said trying to mask his disappointment.

"What's wrong?"

"I'm sad to see it come to an end. You should have more than seven experiments. I feel like I can keep going. There should be no end, really. There should be an eight, a nine, a ten—it could go on forever."

"Perhaps you will take up the baton, my friend."

Gary nodded his head in agreement. "Perhaps."

"Okay, experiment seven. As I alluded to, you're going to use your mind to do something you never dreamed was possible."

Gary had anticipated Bob's words. "Move things with my mind?" he said.

Bob pulled his head back. "How'd you guess?"

Gary flashed a knowing smile. It wasn't a guess at all. He had simply become adept at moving into others headspace, seeing, experiencing and feeling as they did. It was like watching a motion picture complete with color, shape, and dimension. As for the minds he invaded, they never knew. Bob was oblivious. It was a game to Gary—a fun, amazing and sometimes creepy game. Other people's thoughts weren't always pleasant ones.

"Well, It's the next logical step," Gary said.

"Yes, and it's the final and most important one too."

"You know Bob, I feel like my mind has been going through a transition; it's like the first six experiments have prepped me for this very type of thing. Each one reshaped who I am and how I think."

"Yes, that's right. You have the belief and that belief is the secret ingredient to obtaining anything you want. Can you conceive of it, Gary?"

"Of course."

"Now, see it. Believe it has already happened."

"Yes, I believe."

"Now watch it come to pass. You're to start with something small. Turn the page."

"What's that?"

"Get a book, any book you want. Open it, and then turn the page..." Bob leaned in close to Gary and whispered, "...with nothing but your mind. Can you do that, Gary?"

"I can do that," Gary answered smugly.

"You seem confident."

"I am, and why shouldn't I be? Every experiment has worked." Gary paused and scratched his goatee. "Well," he continued. "Everyone except experiment four."

"Oh? What happened with four? I thought the plants were growing nicely for you."

"Yeah, they were. The right side that is, the side I prayed for, but now they've stopped, and the left-side has overtaken the entire egg carton. They've become a fuckin' jungle."

Bob scratched the top of his balding head. "And how do you account for this?"

"Sarah," Gary answered coldly.

"What? Sarah?"

"She doesn't like the experiments, Bob. She thinks it's the work of the Devil, so she's tried to sabotage them."

"How?"

"I don't know," Gary said before downing the rest of his scotch. "She gave the left-side Miracle Grow or something. I don't know for sure; she denies it."

"She really thinks the experiments are the Devil's work?"

Gary smiled. "Well, I'm exaggerating," he said. "I suppose I haven't helped much. I've stopped being as Christian as I once was. I haven't been going to church. Do you know I lost my position?"

Bob nodded his head. "Yes, I heard."

Gary raised an eyebrow. He hadn't told anyone. "And how did you hear this?" he said.

"Sarah told me."

"God damn it," Gary said slamming his glass on the table. "I wish she'd mind our own business. Has she been blabbing all over town about how her husband's a thief? I didn't steal that goddamn money, Bob. You know that, right?"

"Don't be mad at her. She was just concerned."

"And what did she tell you?"

"Well," Bob shrugged. "Just that you've been struggling."

"Struggling? How?"

"With your faith. Like you said, you're not as Christian as you use to be."

"And what the Hell is that supposed to mean?"

"I don't know, Gary. You said—"

"If that means I'm no longer a fool who repeats what other Christians say, then you're right about that. I've disavowed that way of thinking and distanced myself from that world. But you know something, Bob, my spiritual convictions are stronger than ever. I'm more convinced of the existence of a higher power than I ever was. How else would I be able to manifest the life I've always wanted, to achieve what I've always deserved? Isn't that right, Bob? Isn't that what you believe?"

"Of course, but—"

"I mean Christians talk about an angry, vengeful God, and they love to talk about sin. What a joke. What is sin, and why is it so important? I'm human. I sin. What of it? You know what sin and forgiveness have done for me?"

"No."

"Nothing. Not a god damned thing. What does sin have to do with our spiritual life? Everyone sins. So what? How can you avoid it when a mere thought can constitute sin? Did you know thinking about a woman with lust in your heart is a sin?"

"Yes, but Gary, as you now know, mere thoughts can take on physical form. Christ said that we must control our thoughts because they can manifest into our reality."

Bob's argument was good, but Gary wasn't backing down. "Who are you?" he laughed. "Seriously, who the fuck are you? And whose side are you on, Mister—we—need—to—fix—Christianity because it's broken bullshit? Well, I agree with you. Christianity is broken."

Bob shook his head. "I'm on no one's side, or rather I should say I'm on the side of truth. Christ was speaking the truth. I merely pointed it out."

The two men engaged in a brief staring contest, neither said a word, neither wanted to back down. It didn't last long. Gary was the first to avert his eyes and speak. "Yes," he said. "But this so-called truth has been perverted by Christian ideology over the past two-thousand years."

"Perhaps," replied Bob. "Certainly, by the Christian right."

"So what's this concern written all over your face? Several months ago, you were trying to convince me that Christianity rang hollow and lost its original spiritual message. Isn't that right?"

"Yes, that's right."

"So, now I agree with you. What's the problem?"

Bob clasped his hands together. "These experiments," he began. "They were designed to enrich people's lives, your life, Sarah's life. In fact, I designed them to benefit society, all of mankind."

"Yes, Bob. And they have enriched my life."

"Good. Good. Good. That's all well and good, but I'm afraid you may have lost your rudder, your faith, my friend. Do you understand?"

"No, you're wrong. My faith is stronger than it's ever been."

"Yes, but in what?"

"Well, in God, in the Universe or whatever you want to call it. Isn't that the point of all of this?"

"Yes, of course, it is. But to what end?"

"To what end?" Gary replied incredulously. He laughed, threw up his hands and slammed his index finger against his chest. "To my end," he concluded.

Bob shook his head from side-to-side. "No," he said. "To mankind's end, to societies' benefit."

Gary looked around the library. "Bullshit," he announced. "I'm calling bullshit on that, and I call bullshit on you."

"Why do you say that?"

"Look at you," Gary said extending his hand towards Bob. "You sit there in your twelve-hundred-dollar leather chair, living in a one-million-dollar mansion with your trophy wife, and enough toys to make a millionaire blush. These experiments are designed to benefit the practitioner, not mankind. No, my friend, don't get sanctimonious with me. Please. You practiced these experiments to the benefit of Bob Harris, and you know what I say? Good for you. You were looking out for you and your wife, and I say good for you because if you don't look out for yourself, no one else will. Trust me. I know."

"Yes," Bob agreed. "I picked up a few things along the way, nice things. You're right about that. But I helped myself so that I might help others. You've been helped by these experiments, but I'm afraid they've hurt you too."

"How? How have they hurt me?"

"Perhaps they've put a rift between you and your wife, or you and your Christian beliefs? I never meant for that to happen."

Gary waived his hand dismissively and smiled. "This rift, it was already there. I did well to hide it, a bit too well I'm afraid. The experiments, well, they've only accelerated the inevitable. Look, I'm sorry if I came off as a bit of an asshole—"

"You're fine," Bob said cutting him off. "You know I just want the best for you, my friend. I'd hate to see you and Sarah unhappy and to know I may have had some part of that."

"Unhappiness?" Gary chuckled. "You don't understand. I've never been happier."

"Is that right?"

Gary smiled and pointed at his empty glass. "More please." Bob refilled the glass and Gary immediately raised it to his lips. Before taking a sip, he looked at Bob and repeated, "I've never been happier."

"I'm glad to hear it. Now, it's time to turn the page, Gary. I'm giving you two weeks to make it happen. Think you can do it?"

Gary winked and said, "I can do it in a day."

CHAPTER TWENTY

Gary lowered his nose into the yellow, dog-eared paper and inhaled the musty scent of his childhood. "so long ago," he whispered into the fragrant page. With the bitter-sweet memory fresh in his mind, he closed his eyes and focused on the rhythmic rise and fall of his breath.

Several hours had passed, but to Gary it was just a moment; when he opened his eyes, he looked at the page as if seeing it for the first time. The once static ink now appeared fluid and breathed with a life all its own. The letters moved and rearranged themselves to form new words or plain gibberish. It made him laugh.

With great concentration, Gary floated his hands an inch above the page. Instantly, he felt a static charge pulsating at his fingertips. It felt good, and he enjoyed the rush it provided. He waited and watched carefully, anticipating the slightest movement. Suddenly, the energy in his hand spiked and he saw a nearly imperceptible twitch. Then, as if directed by a ghostly hand, the page turned. Gary looked around for a witness, but of course, there were none. He was alone in the bedroom.

"It's alive!" Gary laughed. "It's alive! It's alive!"

.   .   .   .   .   .

Time lost all meaning when the automatic writer appeared; he couldn't be sure how many hours had passed—two, perhaps three, maybe more? During this time, he heard several half-hearted knocks on his office door, but he ignored them all. He had missed his class but could care less. Work, and life had lost its meaning. There was only one life he wanted to live, and he was already living that one to the fullest. There was no room for anything else, and no reason to change.

Gary continued to write, and there was another knock. This one was sharp and reverberated throughout the office like a metal gong. It brought with it an urgency that broke the spell he was under.

"Who is it?" Gary yelled. "Go away. I'm busy. I'm not feeling well."

"It's me," a voice on the other side said softly.

Gary focused hard. He had grown proficient at seeing the face on the other side of a closed door, or phone calls from unknown numbers, knowing the faceless person before they identified themselves, but now, he drew a blank, seeing only a cold, pale figure where a human body should have stood.

"Who are you?" Gary demanded.

"It's Lucas, the bookseller."

"Go away," Gary snapped. "You've already looked at my books."

"Ah, but I may have missed some."

"Go away."

"Let me in."

Gary was about to stand but remembered there was no need. He concentrated and watched the door slowly swing open. There, on the other side, stood Lucas wearing a bemused expression on his face. He looked at Gary, then at the door, and then back at Gary.

"Parlor tricks," Gary answered in reply to the unspoken question.

"Very impressive," Lucas said. "May I come in?"

"The door is open. Step in if you must."

Lucas walked into the room. He had an odd gait. It reminded Gary of a holiday float hovering inches above the ground. Lucas came to a stop at Gary's side and stood rather close—too close for Gary's comfort. Lucas' tall, spindly frame towered over Gary's seated body.

"Sorry to disturb you,' Lucas said. "I hope I'm not troubling you."

Gary pushed off with his toes and sent his wheeled chair backward several inches to recover some personal space.

"You are troubling me," Gary insisted. "What business do you have here? I told you; you've already looked through my books and purchased the ones that had value."

Lucas glanced at the ragged book sitting on the desk. He gestured towards it and said, "May I?"

Gary hesitated, but deciding there was no harm, gave Lucas permission.

"Ah," Lucas said, his face taking on a warm glow. "Jules Verne. You like Jules Verne?"

"No. I <u>love</u> Jules Verne."

Lucas ran his fingers across the cover, feeling its texture and admiring the craftsmanship that went into its making. He ran his thumb up and down the spine, pressing lightly as if stroking a cat. "It's old," he said.

"My mom—she gave it to me when I was a boy."

Lucas opened the book. The ambient light reflected off the page and into his face turning his already pale skin a stark white.

"Look," Lucas said excitedly. "It's a first edition. Your Mom got you a first edition."

"Really? I hadn't noticed."

"See?" Lucas said pointing to the copyright page. "There it is."

Lucas lowered the book and turned it so that Gary could peer into it. "So it is," Gary said in a matter of fact tone.

"Your mother, is she still alive?"

"No. She passed some time ago."

"She must have loved you very much."

"Look," Gary said in a raised voice. "She was my mother. I suppose she loved me as much as any mother loves her son. Now, if you'll excuse me, I have work to do."

"I'm sorry. I've upset you. Of course, you are a college professor. You have classes to teach. I'll leave you be, but first, would you be interested in selling this book?"

Gary thought it over. The Jules Verne novel was a cherished gift from his mother, and Gary loved his mother. In fact, she may have been the only woman or person that he had ever loved, and he was sure she felt the same about him. Despite this, Gary had read it several times, and Lucas was always good for some extra cash.

"How much?" Gary said. Lucas opened his mouth, but before he could answer, Gary spoke for him. "Wait. Don't tell me. Four hundred?"

The corner of Lucas' lips turned upward into a slimy smile. "How did you know?"

Gary grabbed his journal and held it up to Lucas. "Because," he said. "I have it written here." Lucas reached out as if to take the journal but was stopped by Gary's bark. "Keep your fucking hands off my journal," Gary said. "No one but me touches this."

Lucas pulled his hands away in an act of surrender. "My apologies," he said. "So, do we have a deal?"

"Four hundred? Do you have a check?"

"I don't do checks. I have cash."

"You carry around four hundred dollars in cash?"

"I only deal in cash."

"You better be careful," Gary warned. "Some desperate freshman will likely roll you for the fifty bucks in your pocket let alone the four hundred."

"Oh," Lucas laughed. "I'm not worried about that."

Lucas reached into his coat pocket and pulled out a wad of cash. Gary's eyes grew big as he watched the book seller peel away four, freshly minted one-hundred-dollar bills and lay them slowly and gently on Gary's desk. When he had finished, he caught Gary's gaze and held it. "Four hundred," Lucas said pushing the bills closer to Gary.

Gary reached out and with both hands, pounced on the cash. It looked real and smelled real. With trembling hands, he gathered the money into a crumbled mass and shoved it into his pocket while Lucas placed his book into a tattered canvas bag.

"Let's talk about parlor tricks for a moment shall we?" Lucas said.

Gary wrinkled his nose at the stench coming from Lucas' mouth. It was an unpleasant aroma that reminded Gary of coffee, cheap wine, and stale salami. "How 'bout we not?" Gary replied. "How 'bout you go already and leave me to my work?"

Lucas smiled. "Parlor tricks are fun," he continued ignoring Gary's rebuke. "But in the end, they serve no real purpose, do they?"

What an arrogant prick, Gary thought. "And what would you know about parlor tricks?" he demanded.

"Flipping pages, turning metal rods like trained dogs, and conjuring a few bucks here and there is great fun, but you're thinking too small."

"Am I now?"

Lucas nodded. "Yes. Look at you. You're quite pleased with yourself, sitting in this tiny office with the few hundred bucks stuffed into your coat pocket as if you achieved something great."

"That few hundred may not be much to you, but it's a lot to me."

Lucas' face broke into a sympathetic grin. The lines and crows' feet around his cheek and eyes grew thick and aged him by a hundred years. "Excuse me. I didn't mean to sound harsh. You have done well for yourself, but there is more to be had. If you're going to attempt tricks, why not make them bigger, more grandiose?"

Lucas now had Gary's full attention. "Such as?"

Lucas raised a single eyebrow. "Well, let's start with your career. Did you know State College is looking for an assistant professor of theology and divinity?"

"No, I didn't know that. State is a first-tier University. They'll be a hundred applicants for that position, maybe more."

"Where's your journal?"

"It's here," Gary said nodding toward his desk.

"Good. Draw yourself standing in front of a crowded lecture hall at State. You can flip pages with your thoughts and open doors; a few rivals shouldn't stand in your way. The starting salary is eighty-six-thousand dollars, nearly double your pay at St. Mary's."

"Is that so?"

"But that's just the beginning, my friend. There is more, so much more."

"Like?"

Lucas' hands were animated as if he were trying to paint a picture for Gary. "Use your imagination," he said. "Ask yourself what is not possible. There is nothing you cannot accomplish, my friend, not one thing is beyond your grasp. The laws of the universe will bend to your will. You just have to give the command. Press the right buttons as it were."

A single thought formed in Gary's head. "Belle?" he said.

"Ah, you like Belle?"

"Who wouldn't? Those breasts, her legs—they scream sex."

"Then take her. She is yours."

Gary smiled and shook his head. "She belongs to Bob, and besides, she has no interest in me."

"Belle belongs to whomever she wants. She is a free spirit who will grab her meal ticket like a ravenous wolf latches to its prey."

Gary tried to make sense of this odd man. Lucas had something of the used car salesman in him that reminded Gary of weasel. Furthermore, he looked strange, and he sounded stranger, and yet, he knew things he could not possibly know. Gary was beguiled by this book salesman.

"I don't know about that," Gary said.

"Yes, but I do. Did you know your friend Bob has a life insurance policy, with a rather substantial death benefit, and Belle would stand to gain a fortune in the event of his death as untimely as it may be?"

"Why are you telling me this?"

"Are you dense? Why do you think Belle would marry a broken down old man like Doctor Harris? Love?" Lucas laughed and flashed a set of yellow, crooked teeth. "She's waiting for him to pass so that she can have a big payday. She thought the Cancer would have done its job by now, but that fool proved tougher than she ever imagined."

"I didn't know."

"Now you do. Perhaps you should give Belle more credit. She's smarter than she looks, but perhaps she needs a helping hand?"

"A helping hand? How?"

"Remember what I told you? You are no longer bound by human limitations. You are God, Gary Miller, and you posses all the powers that come with the title."

"I don't understand."

"So you're interested?"

Gary sat up straight. "Of course I'm interested," he said. "Who wouldn't be?"

"Then you need to practice, hone your skills, refine them."

"But how? On what?"

"It's the same as you've been doing, only now you'll give yourself greater and greater challenges to reach a level of unparalleled faith. With this faith, you will achieve anything you can imagine and things you can hardly imagine but are there—there stored deep within the recesses of your mind. You only need to reach back and pull them out."

"Yes, but what kind of challenges?"

Lucas' face buckled under the weight of his smile. "A man once walked on water," he said.

Gary formed a mental image of Christ walking on the sea. "But I'm following the experiments," Gary said. "Bob and I haven't gotten that far yet."

"And you never will. Do you think Doctor Harris wants you to surpass him?" Gary hesitated. "The correct answer is no," Lucas said. "Why would he? He wants to keep you subservient, beneath him."

"Why would he want that?"

"For the same reason society has kept you down all this time, relegating Gary Miller to the bottom depths so that richer, more powerful men can prosper off of your blood and sweat. Dr. Harris is not your friend, not your real friend."

"Is that so?"

"That is so. Why do you doubt me?"

Gary was conflicted. He had no reason to doubt the book seller. Lucas appeared wise and was merely saying things Gary had already believed. Still, Bob was a good friend. "I don't know," Gary said. "Doctor Harris introduced me to the experiments. I owe him a great deal."

"Well, believe this. You are a powerful man, Dr. Miller. Now, start using your power for greater things. Remember, nothing is beyond your reach. Look in your journal. I left something there for you." Gary picked up his journal and opened it. "Turn to the last entry," Lucas instructed.

Gary was hesitant but did as he was told. He flipped to the end and began reading an entry written in red ink, and penned by a different hand than his own.

"What is this?" he asked.

"What does it look like?"

"More experiments—eight, nine and ten?"

Lucas smiled. "That's right," he said. "You asked for them. The experiments Harris would not tell you about. Take particular note of ten."

Gary studied the entry, then looked up at Lucas and met his gaze. "Where did they come from?" he said.

"Never mind where they came from."

"You put them there, but how? Who are you?"

"Me? I am Lucas, a humble book salesman at your service."

Gary knew this was a lie. Lucas was a man Gary could look up to and aspire to be one day, but there was nothing ordinary about him. "Humble book salesman my ass," Gary smirked.

The two men gave each other a knowing smile. "One last thing before I go," Lucas said. "You should be careful about that wife of yours."

"Sarah?"

"That would be the one."

"Don't worry about her. She'll not bother me."

"She may be more bother than you think. You should take care of her. Do you understand?"

Gary nodded his head even though he didn't understand. Sarah was a nothing, a nobody, and more of pest to him than anything else.

"I must be going now," said Lucas. "Tell me, do you have the time?"

Gary lifted his wrist to read his imaginary watch but was stunned to see there was nothing imaginary about it. It was as real as anything he knew to be real. It had form, weight, and dimension, and the time glowed brilliant blue against a black matte background.

Gary looked at Lucas with an open mouth and an incredulous expression. Lucas returned Gary's silent question with a laugh. "What's this?" Gary said.

"It's a watch. You asked for it, remember?"

Gary thought back to his journal. He did remember. Gary asked for a watch, a nice watch, and now it sat on his wrist like it had been there all this time.

"But how?" Gary said.

"It's called manifestation. You wrote about it, drew pretty pictures, and, well, here your are and there it is."

"But I haven't done anything," Gary protested.

"I gave you a bit of help," Lucas said smiling. "Call it an assist."

"But that's impossible. Things don't just appear from thin air. That's not how the world works."

"I'm afraid Doctor Harris didn't teach you that lesson. The world works differently for people like you and me."

Gary looked back at the watch to make sure he wasn't dreaming. He was fully awake, and the watch was real. There was no mistake about it, but he couldn't reconcile this fact with his knowledge of the world. "No," Gary said shaking his head. "It's a trick. You slipped it on me when I wasn't looking. I mean thanks and all. I really appreciate it but—"

"It's no trick," Lucas assured him. "You asked for it, and the Universe responded. As I've told you, the Universe is here to do your bidding."

"But how?"

"Read experiment nine in your journal. It will explain this and more. Just follow all my instructions. Carry them out without delay, and leave no stone unturned. Do not question any of it. You may have reservations, but believe me, it's for the best. And when you have finished, the experiments must be destroyed, and every last living trace to them must be eliminated."

"What? I don't understand."

"This power you have, it can't be released to the general population. That's what Doctor Harris plans to do, and that would be a huge mistake; if others knew, then your power will be diluted. Read my journal entries. They explain everything."

"Yes, yes, of course, I will."

"Good. I'll be taking my leave now, but one parting gift before I go. He's coming down the hall now."

Lucas left Gary's office and shut the door behind him. Immediately afterward, Gary heard a knock and recognized a male presence standing on the other side. It was a student of his.

"Come in, Brandon," Gary said.

The door swung open and in walked the nervous teenager. "How did you know it was me?" Brandon said.

"Oh," Gary said pointing his index finger at Brandon. "I was expecting you."

"But, I didn't have an appointment."

"I was expecting you notwithstanding." Brandon looked confused. "Parlor tricks," Gary continued. "You wouldn't understand."

"I'm sorry," Brandon said turning towards the door. "I didn't mean to bother you."

"It's quite alright," Gary assured him. "Come in and close the door. Have a seat next to me."

Brandon walked over and took a seat next to his professor. Gary opened his desk drawer. and pulled out a pair of black, sheer stockings. Brandon watched intently; his eyes filled with trepidation. "What are those?" he said.

Gary flung the stockings around the back of Brandon's neck and lassoed the boy's head towards him. "Put these on," Gary whispered.

CHAPTER TWENTY-ONE

From the Journal of Gary Miller, May 10th

No more bitching or whining about how things should have been or could be. It is time to act. The path has been laid before my feet, illuminated by a guiding light. No more guess work, no forks in the road, no doubt, just do what I know to be true. Follow my Dharma. Know what my Dharma is. Bob told me about Dharma. For all these years, I've followed someone else's dream, not my own. And now, I'm tuned in, plugged in as it were to the Universal consciousness. I am living the Tao. The Tao lives through me. My only regret is I didn't start sooner, but even that isn't impossible to rectify. I almost think I can, in time and with much practice, go back, and re-write my story. I would have thought myself or anyone else mad, for thinking such thoughts, but I no longer feel that way. I see things differently now. I see nothing is impossible. I literally have a vision of the world around me. It's no longer made up of the ordinary, and the mundane. My world is EXTRA-ordinary. I realize no one else see's it. No one else can. Time, space, dimension... well. it works differently than what I first thought. Some people grasped the concept. Einstein with his theories of space, time, Hawking. Physics gave them a glimpse. Their numbers gave meaning, shape and form to the universe and a sense of order. But I—I ACTUALLY see what their numbers told them. Gravity has shape and form, and color. I see that. It's like a painting made up of infinite brush strokes. For most people those strokes are colorless, just blobs of grey and black. For me, the painting glows with every hue and with infinite brilliance. I can control what physical laws dictate. I am the keeper of the law. The experiments unleashed something inside of me, opened up doors that were previously closed. A famous Olympic athlete said that your mind contains the power to make or break you. He used the power of his mind to win gold. Now, I know exactly what he meant. I can use the power of my mind to achieve success. I laugh when I think of the past. I use to tell people they should rely on God, that God will provide for them. Lots of Christians said the same thing. It was part of common Christian speak, the platitudes that were carelessly spread about like dust in the wind. I realize how wrong I was. That mentality of relying on God just led to ultimate failure because God is unreliable. RELY ON YOURSELF. Make your own way in this world. You are God. I am God. If God is everywhere, he is in me. How can he not be? I'm perfectly capable of getting what I need and want through the God powers that reside within me. I simply needed a way to tap into this power, and I have found this way. It's like plugging into an electrical outlet. There's no need to rely on anyone but yourself. If I need a job that pays more money, then I can get one on my own. Sex, food, water, clothes, homes and cars… there's nothing I can't achieve, and without God's help. I sat around all those years, waiting for God to answer my prayers. That really fucked up my life. Get this; I use to pray to God to send me a wife. Night after night, I would lay awake at night, tears in my eyes, begging he would bless me with a beautiful woman I could hold and love, and make love to every night. He sent me Sarah. What the fuck, I could have done better on my own, and I would have too if I had more guts to go out and meet a beautiful woman, talk to her, bed her. Instead of praying, I should have been searching. I'm sure I could have done better than God. Ah, what's the use? What's done is done. Time to move forward. Time to make things right.

I am excited about what I've accomplished thus far, but this is just the beginning. I can barely imagine what it will be like, almost too wonderful to imagine, but every piece seems to be falling into place. These past four months have been incredible, like no other stretch of time that's ever come before. I'll look back at this time as a seminal moment in my life, a stretch that completely transformed my life for the better. I needed this. I needed a win. I was in a bad way before and now I feel I can put my fist through a brick wall; tear down the wall if need be. Nothing is a challenge anymore. The problems I once struggled with have now turned to ashes. I regret I ever gave them much thought. I can do as I please. Go where I want to go, say anything, penetrate anyone—students, teachers, men, women, cats and dogs if I were so inclined. Sexual liberation is unbelievable, fantastic and without a single hang up. It's sex as it were meant to be, as it was created by God, for the utter pleasure of mankind and well, procreation, of course. Now, I can experience it like I've never had before, without the religious constraints and fuckin' dogma that bound me once so tight. It's wonderful to have discovered freedom because it's been freedom that I've craved all along. It's what all mankind craves. Sure, money is nice and it goes along with freedom (the more money you have, the more freedom it provides). But the ability to do what I want is intoxicating (as any opioid created by man).

Humanities hired a new Spanish professor this past fall. Her name is Barbara. She's a thirty-something long-haired brunette beauty whose face glows like a goddess; her curves remind me of what a woman should look like. She has beautiful tits, and her tight-fitting slacks wrap her ass tight like a piece of cellophane. I walked behind her one day, about a foot away, and I took in her scent. I got so hard. Sarah is nothing more than a shapeless blob compared to, well, compared to anyone I suppose. Barbara on the other hand, she's a goddamned thoroughbred. Her boyfriend came to visit her one-day. I could hardly believe it; ugly as fucking sin, a short fat fuck. I'm thinking to myself, how the fuck did a monstrosity as him wind up with a gorgeous bitch like her? He must be one hell of a talker, or must be a practitioner of the experiments because by God's natural laws should a brute such as he be with someone as beautiful as Barb. Well, I just had to fuck her, and so I did. I called her into my office and watched as she dutifully undressed in front of me, starting first with her top and bra, she stood before me, her swollen breasts and erect nipples staring straight at me. I salivated like a dog. I did. I swear it was all I could do from coming in my pants; oh god that beautiful curvaceous body peeled like a banana before my eyes; it was one of the greatest sites these eyes could have witnessed. Then she removed her bottoms; her pubic hair was dark and there was a lot of it. She stood in front of me naked. She turned slightly and I caught sight if that chubby ass or hers. It was round, white and wonderfulful and I pictured myself pounding her ass and watching her skin ripple in waves as I fucked her from the rear. The funny thing is she had no idea why she was doing what she was doing. I laughed as I read her thoughts. Why am I doing this? My God, I'm happily engaged. But she couldn't. It's like raping a woman without laying a hand on her. It was remarkable actually. I had fucked her many times in my mind before, and now as she stood naked before me, I nearly stopped myself, thinking that seeing her nude was good enough. But then I thought I would regret it forever if I had this vision in front of me and I didn't take her. She looked awesome in the black stockings. Her thighs were so fleshy, yet shapely and the big black mound of grass dangling from her crotch and accenting the black nylon was pure bliss. She was a great fuck, but she made a lot of noise. Several times, I had to tell her to shut the fuck up. I even slapped her hard about the face and head several times but that just made things worse. She seemed to like it. I boned her hard for several minutes straight. I didn't think I'd be able to come, but finally I did, exploding inside of her like a canon. It was fun. She now gives me dirty looks when I pass her in the hall. Fuckin' bitch. It was the best fuck she ever had, and she knows it (I read her mind. She really does know it LOL). No matter, the semester will be over soon, and I'll be off to my new life. I'm thinking about giving her a goodbye fuck before I leave. Yes, I think I will.

Then I bagged the Physics professor, Doctor Daly. She's a cute little blonde with small, but shapely boobs. She's in her sixties, but I didn't give a shit. She looked good to me and she could fuck too. I was a little surprised, she has a bit of the schoolmarm in her, and looks like she hasn't had sex in years—she probably hasn't. I heard women her age are dry as a bone, but she got real wet, and I slipped it in easy. She looked great in the black stockings. I railed the fuck out of Ms. Daly in her office. I fucked her twice more in mine. She's been real cool about it too. Unlike Barb, Ms. Daly gives me a knowing smile when we pass in the hall. There's been other's too. Some staffers. I fucked two academic counselors. I forget what heir names were. I think one was called Connie and the other Joan or Jane or something or another. They were both in my office at the same time (I bought another pair of stockings). I took them one at a time, first the blond. When I was on the brink of coming, I pulled it out and then slid it in the brunette and railed her until I was about to come. Then I repeated this several more times before I finally shot my load inside the brunnete. She was the pretteier of the two. I want to try them again, this time finishing in the blonde. They were both nice.

I've I did more fucking in the last month than I have in all my years' prior. It's been wonderful. It's not just women. Why should it be? I like men. There, I've said it. So what? A man can please me as much as any woman, more so if I'm being honest. It takes another human in possession of a cock to know how to please that cock, and how much pleasure it brings. Fuck anyone who says it wrong. They don't know. They don't know anything. My cock doesn't know if its male or female, couldn't give a fuck. I can fuck anyone I want, and I don't need drugs or alcohol either, just the power of my mind. I am the envy of every serial rapist that ever drew a breath. One cunt, one mouth, after another, after another, after another. They're all different too, no two cunts exactly alike, different shapes and sizes and colors and they all taste different too. I want to fuck as many cunts as I can before I die. I want to see how many I can fuck before I die. I do not worry about Christian legalism and rules anymore. Sex is so much better without all that shit weighing me down. Worrying about sin and virtue. BULLSHIT. It makes sex seem so awful a thing. Waiting until marriage does NOT make you more virtuous. Having sex does NOT make you a sinner or anymore a sinner than what you already were. Sex is just a thing, like eating is a thing, and drinking is a thing. FUCKING IS A THING. It's a thing we humans do. It's what all animals do to continue the species. Big news flash: we're not that special. If someone else reads this, you're not special. God doesn't care. It's fucking. That's all it is. And hey, if you want to wait because you don't want to get pregnant, or catch disease, then go ahead and abstain, but don't tell people God has anything to do with it. He doesn't care where you stick your dick, or what you do with your cunt. Stop telling people that a marriage license makes it okay, not a sin. What a joke.

Weed and sex is fucking awesome. It's mind blowing. It's like the fuckenest best hard on I ever had, like my skin is stretched so tight it feels like its going to burst a seam. It feels so fucking good it hurts. I've fucked Belle many times while stoned. My only regret is I didn't discover weed sooner—or Belle for that matter. She's been great. The other women are whores to me. Belle, she's different. She's my soul mate, if I actually believed in shit like that. We talk and fuck, and laugh and get stoned. She's introduced me to a world I never knew existed. She's told me stuff about Bob, too. God, I never knew what an asshole he was, keeping her like a slave in that house, fucking with her mind, and trying to control her. Like real crazy shit. It's totally changed my perception. I'm grateful he introduced me to the experiments, and he is a brilliant individual. I admire him for that, but I despise him as the most worthless human being to take a breath. What he's done to Belle. It's no wonder she wants to leave him, to get out as soon as possible. She would have left sooner, but she needed my help. I had to talk her into waiting a bit longer. "soon," I told her.

The planted seed is taking root as I write this. Growing and festering and stinking up the host. Once it takes hold, pays its load, does its damage, then there's no turning back. No drug will be able to undue what I have done. Chemo, a surgeons knife, nothing will help. It will take no more than a few days, a week at most. Belle and I have a home, money, everything I've always wanted.

Funny, having no problems, no barriers, no one to say no to you, is in fact, a problem in its self. It's like the challenge in life is no longer there. I never thought I'd miss it. In fact, I've always dreamed of such a life, a life of bliss, no worries, but I've found it has lost some of its luster. Being broke sucked but it was oddly and wildly exciting. Imagining I was fucking the new hire was fun. Actually fucking her was fun too, but not in the same way. It was as though my imagination was almost as good as reality, maybe in some ways better. Funny, I'm not sure I can tell the difference anymore. I'm not sure it matters, either. Don't get me wrong, I'm very happy. I'm not complaining. Well, I guess I shouldn't complain. I never want to go back to that old life, that miserable man I was, rolled over by every authority figure I've ever met because that's what authority does. I'm the authority now. It's good to be the authority, the hammer and not the nail. Freedom is a drug, like I need more of it to get me high. I guess I'm an addict. I guess I don't care.

Belle, Sweet Belle

By Gary Miller

I want to inhale your lips into my mouth and chew them like bubble gum, sucking and chewing on them until red juce flows from your lips into my mouth like cotton candy.

May 14th

Experiment 10:

Me and a man named Jesus Christ. He was no more a god than I am. This I know. He was spiritual to be sure and way ahead of his time. It would be like me going back two thousand years and showing people my cellphone and telling them I was God. I suspect they would believe me, worship me, and write stories about me. The stories would grow more grandiose with each retelling. I give Jesus a lot of credit, however. He used his parlor tricks to great effect. Good for him. But it shed light on reality for me. What he was, and who I am, we're not different. We both stumbled upon something fantastic, and we both used that very thing to gain fame (he was too stupid to go for the fortune). Pity he was crucified for it. Allowing death to fulfill some daft notion in his mind about being the son of god. He could have commanded the skies to open up on the fools. He could have sent a million volts to spark their asses. Instead, he chose to lie flat on a wooden cross resigned to some meaningless fate. Not me. No one is crucifying me. I'm not here to save mankind. I'm here to save myself.

There were a number of fits and starts before today, stepping into the murky Chadakoin; it was unable to support my weight, and it only served to make my shoes wet and muddy. As my faith grew so did my ability to remain afloat. At first, it was a few steps, then a few more. Today, I made it nearly across. I got half way before I noticed I was beign watched, a boy at the top of a foot bridge gawking as though he saw something miraculous (well, I suppose he did). I smiled at him. I was showing off and in full swagger. Then he gave me this look; it was a look of horror; his face turned ashen as if had seen the impossible. His doubt became mine. I could feel it, invading my mind like poison. My legs, my body quivered. I lost my focus, my belief. I looked down at the murky water, and it dutifully swallowed me whole.

That kid. What was he doing there? I picked that spot for its seclusion. I feel sort of bad, but not really. It was his fault for being there. He wasn't supposed to be there. I do feel a little bad. It wasn't supposed to go down that way, but I suppose sacrifices must be made.

Fuck. I was so close. But still I did it, if for only a brief moment. Most importantly, it showed me. It showed me what I can do.

CHAPTER TWENTY-TWO

Snowball's ears perked up at the car door slam. He started out in his usual manner, a playful romp towards his friend, ready to slay the dreaded laces; then he froze; His back curved into a C and his hair stood on end like porcupine quills. Snowball cocked his head to one side and then the other as he stared at the rail-thin body rapidly approaching.

He paused for a moment as if trying to decide whether to pounce or play safe. The cat wiggled its ass and coiled its hind legs. A couple of short, hurried steps positioned him within striking distance. In an instant, Snowball flew through the air taking dead aim at the offensive black lace. His timing was flawless, and his leap would have placed him perfectly on Gary's instep. But Gary had seen the attack coming, and at the last moment, he lifted his right foot several inches off the ground causing Snowball to hit the cement with an embarrassing flop. Snowball rolled onto his back and laid there, his belly facing up and in full view of Gary's hard leather sole.

Gary thought it over. Then, in one violent, downward motion, he stomped his hard leather heel onto Snowball's face. There was a sickening thud like a watermelon smacking the ground after a fall. The blow landed like an anvil, crushing the thin cranial bone like a cracker and breaking teeth into sharp, useless shreds. After that, there was an eerie silence, soon followed by the sound of black, screeching crows from the trees above. Gary could see himself from their view, looking straight down at his own smiling face and the twitching cat.

Gary slowly lifted his foot and inspected his work. Clinging to the bottom of his shoe was a grotesque mass of white fur, mixed with dark, red blood, which oozed from the corners of Snowball's mouth like fruit jam. Gary balanced on one leg as he viewed the remains. His expression never changed. It was the face of a man preoccupied with nothing more than the weather. Satisfied the cat would no longer disturb him, he continued down the cement walk leaving a faded trail of red footprints behind.

He knew he had to work quickly. It was Tuesday; shopping day. Sarah would be home soon. He flew up the stairs and stepped into his bedroom. He caught his reflection in the dresser mirror and recognized what other people had been saying about him. He liked what he saw, long and lean with a narrow waist, and the black goatee, well, it was stunning by his own estimation. It gave character to his face. He looked like a somebody, dark, brooding with a bit of don't-fuck-with me thrown in.

When he finished admiring himself, he turned his head and saw his journal lying on the desk. It was tied shut but was missing its signature bow. He was angry at himself. God damn it, he thought. How can someone as smart as me, be so stupid? He found his suitcase and began filling it.

Something caught his attention and made him stop. Sitting on the nightstand was a stack of old magazines. Gary recognized them. He grabbed a handful and began rifling through them, studying the erect cocks with a sense of excitement and outrage. A smirk spread across his face as he placed them into the case along with his clothes.

A voice from behind startled him. "Yes," Sarah said. "You wouldn't want to forget those, would you?"

Gary wheeled around and faced his wife. "Ah," he said in a raspy voice. "Sneaking up behind me?"

"I'm not sneaking. This is my house too. I may go where I please."

Gary studied Sarah carefully. She looked different though he couldn't say what it was for sure. Her hair was fancy, or maybe it was her makeup. She was leaner with a thinner waistline that accented her bosom. Whatever it was, Gary liked it and thought a goodbye fuck might be in order.

"Oh? I think you've been doing a lot of sneaking around lately," Gary said.

"Well, I was doing some cleaning and found your magazines tucked away in your underwear drawer. I thought you might like to take them with you. You do plan on leaving me, right?"

Gary's face twitched uncontrollably. It was new habit of his, a rather disturbing one that he couldn't get a handle on.

"You've been reading my journal," he said in a calm voice.

"I have not."

"How else would you know I was leaving you?"

"Because—because your leaving has been evident for some time now. In fact, you all but left me several years ago, and besides, why else would you be packing?"

Gary wanted to explode, but he held off. Instead, he smiled warmly and said, "Don't lie to me you fucking cunt."

"I'm not—"

Gary rushed towards Sarah, and before she could move, his right hand sprung forth like a cobra. His long fingers snaked around her neck; he pushed hard, lifting her body and pinning her head against the wall in one motion. Sarah gasped for breaths as her feet twitched and her toes desperately sought solid ground.

"Don't lie to me," he repeated.

Sarah managed to choke out two words. "I'm not." Gary smiled and slowly lowered Sarah to the ground. "Who are you?" she said after regaining her voice.

"Me? I'm Dr. Gary Miller."

"No," Sarah said shaking her head. "You're not. You're not the man I married. The man I married was righteous and kind. He had his faults—"

"The man you married was weak, I'm sorry to say—some sniveling…some whining…he disgusts me. I'm the new Gary Miller, the new and improved version."

"Does the new Gary Miller like porn?" Sarah said nodding towards the stack of magazines lying in the suitcase.

"Porn my ass," Gary said waving a finger in her face. "You want to know what fucking porn is, Sarah? Porn is one percent of the population having ninety-nine percent of the wealth. Our government is porn. Our president is porn. Christianity is porn, poverty is porn, society is porn. That's what porn is, Sarah, the real kind, the kind that destroys a man, and a society."

Sarah ran her fingers across the swollen islands that covered her throat and a wave of empathy filled Gary. "How's your neck?" he said gently.

"I'm having trouble swallowing."

Gary reached out towards Sarah, but she recoiled at his touch. "It's okay," he said. "I won't hurt you. I promise."

Sarah turned her head allowing Gary to place his hand on her bruised neck. He ran his fingers over her skin causing goose bumps to magically appear where his hand passed; her skin turned warm and red; she closed her eyes and steadied her breathing while Gary worked. After a few seconds, Gary lifted his hand away.

"There," he said. "That should feel better."

"Thank you. It does."

"Yes, well, I better finish packing."

"Can I ask you a question, Gary? Promise you won't get mad?"

Gary nodded. "Sure," he said. "Ask me anything."

"The magazines—when did you start liking boys?"

The corners of Gary's mouth turned down and his voice rose in pitch as he spoke. "I'm not gay," he pleaded.

"I didn't say anything about being gay."

"Then what are you saying?"

"Well, the magazines, Gary. They're yours. You like looking at naked men?"

Gary bit his lower lip as he searched of a response. "Yes, I suppose I do, but that doesn't make me a fag, or a faggot as the Monsignor called me."

Sarah reached out and placed her hand on his shoulder, but he shrugged her off. "Why didn't you tell me?" she said.

"Well, it's not the kind of thing you brag about to your wife, is it?" Gary chuckled.

"No, I suppose not."

"Besides, I could never bring myself to admit it. Brought up in the Catholic Church and all, the shame, the guilt, the horror of it, being a sin and all that. Then becoming born again, it was the same thing, an abomination."

"And now?"

"And now," Gary shrugged." I just don't care. It's who I am; you see?"

"And cat mutilation, is that who you are too?" Gary did not reply. Instead, he turned his back and went to work filling his suitcase. "My God, how could you?" Sarah continued. "What did that poor little creature ever do to you?" Sarah fought back the tears. "And what's to become of me? What about the house, the mortgage?"

"I'll continue to pay the bills," he said with his back still turned. "And give you some money until you get on your feet. There's a lot of equity in the house. I wouldn't want to lose that."

"But how are you going to manage two households? You can barely afford the one."

"Well, I turned in my resignation if that makes you feel any better."

"What?" Sarah said her voice cracking. "Gary, why would you do that?"

"Oh, don't worry yourself. I have a plan."

"Gary, don't do it. Listen to me, honey. Listen to me. What you're planning will destroy you. You think it will make you, but it won't. It will ruin your life, and worse yet, it will damn your soul."

"Oh, is that right?"

Sarah's voice shook as she pleaded. "Gary, I know. I have a feeling, a knowing about this. If you go ahead with your plan, it will turn out bad for you, very bad."

"And how exactly would you know what I have planned?"

"I know…" Sarah bit down hard on her lower lip before finishing. "…I know whatever it is, it can't be good."

Gary walked over to his desk, picked up his journal and carefully placed it in his suitcase on top of his scattered clothing. He then made several more trips to his closet, returning each time with shirts and pants, and stuffing them into the suitcase until it was overfilled. Then, with much difficulty, he managed to close it and latch it shut.

"I'll come back for the rest of my things later," he said. Gary walked toward the door, suitcase in hand. He turned to Sarah and gave her a military-style salute. "Well," he said. "It was fun."

He turned to leave but Sarah's voice stopped him. "Gary," she said. "His name was Bobby."

A chill went down Gary's spine. She knew, but how? How could she? Gary tried to tap her brain, but it was no use. He had tried and failed before and it was as impervious as ever.

"His name was Bobby Lawton," Sarah continued. "Bobby Lawton. He was a boy, Gary, just fourteen years old. He wanted to be a biologist when he grew up. He went to Falconer middle school near the Chadakoin River. They found his body washed up on shore."

Gary's body froze. How much did she know? He stood there trembling, his back turned to Sarah. He didn't dare show his face. His face, he knew, would tell her everything. Instead, he shook his head and proceeded out of the bedroom.

"I'll pray for you," Sarah yelled after him.

"You do that," Gary yelled back.

"I love you," Sarah whispered. "I mean, I loved you. God rest your soul, Gary Miller."

CHAPTER TWENTY-THREE

The room reeked of human excrement and foul breath. It reminded Gary of a nursing home where the old and the sickly lay, one foot in the grave and the other clinging to life—parched leaves on a winter's day, as Gary called them.

Gary's eyes grew accustomed to the light, and he saw the familiar chair in front of the book stacks. In it sat a shrinking figure; it was hunched, frail-looking and covered with a blanket to protect against a nonexistent chill. The body sat nearly motionless, and if it weren't for the slow rise and fall of its shoulders synced to its labored breathing, Gary would not be able to tell if it were alive or dead.

"It's very dark in here," Gary said in a hushed voice. "Shall we turn on the lights?"

Gary raised his hands towards the ceiling as if he were about to conduct an orchestra. The lights slowly turned on and grew in intensity until they reached full power. Every corner of the library was now lit.

"Let there be light," Gary said laughing as if he were the only one privy to a joke.

Gary helped himself to a seat across from the figure. The poor creature was so far removed from its original form, Gary did not recognize him at first. His eyes were sunken. His skin draped its skeleton like a poor-fitting suit. It was inert and lifeless, a soul in need of a useful body.

"Good God," Gary said. "Doctor Harris?"

Bob slowly lifted his head. "Gary?" he said in a thick and raspy voice. Gary stood frozen for a moment, staring at the emaciated body while trying to think of something to say. He was fascinated. As for empathy, he had none.

"Look at me," whispered Bob. Gary looked into his Bob's eyes. There was no spark, charisma, his essence gone.

"I—I…" Bob began. Bob wanted to finish the thought, but his mouth was dry, and his swollen tongue stuck to the roof of his mouth like cotton candy. Crust formed around his lips and entangled themselves in large clumps through his beard and mustache. His lips stretched back forming a smile that made him look like a deranged clown.

"Well," Gary said smiling. "I'd ask how you are, but that's rather evident. You're not doing well, are you?" Bob shook his head. " I wasn't expecting this, but I suppose death isn't a pretty sight, is it? I didn't realize it would be this bad..." Gary paused and then shook his head before continuing. "...but I suppose I didn't care either."

Bob straightened his back and said, "I need—I need…" he swallowed hard choking down what little spit remained in his mouth before gasping out the rest. "…your help, friend. I'm not well."

"Oh?" Gary replied. Though he knew the answer to his next question, he asked it anyway. "What seems to be the matter?"

Bob found some air and wheezed out his reply between short, labored breaths. "I'm sick, my friend, very sick. I am having trouble catching my breath, and I'm weak, and can't hold anything down."

"Was it something you ate? Because you look thin. Have you been eating well and where is Belle? She should be taking care of you."

Bob shrugged. "I…I…I…"

"Take your time old man. Find your words."

Bob swallowed hard and then spoke. "I don't know."

"Huh," Gary said shaking his head. "She really should be here, taking care of her husband."

"She—upstairs."

"Yes, I'm sure she is."

Bob hung his head low and shifted his eyes back and forth as if he were looking for something. Then, he set his focus straight ahead and pleaded with Gary. "Look at me," he said. "Look at me."

"Yes, I see you. You are not well."

"I don't know what's wrong with me."

"You're dying."

Bob's eyes swelled to the size of half dollars. His breath came harder than ever as he coughed out a reply. "Dying?" he said.

"Yes. It's lung cancer. It's returned."

"How do you know?"

"Well, what else could it be?"

"Take me to a doctor."

Gary shook his head from side-to-side and smiled. "No, you don't need a doctor."

"What do you mean?"

"Perhaps a nice cup of tea? I'll get us both a cup. Where did you say the kitchen was? I suppose I should find out since I'll be living here soon enough."

Bob coughed hard and hacked-up red-speckled, opaque, yellow globs into his hand. "What are you talking about?" he said after regaining control. "I'm sick."

"No, my friend," Gary said shaking his head. "A doctor won't help. You're beyond medical attention. It's far better for you to go gentle into that good night."

Bob forced his eyes wide open. "Gentle into that good night?" he said. "That's a poem, by, by, by… Robert Frost."

"Dylan Thomas, actually."

"No," Bob said thrusting his thumb into his chest. "I'm a fighter. I beat this thing before. I'll beat it again. Where is my cell phone? Do you see my phone?"

"Not this time," Gary answered calmly. "Your cancer is advanced, stage four. As I speak, cancerous cells are marching like a ravenous army. They're coming for you, Bob, and they'll devour every healthy cell in your body. I can close my eyes and see them as I speak. You'll succumb in a few days. Neither surgery, nor a sea of chemo will save you."

"Where is my phone?" Bob blurted out, his voice stronger now, but shaking with anger. "Why are you saying this? How do you know?"

"Because, the cancer in your lungs, the tumors eating away at your tissues…"

"Yes?"

"I put them there."

It was as though all the air had been sucked out of the room. Both men stared at each other in silence, Gary with a wide, self-important grin, and Bob with a look of stunned disbelief.

"You did what?" Bob rasped.

'You heard right. The cancerous cells eating away at your lungs, sucking the very life from you as we speak—I grew them."

Bob managed a full breath for the first time in a long while. The effort, however, caused a sharp pain that made his face grimace. "Why?"

"Insurance. I'll be a rich man when you pass from this earth."

"That's not true."

"Why do you say that?"

"The insurance policy, Belle is the beneficiary."

Gary nodded his head in agreement. "That's right," he said. "Belle will have the million, and I shall have Belle."

For the next several minutes, neither one spoke. The only sound came from Bob's labored breathing. Gary watched the withering man and thought about the chair he sat in. It needs a good scrubbing. Gary looked around the room and decided the entire library needed cleansing. Cancer wasn't contagious, but Bob made an awful mess.

"Why would you do this?" Bob finally asked. "We're friends."

"Oh don't take it so personally, Bob. I still consider you my friend. In fact, I owe you a lot." Bob interrupted Gary with a loud cough. Gary poured himself and Bob a glass of scotch. He handed Bob his glass and then took a swig from his own before continuing. "You see," Gary said. "I consider you my mentor, my teacher, and dare I say you have been my savior? Before you introduced me to the experiments, I was lost. In fact, it's only now that I realized how bad off I really was. And now, the entire universe lies prostrate at my feet. It conspires to give me what I want. I defer to no man. They bow to me, and I have you to thank."

"The experiments?" Bob mumbled.

"Yes. You remember, the seven experiments?"

"Yes, the experiments. Which one are you on?"

Gary laughed. "I've gone beyond way past what you've prescribed."

"You have?"

Gary closed his eyes and concentrated. The lights turned dim until the room went dark, and then in another instant, they flashed back on."

Bob looked around the room. "Did you do that?" he asked.

"I did," Gary said proudly.

"Impressive."

"Parlor tricks."

"And this mind of yours—it can manipulate human flesh? You can cause tumors to appear and disappear?"

"I can grow them the size of grapefruits, bigger if need be," Gary boasted.

"Prove it."

"What?"

"Yes. You said you caused my illness; now make me better. Remove the tumors."

Gary laughed. "No, no, my friend. I put them there, and there they shall stay."

"Ha, like Dorothy's slippers."

Gary opened his mouth, and the wicked witches' voice came pouring past his lips. "And your little dog too," the female voice cackled.

Bob smiled. "And Toto too," he replied, echoing the high-pitched tone.

"So you see," Gary said. "You have taken me far, but I have advanced further than even you conceived."

"Well, this is remarkable."

"Is it?"

"Why yes. I'm happy for you."

Gary didn't believe a word of it. "You are?"

"Of course I am. This is what I wanted for you."

Gary finished his drink. He poured himself another and lifted his glass. "You haven't touched yours, Bob. C'mon, man, join me. A toast—to me."

Bob picked up his glass with two shaky hands and placed it to his lips. He tilted it back allowing the liquid to flow down; half of it spilled into his mouth, the other half dribbled over his chin and onto his shirt. When he finished, Bob placed his glass down and smiled at Gary.

"So, you have everything you want?" Bob said.

"Almost," Gary explained. "Most everything. There's still more to be had. I have a list—a rather lengthy one—I will get there in time."

"And that's a good thing?"

"You see, Bob, you're a brilliant man, quite brilliant. I could never hold a candle to you in intellectual prowess."

"Not many who can."

"True enough, but there is a fundamental flaw with your philosophy and your experiments."

"And what is that?"

Gary leaned in and in a stern voice said, "They don't go far enough."

"Is that so?"

"Right. You've taken me so far, but there's another step, quite a few actually, that reach far beyond either one of us imagined."

"Tell me about these steps, Gary."

Gary looked into his glass and swirled the liquid with a circular motion of his hand. "Well," he replied. "The little tricks Christ performed while he was on this earth, walking on water— let's take that for example."

Bob's eyes lit up. "What about it?" he asked. Gary did not answer. Instead, he nodded his head up and down rhythmically. "You've walked on water?" Bob asked.

Gary took another sip. "I have. For a brief moment anyway."

"You're mad. You're out of your fucking mind. Can't be done."

Gary shook his head from side-to-side and raised his eyes to meet Bob's. "I am not mad," he said. "And yes, it can be done. I did it."

"Where? Where did you walk on water?"

"On the Chadakoin River. I had faith I could do it, and well, I did it."

"You walked across the river?"

Gary closed his eyes and relived the moment, the spring breeze, the water so thick it could support a man's weight. He remembered the fall, swallowing water, gasping for air, and grasping for a hold, anything that would keep him up—a floating tree trunk, a human arm, anything.

Gary opened his eyes. "Not quite," he said. "There was a boy. He saw me; our eyes met, and I got scared. Disbelief crept into my mind. I fell."

Bob lifted a frail finger and pointed it at Gary. "You," he said. "You have transcended the physical realm?"

"Yes. Isn't it wonderful?"

"There are no limits to how you can help mankind. You can cure cancer…" Bob struggled to find his breath. "…you can do so much to help… to help your fellow man… and yet…"

"And yet what?" Gary growled.

"You choose this?"

Gary's face twitched. He looked at Bob's chest and Bob clutched his heart. His eyes rolled back into his head and looked like two, white slits. His jaw fell open as if he were going to scream, but the only sound he made was a gurgling breath. His mouth opened and closed repeatedly, gasping air like a fish out of water. Bob lifted his arms above his head and was finally able to draw a nice lungful before blowing it out in one hard breath. Gary lowered his eyes, and Bob's face relaxed.

"You did that?" Bob said between breaths.

"Do you still doubt me and my power?"

"Power. You have no power."

The audacity, Gary thought. It must be his delirium. "What did you say?" he answered in a quiet, even tone.

"Real power doesn't come from hurting people, and it doesn't come from money. Those things are of the physical world, and they are doomed to dust. Once they have passed, so has your so-called power."

"You think so?"

"I know so."

Gary stroked his goatee slowly. "Do you feel that?" he said.

Bob doubled over in his chair and drooled bile onto his lap. Again, he sought a big breath that never came. Instead, he settled and was grateful for the small puffs of air he managed to suck in. He lifted his head and met his tormentor's fierce eyes. He could not speak but was able to communicate a solitary word. "Please," he murmured.

Gary released the hold. Bob relaxed and bowed his head and the sweat poured down his face and into his eyes.

"Tell me," Gary said shaking his head. "Are you a glutton for punishment? You haven't felt one-third of what I'm capable of, not a third. Would you like to feel what I'm truly capable of? I could put you in a state of infinite pain, pain like you can't even imagine, twenty on a scale of ten, and furthermore it will last forever. I'll keep you alive so you can suffer every minute of it. I'll make sure of that."

Bob shook his head and waved his hand in front of his face. "No. No, please," he said.

"Then stop giving me this bullshit about true power. I know more of this than you. I am a spiritual being, the most spiritual being you'll ever meet. Like you said, I have transcended the physical world. The laws of this universe don't apply to me as it does you and others. Furthermore, don't talk to me about the sin of material wealth—you with your big mansion and the Tesla parked in your garage and your four-thousand-dollar globe, or whatever else you've purchased to soothe your soul amidst a loveless marriage and the rubble of unfulfilled dreams. If money has no true power, you've gone out of your way to surround yourself with it. Haven't you?"

"Yes," Bob agreed. "Yes, I see that now. You're right. I can see you're far superior, but please, just tell me how, and why? I'm not judging. As a scientist, I just want to know."

Gary saw through Bob's thinly veiled attempt at mercy but decided there was no harm. Besides, he liked talking about his accomplishments and would tell the world if Lucas' warning didn't ring so true. "What do you want to know?" Gary said.

"Tell me what it feels like. It must be amazing, being able to walk on water? Tell me about that. What was it like?"

"Eh," Gary shrugged. "It was like walking across this fuckin' floor.

There wasn't much to it, actually."

"But you fell? You got wet?"

"Yes. I lost my focus. And when I did, the river swallowed me whole."

"You've reached another level of consciousness, Gary, a level unknown but to a few rare individuals."

"I am a rare individual, Bob. I walk the earth as Christ walked it, Buddha, Lao Tzu, and the other great spiritual men. I am free."

"This is fantastic, Gary."

"Yes, it is."

"Yes, you are an incredible human being, Gary Miller. In fact, I want to learn how you did it. I could help you."

Gary was suspicious. "Help me, how?"

"Well, I could document your success. I could—"

"Stop," Gary said. "There will be no documentation. There is no need. No one else has to know what I did or how I did it."

"But Gary, the good you can do for society."

All of Bob's good-for-society-rhetoric, Gary thought. He listened to it ad nauseum; he was tired of it. "What good?" Gary said. "The only good I'll do is for myself. That's the way the world works. You help you and yours and to Hell with everyone else."

"No," Bob replied. "I don't believe that."

"Look at you, Bob. You sit there with one foot in the grave. You grovel and suck up to me with the hope I will spare you. Why?"

Bob eyes welled with tears. Large, wet drops slowly trickled down his cheeks before falling onto his chest. "Because I want to live," he answered in a trembling voice. "I want to live."

"Because you want to live?" Gary sneered. "Despite your pain? I know how much this is hurting you. I've tapped your brain for as long as I could stand it. It's unbearable, like a searing hot knife buried in your chest. Isn't that so?"

Bob clenched his teeth and a high-pitched wail sounded from the back of his throat. A minute passed while Bob's hands tore at the armrest and his body shook the chair like a man being electrocuted.

"P…p—please," Bob managed to screech out.

Gary relaxed his mind and watched his friend slump in the chair. "No," Gary said. "There will be no documentation. Our little secret ends with your life."

Bob nodded his head. "I understand. Won't you tell me how? The scientist in me wants to know, one last mystery to solve before I pass."

"You already know, Bob."

"I do?"

"Of course you do," Gary said. "After all, you are the architect of all of this. See, Bob, you didn't take the experiments far enough. You underestimated the power of the human mind and the power of our will, the power of my will."

"I see that."

"Your concept is accurate. I have no doubt of that." Gary tapped the side of his skull repeatedly with his index finger. "Think it. Believe it and see it come to pass. It's so simple. I can't believe I didn't discover it sooner of my accord. It took you to show me. However, I have gone beyond simple trickery and mere possessions. I've taken it to a new level, one you could hardly believe. I hardly believe it myself."

"May I ask a question?"

"Of course."

"You won't get angry? I mean you won't cause the pain to come back?"

Gary deliberated. "For now, I will not inflict any more pain."

"Promise? I don't think I could handle any more."

Gary flexed his mind, flooding Bob's brain with endorphins. Bob's face relaxed, and Gary knew it was working. "There," Gary said. "That should help."

"Thank you," Bob said.

"No problem."

"These things are fantastic. But what good are they without compassion?"

Gary's forehead wrinkled. "What do you mean, compassion?"

"Well, you said you walked on water, and I believe you did, but yet here I sit in my home, dying, hurting so bad I can only pray for death sooner than later. How does this benefit me?"

"How does this benefit you?" Gary laughed. "Well, clearly it doesn't, Bob. It doesn't benefit you at all. It benefits me."

"Yes, but don't you care about me? I helped you? Remember? I was your friend? I volunteered my help without you even asking? What's happened to you, Gary? The Gary I knew was a Christian, committed to helping others. He would never hurt anyone even at his own expense. Where has that Gary gone?"

Gary rested his chin on his fist and pondered the question. It wasn't the first time he had heard it. People—his wife, deacon, co-workers—asked where the old Gary went. He knew what they meant; he didn't understand why they cared. The old Gary died, and this was good. New Gary was, well, better. New Gary walked with his head high, proud, unafraid. He was taller and leaner; he was in control and didn't answer to anyone.

Still, he wondered, where was the old him? Was he inside, buried deep and desperate to return? Why would he want to return? Better off dead.

After several silent seconds passed, Gary answered honestly. "I don't know," he said.

"You don't know?"

"I'm not trying to be coy. I really don't know."

"Have you thought about it much?"

"A little. As part of my religious training, I was taught to counsel people, to help them overcome their problems, addictions, marriage issues and the like. I know a little about the human psyche, what makes us tick."

"Yes?"

"Well, we have a side to us where all the rage and hate and envy and the terrible things are kept, but we're able to keep a lid on that side. That lid is what prevents us from unleashing a monster into our world. It lets us co-exist peacefully."

"So what's happened?"

"I don't know," Gary said, shaking his head. "My lid must have popped off."

"Why?"

"I don't know, man," he said his voice growing tense. "It was a process. It didn't happen overnight. It's been years in the making, even before the experiments. It's like a hot gas inside of me has been slowly building, exerting more-and-more pressure on my overworked brain. The experiments merely added the impetus to totally dislodge the lid."

"So you know, Gary. You know that what you're doing isn't right? It's a bad thing, not good."

"It's good for me," Gary reasoned.

"Yes, but not for others. Hurting people is bad."

"I don't care," Gary said. "I'm just tired—"

"Gary, you could stop this right now. You put the tumors there, the pain. You can take them away."

Gary saw the trick, a sick man pleading for his life, trying to talk to the good still inside of him. Gary looked at the frail man and thought about going back, reversing what he had done. It wasn't too late. He would be forgiven, life would go on. That thought came and went quickly. There was no going back.

"No," Gary said shaking his head "The tumors have been there for weeks. The damage they've done to your organs is beyond repair." Bob sat in his seat in stunned silence. "Oh, don't look so horrified, Bob. And don't take it so personally. It's nothing personal."

"It's not?"

"No. We all have to die sometime. So you'll be dead sooner than later."

"That's for God to decide," Bob said softly. "Not you."

Gary leaned in close to Bob and whispered, "I am God."

Bob covered his head with hands and said, "My God."

The two men sat silent for several minutes. Gary looked at his watch, checked his phone and sent a text message. He looked around the room making mental images of each item and wondering if many changes needed to be made. Bob had a good sense of style and décor. He could live with it for now.

"If it's any consolation to you," Gary said. "Your disease is highly advanced. You're not going to make it through the night. By morning, you'll be dead."

"Thank you," replied Bob nodding his head up and down. "That's so thoughtful."

"Well, it's the best I can do."

"Why is that? With your power, you could strike me dead as I sit here. Do that, and it will put me out of my misery."

Gary bowed his head and lowered his eyes. "No," he replied. "I cannot."

"Why?" Gary sat quietly and avoided Bob' steady gaze. "You're afraid?"

Gary stood up. His wiry body appeared much taller than his six-foot frame, and he towered over Bob. "Think what you like," Gary said. "I must be going now."

Bob looked up at Gary, and saw Belle standing just off his left shoulder. "Belle," Bob said. "Where have you been? I couldn't find my cell phone. I need help. I need a doctor. Please." Belle was silent. Gary and her exchanged glances. "Belle. What is wrong with you? Look at me. I'm sick. Help me."

"I have your cell phone," Belle said.

"Call a doctor. Terrible pain." Bob pointed at Gary. "He's a monster.

He did this to me."

"I'm sorry to interrupt, old man," Gary said. "But we must be going. The Tesla's charged and waiting."

"What?" Bob said. "Who's we? Where are you going?"

"Belle and I. We're going to Niagara Falls, a honeymoon of sorts."

Bob shook his head. "What are you talking about? Belle is my wife. Tell him, Belle. Tell him. Go ahead, tell him. He's gone mad, or I have; I can't tell anymore."

Belle said nothing. Instead, she took a step towards Gary's side and the two held hands.

"Oh," Bob said lowering his eyes. "I see."

"Come on, Belle," Gary said. "We must be going. It's time to leave Bob alone."

"Belle, wait," Bob pleaded.

Gary turned to leave. "C'mon."

"Belle, wait, please."

"Let's go."

"Wait one moment," Belle replied.

"Come on Belle. The weather is turning—"

"I told you to wait a moment."

Belle walked over to where Bob sat slumped in his chair. She pulled a pipe and a small plastic bag from her purse and placed it on the end table next to Bob.

"I'll leave this with you," she told Bob. "It will help with the pain. Do it just like I showed you. There's a lighter in the bag too."

"Belle, please," Bob cried. "Please don't leave me here. I'll die."

Belle leaned over and placed a kiss on Bob's wet cheek. Then she whispered into his ear. "You deserve better than me."

"Belle, let's go," Gary said.

The lights dimmed; Belle and Gary exited the library, leaving Bob alone in the dark.

CHAPTER TWENTY-FOUR

The red Tesla sped down route 90 as the Western New York scenery swept past the windshield in a blur of dark greens and earthen browns. A light drizzle coated the windshield and was wiped clear by intermittent swipes of the windshield wiper. The summer sky, which had been bright and sunny moments earlier, was now saturated with purple, and pink hues that echoed the couple's mood.

Belle sat in the passenger seat; she took a long drag from her bowl and blew the smoke into the air in white, puffy plumes that smelled like a mix of skunk and wet leaves. "Why did you take the car?" she said. "It's too soon. He's not gone yet."

"Oh stop your bitching," Gary replied. "He'll be dead soon enough. Besides, I've been waiting my whole life. I'm done waiting. I'm taking what's mine."

"It looks bad, that's all I'm saying."

"So it looks bad."

Belle took another hit. "Regrets?"

Gary drove in silence and contemplated Belle's question. Regret was not an option, he thought. It's the only thing that could derail his plan. "No," he answered.

"I just wish you could have put him to sleep—stopped his breathing or something. No pain."

Gary pressed lightly on the pedal. With an acceleration he wasn't expecting, the car lurched forward, passed slower traffic to the left, and then deftly darted back to the right lane.

"Holy shit," Gary said. "This is unbelievable. I never thought an electric motor could do that."

"Will you slow down? I'm smoking dope, do you want to get busted?"

"That's not going to happen. Give me a hit."

"You're driving."

Gary laughed. "You're blowing so much fucking smoke in the car, I've already got a contact high."

"Well, that's enough for you, then."

Belle and Gary rode in silence. For a long time, the only sound came from the big raindrops pulsating against the car, the rhythmic swish of wiper blades and the sucking in and blowing out of pot smoke.

"Too many questions," Gary finally said. "Stage four cancer will answer all of them. He'll pass quickly. You got a good look at him?"

Belle closed her eyes and bit her lower lip. "Yeah," she said. "I saw him."

"He'll be gone soon. He might be gone already, by morning for sure."

"Oh? I'm not so sure. He's a tough little fucker. Cancer had tried before, and he beat it."

Gary closed his eyes and saw the tumors in place, and growing, looking more like exotic sea urchins than human tissue. "Yeah, he beat it with surgery and drugs and everything medical science had to offer. He's got no chance now."

Another long stretch of silence ensued. The sun dipped below the tree line, the light faded quickly, and the rain fell more intensely. The wipers worked overtime in a futile attempt to clear Gary's view. Without the competing conversation, the raindrops slammed the windshield, thundering like glass marbles on a metallic roof.

"You did something to me, didn't you?" Belle said. There was no response from Gary, so she tried again. "I'm not acting of my own accord, am I? It's okay. I just want to know. Am I really capable of this, or did you do something?"

Gary kept his eyes glued to the road ahead. "If it makes you feel better about yourself, go ahead, blame it on me."

"I'm not sure it makes me feel better at all. I just want to know if I'm in Bob's car, driving to the Falls with you because I really want to, or because you want me to?"

"Well, I really want you here with me, and as for you, I think you want to be here too. You never cared for him. You were only after his money. You just needed a little push, that's all."

Belle nodded her head. "I see," she replied. "Did you know he was a professional baseball player?" Belle said.

It was hard for Gary to imagine a young, athletic Bob Harris. Bob was frail and highly intellectual, the antithesis of an athlete. "Yeah, he told me."

"He struck out Thurman Munson. I don't know who Thurman Munson is, but he made it sound like it was a big deal. Bob was quite the man, and you're wrong. I did care for him—a lot."

"Is that so?"

"Yes, that's so."

Gary smiled sympathetically and said, "It will be over quick. There won't be much pain. I made sure of that. He just looks a little worse for wear, that's all. He's actually quite comfortable."

Belle let out a long, audible sigh. "Slow the fuck down," she said. "I want to arrive in one piece."

Gary smiled and thought about the next forty-eight hours. He had reserved a hotel and a room with a view of Niagara Falls. He and Belle would have the entire week together.

Gary glanced over and caught sight of Belle's cleavage.

"This is going to be the best vacation ever," Gary said.

"Is that so?"

"Niagara Falls will be fantastic. Though we'll be in the hotel most of the time, we probably won't be seeing much of it. You know, Belle, for the first time in my life, I'm truly happy."

"Oh?" Belle said. "You mean you've never been happy before?"

Gary cocked his head. "Maybe when I was a child. There were times I thought I was happy as an adult, but it was just a front. I've never been as happy as I am now. It's like I'm free, and freedom's a drug. It's changed the way I look at life and how I walk through this world."

Belle took another drag from the pipe and held the smoke in her lungs. Then, in a sudden burst, she expelled the smoke with a series of violent coughs that sent a white cloud into the car's interior.

"What did you have to be unhappy about?" Belle said after recovering her voice. "You had a lot going for you. So many people out there are suffering, truly suffering."

"You don't know what it was like," Gary snapped.

"So what was it like?" she said. "Tell me of your misery. How does it compare with all the pain others have suffered throughout this world? Did you survive round after round of chemo and radiation treatment? Perhaps it was like the Holocaust? Did you survive a Nazi concentration camp?"

Gary felt the familiar hot burn on the back of his ears and his neck. "Oh, shut the fuck up," he snapped.

"I'm just saying you're a college professor living in the suburbs. You have first world problems. They couldn't have been that bad."

"Now you sound like, Sarah." Gary laughed. "That's not a good thing."

Twenty miles of I-90 and countryside quickly peeled away in the rearview mirror. It was darker now, and the rain intensified forcing the wipers to work overtime, but they could hardly keep up with the cascading river flooding the windshield. Visibility was poor and getting worse with each pound of pressure placed on the accelerator.

"Slow the fuck down." Belle said. "Are you trying to kill us both?"

Gary laughed. "No need to worry my dear. I'm in complete control of the car like I'm in complete control of everything else."

"Uh, huh," Belle said nodding her head. "That's what I'm worried about."

"I'm so looking forward to tonight. I want to inhale you and make love to you forever. I want to suck your fat lips into my mouth and chew them like bubble gum." Belle took another hit of her pipe. "Hey, give me some," Gary said.

"Nope, you're driving."

"C'mon. I'll put it on autopilot. This thing can drive itself."

"Seriously?"

"Sure. Your husband had expensive tastes. He ordered the fully autonomous model. You don't even need a driver."

"I don't trust it. It's raining too hard."

"That doesn't matter. The computer and the sensors will know what to do. In fact, it's probably safer than me driving. Besides, I'm right here in case anything does go wrong."

Gary reached forward and pushed a button. He slowly lifted his hands from the steering wheel to show Belle he was no longer driving the car. The mechanical mind mimicked the brain of a human driver and the car slowed and sped up in response to surrounding traffic.

Gary leaned back in his seat and smiled. "See?" he said to Belle. "Genius—pure fucking genius of the human mind. There is nothing a human brain cannot do. If we put our minds to it, we can achieve great things, anything we want is ours, and it all begins with a single thought."

"Yes," Belle agreed. "And even things we don't want."

"Belle, we shouldn't mention anything about this, not a soul."

"About?"

"You know, the experiments, and what I'm capable of."

"Oh that," Belle said with an air of disdain. "I wasn't going to."

"Because if anyone found out, they would try to do the same. Right now, I'm special. I might be the most special person alive on this planet. I dare say I am."

"Uh, huh."

"I walked on water, you know. You know that, Belle?"

Belle shook her head. "I'm sorry. I'm really stoned right now. It sounded like you said you walked on water."

"That's right," Gary nodded. "Doctor Gary Miller and Jesus Christ himself. The only two souls to ever do so."

"I don't believe you."

"Why not?"

"Because you're such a liar. I can never tell when you're telling the truth or lying."

"I'm not lying. I really did walk on water."

"Prove it."

"Alright, I will."

"We'll fill up the bathtub in our hotel room, and you can walk on top of that. Or better still, our hotel has a swimming pool, perhaps you could demonstrate there, or Niagara Falls, now that would be..."

"Shut up, would you?"

"...truly fucking amazing."

"Oh shut the fuck up," Gary yelled. "I should have known better than to confide in you on spiritual matters. You're not very spiritual you know? Not like me."

"Is that so?"

"C'mon, give the pipe here," Gary said reaching to grab for it.

Belle took one last drag and then passed the still smoldering bowl to Gary. He took a long, hard drag. Instantly, a cloud of hot, smoke filled his lungs causing the back of his throat to burn. He began to choke and cough violently as he let the smoke escape his mouth.

"Oh my God," Gary said in a raspy voice. "No wonder the government made this shit illegal."

"You're so white bread," Belle said.

Gary rested his head back in the seat. His mind and body were relaxed, and his face melted into a perma-smile. He fell asleep for a brief moment but was startled awake by a sudden acceleration that pinned his skull deep into the headrest.

"We're moving faster," Belle said.

"Yes, I know."

"Why?"

"I'm not sure."

The Tesla found a higher gear and lurched forward with another burst of speed. Gary and Belle were pressed into their seats as if a heavy weight were pushing on their chests.

"We're going too fast," Belle said. "Make it stop, Gary."

"It's okay," Gary assured her. "The computer is in control. It knows what it's doing."

"Fuck the computer. Take it off autopilot."

The car found yet another gear and was speeding toward the rear lights of a tractor-trailer. The lights grew larger coming at them as if in a dream. A crash looked inevitable, but a last-minute turn of the steering wheel jerked the Tesla into the passing lane and bought them a reprieve.

Gary's eyes were wide and unblinking. He scanned the car's control panel and when he found the right button, he pushed it repeatedly.

"God damn it," Belle shrieked. "Take it off autopilot."

"I'm trying," Gary said.

Gary did his best to regain control of the car, but his brain wasn't working right. He was panicked and flailing like he did in the Chadakoin, only there were no lifesavers to grab hold of. He pushed buttons frantically and without reason; nothing worked. The car sped forward as if it had a mind of its own. The breakneck speed, the windswept rain, and the dark sky conspired against the occupants. They were captives on the roller coaster from Hell.

Gary looked up and read the sign in front of him: *How is my driving? Call 1-800-382-5963.*

CHAPTER TWENTY-FIVE

Bob sat slumped in his chair, motionless and rigid as a corpse. He felt like one too. It wasn't his habit to pray, but with his life in the balance, he scanned the vaulted ceiling in search of a deity—Jesus, Allah, he didn't care; any one would do. He just wanted relief, to be healed, or to pass quickly.

He had tried to manifest his well-being through his own experiments, to clear the cancerous growth with mind over matter. He had reasoned that if a human thought could plant and grow cancerous cells, then a human thought could make them disappear.

He was wrong. In his state of delirium, he could not concentrate. He was powerless to manifest the smallest thought let alone a monumental one to save his own life. He was going to expire, alone in a dark mansion, surrounded by a bunch of books, and a wealth of knowledge he now deemed useless. *What good was any of it*, he thought? We live, we accumulate wisdom and possessions, and then we expire like milk, never leaving more than a trace of our existence behind. We will be remembered less-and-less with each passing generation. One day, there will be no one left who remembers us. Was there something more, something he missed and should have been doing? He smiled and shook his head at his own frailty, his own stupidity. It all seemed hopeless, so pointless to him now.

There was silence in the library, but the sound of the double sliding doors startled him to attention. The room was pitch dark, and he couldn't see a hand in front of his face.

"Who's there?" he said.

At first, there was no reply, but in the next instant, the sharp ring of a kitten's meow shattered the silence.

"Gary?" he said his voice rising with excitement. "Gary is that you? Have you come back for me?" His query was met with another high-pitched meow. "Who's there?" he continued. "Who is that?"

This time, there was no audible response; instead, he felt two sets of pads suddenly press against his lap. It startled him at first, but he reached out and found relief at the soft fur beneath his fingertips. He instinctively stroked the creature along its spine and was rewarded with the sound of a purr whirring like a toy motor.

"Hey, little fella," Bob said. "Where did you come from?"

For a moment the only sound in the room was that of the purring cat, but then Bob heard footsteps approach. He couldn't see who it was, but the click–clack sound of hard heels against the wood floor made him think it was Gary. He had come back, Bob thought, but what for? His heart raced. He cradled the cat and stroked it harder and with greater purpose. He heard a voice, but instead of the expected deep, resonant tone, it was the high-pitched soprano of a female voice.

"Yoo-hoo," it said.

The voice sounded vaguely familiar. "Yoo-hoo?" Bob replied.

"Marco?"

"Polo?"

"Marco?"

"Polo."

"Oh, where the heck are you?" the female voice said.

"I'm here. I'm here," Bob shouted out.

"Oh, it's so dark in here. Let there be light."

Like a flash of lighting, the darkness was swallowed, and every inch and crevice filled with light. In front of Bob, stood Sarah Miller, her arms stretched wide and her palms faced towards the ceiling as if commanding the heavens with her fingertips. For all Bob knew, she was.

Her hair was piled up high and tight, and she wore a smile on her face—a huge smile that seemed to fill the room and Bob's heart at once. To Bob's pleasure, she wore a tight-fitting, red blouse. Even in his semi-delirious state, it was a wonderful sight.

Sarah appeared to be twenty pounds lighter than what Bob last remembered. The effect was a pleasing hour glassed shape, which was at once motherly and sexy. There was a soft glow around her head, and for a moment, he did not know if he were alive or dead, or if this was Sarah Miller, an angel, or some psychotropic vision invented by a swollen, and diseased brain.

"Sarah?" Bob said.

"Bob?" she replied. "I see you've found Snowball, or should I say Snowball has found you?"

In his arms, Bob could now see a snow-white cat with an angelic face returning his gaze; its eyes were blue and watery, and it purred softly.

"What?" Bob said.

"His name is Snowball," Sarah said gesturing to the cat. "I saved him, twice now. He was a little worse for wear, but now he's all better." Bob sat dumbfounded. "And I see I have saved you too," Sarah continued. "Just in time I think."

Bob was now fully awake and alert. His words spilled forth in a single, excited breath. "Sarah," he said. "I'm sick. I'm very sick. Gary—He—"

Sarah smiled at Bob and held a finger to her lips. "Hush, Baby. I know all about that."

"But—but you don't know. He ran off, with Belle, and he did something to me. I don't know—It's like magic—black magic almost. He made me sick."

"Sick?" Sarah said. "What do you mean sick?"

"He gave me Cancer, or he made it return. I—I don't know what he did. Just look at me."

Sarah's eyes scanned Bob's body from head-to-toe. "I am looking at you," she said.

"Well, can't you see? I'm hideous—my body—my hands. I'm wrinkled, and grey."

Sarah shook her head and scowled in mock indignation. "What are you talking about? There's nothing wrong with you. You're as handsome as you ever were, Doctor Harris."

Bob's jaw dropped. "What are you talking about?" he argued. "I'm weak; I can't stand; I can barely talk or breathe."

"But you're talking and breathing just fine."

Bob paused; for the first time in a while, he took stock, pressing his hands against his face and his chest. His skin was pliant and bounced back readily to the touch. He looked at his hands. The grey, wrinkled skin was replaced with healthy, pink tissue. Sarah was right. The shortness of breath, the rasped, thin voice, they were gone. Instead, he heard the unlabored breathing of healthy lungs—his lungs.

"I don't understand," he said. He looked at Sarah, and she returned his gaze with warm, compassionate eyes.

"What don't you understand?" she said. "You are alive and well just like Snowball."

"But Gary, he did something to me. He gave me Cancer."

"You don't have Cancer."

"But I do. Gary—"

"I know all about Gary. And you're right. He gave you Cancer..." Sarah paused. "...I gave you your life back."

"You? But how?"

"In the same manner Gary tried to end it." Bob's eyes grew bright and wide. "That's right," Sarah said. "Gary had amazing powers, quite frightful actually. Me? Well, let's just say I'm a bit more amazing and a little more frightful." Sarah threw her head back and laughed.

"He's run away with Belle. They were here earlier. They were going away together."

"Yes, to Niagara Falls. I know all about it."

"You do?"

"Yes," Sarah said nodding her head. "I read his journal. Everything was written down, his plans, his tricks, world domination, his hatred of me, his love for himself, every bitch and every whine, every slight real or imagined were in his little book." Sarah reached into her purse and pulled out the worn, journal held together by a bow. She handed it to Bob and said, "Here, read for yourself."

"What's this?" Bob said taking the book.

"It's his journal," Sarah said smiling. "I swiped it while he was packing to leave."

Bob opened the book and began flipping the pages. He passed quickly over the textual information but went more slowly when he came to the illustrations. He gasped at what he saw. The pictures were dark and brooding and had a gothic look about them. Black ink wasn't so much applied to the pages as much as it was slathered on. The illustrations first appeared to be massive, shapeless blobs that were void of substance. But on closer inspection, each drawing told its own vile, hate-filled story.

"It's my house," Bob said. Then he turned the page. "...and my Tesla, and here's a picture of Belle." Then he turned the page again and stared blankly for what seemed like an eternity.

"What is it?" asked Sarah.

"It's me... like when I'm dead...my corpse."

He turned the journal towards Sarah. She nodded her head solemnly and said, "Yes, that's exactly what it is."

Bob continued to flip through the journal. "He claimed to have walked on water, or at least that's what he told me."

"He could. I can too," Sarah said matter-of-factly.

"What? How is that even possible?"

"It's a matter of faith, an extreme belief in mind over matter. Once you've mastered that skill, then anything is possible."

"I thought he was mad."

"He was, but you know what your experiments have taught me?"

"What's that?"

"They taught me our minds are incredible instruments capable of superhuman feats."

"Gary said you didn't believe in the experiments."

"I didn't at first, but the more I practiced them, the more convinced I became of their efficacy."

Bob scratched his head. "You? You did the experiments?" he said.

"I did. I never told Gary what I was doing. I did them on my own when he wasn't looking. He would share the next experiment with me and I would try it. When he stopped telling me what they were, I simply read his journal."

Bob smirked and pointed at Sarah. "Ah, clever girl," he said. "He never suspected?"

"He suspected alright. He knew I was praying for the left side carton to overtake the right side."

"Oh my God, Sarah. It was you? That's why the experiment failed?"

Sarah giggled, and her face grew flush. "The experiment failed for him," she announced proudly. "It worked great for me."

Bob and Sarah shared a laugh at Gary's expense.

"You are a clever girl," Bob reiterated.

"Well, clever enough I suppose, and a tad devious I'm afraid."

Bob waved his hand dismissively. "Ah," he said. "Sometimes, you have to fight fire with fire."

Sarah nodded her head. "I believe you're right, Bob. Sometimes you do. I'm sorry to say, but it's true. My one regret is I wasn't able to save the boy. I could have, if I had known about it sooner. God rest his soul." Bob flashed Sarah a confused smile. "It's okay," she continued. "I'll explain it later."

"Sarah," Bob said. "I feel terrible. Like I'm responsible for this mess."

"How so?"

Bob looked down at Snowball and shook his head. "I introduced your husband to the seven experiments," he said. "He was a good man, and I unleashed something inside of him. I turned him into what he became."

Sarah approached Bob and held his gaze in hers. "No," she said. "You had no part in this. He did it to himself, him and that twisted mind of his."

Bob was able to feel emotion again, and his emotions bubbled to the surface. "He'll be back to finish the job. He wants my life insurance policy, so he and Belle can live together in my house; in my fucking house."

"No," Sarah said shaking her head. "Neither will return. They will never bother us again."

"What do you mean?"

"On their way to Niagara Falls, they had an accident. Gary lost control of the car. They were decapitated."

Bob cringed at the ghastly image in his head. "Decapitated?" he said.

"The state police said they were traveling at a high rate of speed. Their car, or I should say, your car slammed into the rear of a tractor–trailer. Neither suffered. They both died instantly."

"Oh my God. Belle and Gary?"

Sarah closed her eyes and shook her head. "Both gone; it's quite tragic. I'm sorry for your loss, as I'm sure you're sorry for mine," she said robotically. "Just remember that thieving husband of mine and that no-good whore of yours were trying to kill you and take everything from you."

Bob did remember. "Yeah, that's right," he said.

"But I'm here, Bob."

"You are? Oh, I mean yes you are."

"And I can take care of you. That is, if you want me to."

"Yes, I'd like that, but I'm a broken down old man. I'm sick. I wouldn't want to burden you."

Sarah smiled and shook her head. "How many times do I have to tell you? You're not sick. Here, hand over Snowball." Bob gave the cat to Sarah. "Now, stand up."

Bob hesitated. He placed his hands on the armrest, and gingerly pushed himself to a standing position. His legs wobbled like a newborn deer, but it felt good to be upright again. To his surprise, there was no pain, just the slightest apprehension of the unknown.

"See?" Sarah said. "You feel normal, right?"

Bob patted himself down as if checking to see that his parts were there and in normal working order. Everything seemed fine.

"I feel normal, yes," he said. "In fact, better than normal. I haven't felt this young or alive since I don't know when. Oh, God. I thought I was going to die."

"Die? Don't you remember me visiting you, telling you everything was going to be all right, that I was coming for you?"

"I do remember seeing you," Bob said scratching the side of his head. "I thought I was hallucinating."

"That was no hallucination. It was I."

"My heroine," Bob said smiling. "You saved me."

Sarah blushed. "Your body was a human lab experiment run by a madman. I simply took command."

"Sarah," Bob gushed. "I don't know how to thank you."

"Your well-being is thanks enough."

"We need to tell the world about this, about you and the seven experiments."

Sarah frowned and shook her head. "We'll do no such thing," she said.

"What? Why not? This is amazing. These experiments can—"

"Destroy the human race?"

"Destroy it? It could save it."

"No, Bob. It would be nothing but a curse. Look what happened to Gary, and look what he nearly did to you."

"Yes, but you yourself said Gary was crazy. Imagine what good people, sane people with the right motives could do." Bob reached out and grabbed Sarah by both shoulders. "We could cure disease," he continued. "Terminal illness would be a thing of the past, and that's just the tip of the iceberg. I don't even know the power behind what I've created. Sarah, you need to help me get the word out. I'll write and publish a paper. I'll get to work on it now."

"No, you will not," Sarah said emphatically. "And most certainly I won't help you."

"But why?"

"Because this thing, these experiments, it's not for man to play with. God will heal disease, and God will walk on water if it pleases him. Bob, we should never mention the experiments to anyone ever."

"But Sarah—all the good that could be done. There are still good people out there."

"Yes, and there are plenty of bad people too. Look at the world around us. Not even a college professor and a minister could handle this power. Look at what he was capable of; now imagine what a deranged dictator could do with this power, or terrorists, or anyone of us for that matter."

Bob lowered his head and nodded. "I suppose you're right."

"Though, I fear we're merely placing a finger in the dike," Sarah lamented. "The knowledge will soon get out if it hasn't already."

"Is that so?"

Sarah stared off into space and stroked Snowball's head. "Yes," she said stoically. "I believe our government is doing research into this field for military purposes."

"Yes, leave it to our own government to find a military application for it."

"Bob, I need to tell you something. I'm done with the experiments. I'll not use the power I've acquired. I'll let things be just as they were intended to be."

"I understand."

Sarah gave Bob a satisfied smile. "Good," she said. "Have you eaten yet? Are you hungry, thirsty?"

"Why yes, I can't remember when I've eaten last. I haven't had much of an appetite, but now I'm famished."

"Very good then. I'll fix us both something to eat. This place has a kitchen I presume?"

"Yes, a big one."

"No need to show me. Snowball and I will find it." Sarah placed Snowball on the floor, and he trotted next to her as she turned and walked toward the double doors. Bob watched in bemusement as Snowball playfully attacked Sarah's boot lace.

"Wait a minute," Bob said.

Sarah turned and looked at Bob. "What is it?"

"I just wanted to tell you something, Sarah."

"Yes?"

"I just wanted to say—Well, you're a beautiful Woman, Sarah—both inside and out."

Sarah's cheeks grew flush, and her face lit up. She walked quickly to Bob, and the two embraced. Bob pressed his cheek aside Sarah's and gave her a kiss.

"I brought my things," Sarah whispered into his ear. "You know for spending the night if that's okay? I don't like sleeping alone. I've been sleeping alone for too long."

"Sure," Bob replied. "That would be great. But Sarah…"

"What is it?"

"I—I'm older now, and I'm not what I use to be. Do you know what I'm saying? Belle and I—we hadn't—"

Sarah reached down between Bob's legs and began stroking the inseam of his pant leg. In a few seconds, she felt the reaction she was looking for. "There, now," Sarah said. "Just one last bit of magic."

A huge grin spread across Bob's face. "Oh, God," he said.

Sarah gave Bob a playful pat on his backside and said, "Well then, hold that thought. You get a shower. I'll get us some food, and then you and I will have some fun. Come with me Snowball."

Sarah and Snowball turned to leave. Bob stood and watched as they disappeared behind the double doors. There was a tear in his eye and a smile on his face.

The End

NOTE FROM THE AUTHOR

Word-of-mouth is crucial for any author to succeed. If you enjoyed the book, please leave a review online—anywhere you are able. Even if it's just a sentence or two. It would make all the difference and would be very much appreciated.

Thanks!
Stephen

ABOUT THE AUTHOR

Stephen Kanicki enjoys thought-provoking, reality-based science fiction. His novel, *The Seven Experiments*, explores religious, spiritual and metaphysical themes woven into an imaginative and frightening narrative.

Kanicki is a father, a teacher, and an award-winning photographer. When he's not writing, he likes to run and if his aging body can stand it, he would love to complete his third marathon.

www.stephenkanicki.net

Thank you so much for reading one of our **Sci-Fi** novels.

If you enjoyed our book, please check out our recommended title for your next great read!

Culture-Z by Karl Andrew Marszalowicz

In the year 2190, mankind has made great strides forward in the worlds of technology, science, and greed. However, when all three get together one last time, this oblivious generation may not exist much longer.

View other Black Rose Writing titles at www.blackrosewriting.com/books and use promo code **PRINT** to receive a **20% discount** when purchasing.